"... the perfect book for those who fancy the darker, grittier side of mystery. A hit-you-in-the-guts psychothriller, this is a compelling story of one man's search for truth and inner peace."
—*Mystery Scene*

"Written with building tension and a strong sense of place, *Killing Neptune's Daughter* brings to life the Woods Hole of an earlier time, both its innocence and brutality. This book will keep you enthralled until the last page."
—Sabina Murray

"Gritty, psychosexual exploration of motives and behaviors that's both a real page-turner and an insightful portrayal of a half-dozen characters in a tightly knit fishing community .... What becomes clear as Mr. Peffer's story unfolds is that the relationships among these kids is so tangled that tragedy, sooner or later, seems inevitable."
—*New Bedford Standard-Times (MA)*

"This is a story for those who can handle grit with their detective fiction ... provocative and disturbing portrait of Cape Cod youth running seriously amok. It's worth the turn of the screw on the reader's thumbs, however, for Mr. Peffer's unforgettable characters, startling revelations and haunting New England atmospherics."
—*The Vineyard Gazette*

"*Killing Neptune's Daughter* is not a pretty book but it accurately reflects the darker goings that go on between high school students .... Randall Peffer is a talented writer who gives new meaning to the words vigilante justice."

"A first novel that readers of dark crime will not want to miss."
—*The Constant Reader*

killing neptune's daughter

by

randall peffer

speck press

denver

First paperback edition 2005
Published by: *speck press,* speckpress.com

Book layout and design by: *CPG,* corvuspublishinggroup.com
Printed and bound in the United States of America
Copyright © 2004 Randall Peffer
First published in hardcover by Intrigue Press

ISBN: 1-933108-05-3, ISBN13: 978-1-933108-05-6

This book is a work of fiction. Names, characters, places, and incidents are
either the product of the author's imagination or are used fictitiously. Any resem-
blance to actual events or locales or persons, living or dead, is entirely coincidental.

Library of Congress Cataloging-in-Publication Data

Peffer, Randall S.
Killing Neptune's daughter / Randall Peffer.-- 1st pbk. ed.
p. cm.
ISBN-13: 978-1-933108-05-6 (pbk.)
ISBN-10: 1-933108-05-3 (pbk.)
1. Rock musicians' spouses--Crimes against--Fiction. 2. Married women-
-Crimes against--Fiction. 3. Funeral rites and ceremonies--Fiction. 4. Woods
Hole (Mass.)--Fiction. 5. Friendship--Fiction. 6. Psychological fiction. I. Title.

PS3616.E35K55 2005
813'.54--dc22

2005029692

10 9 8 7 6 5 4 3 2 1

For Lula, Geeter, Charlie D, Dave the Head, Fish, Hep, Reiniger's Raiders, Loeper, Warner, Debbie Jo, Cindy K, Pam, Marla, Violet, Joy Lynn and Sweet Sal, … who kept the faith.

And for Doog: rest in peace, my man!

1

This is no confession, at least not of the strictly criminal sort. But I know how she died, exactly how. The New York papers—even my own—are calling this murder the dark side of the Cinderella story. But they haven't the slightest clue what really happened to her that night ... or a thousand others that led up to it. That night ...

It's a little after nine on the night of October 14 when she decides to leave her house. She lives in one of those Federal-style town houses on Grove Street in the West Village. One of those places the tourists are always parading past during the day on walking tours of Old New York. But when she steps out the door, the street looks empty in the shadows of the streetlights and the trees. Except for the glow in the sky from Manhattan, she can almost picture the scene as a small town somewhere in a romantic novel. A perfect neighborhood. Grove Street is an oasis in the middle of Gotham ... and about as different as you can get from the stink of fish, stale beer, and ferryboat horns where this famous lady grew up.

It's a cool night, and the lights in the town houses are humming into the darkness. Except that a few leaves are falling, this can almost be a spring night. You can smell the change of the year like moist earth, and it feels good just to get out and walk.

The city and the dark never scare her. In fact, it is kind of the other way around. Somehow watching the cars come streaming along Seventh Avenue can bring stillness to a person's mind. The kind that you hear people talk about when they sit at Nobska Lighthouse and stare out at the sea for hours. Sometimes the flash of a drag queen's dress as he rushes down Christopher Street to a club can make you forget every misery of your own life. Other times your mind just drifts in long, smooth circles as the jazz seeps from the doors of bars, the neon buzzes, and headlights dance to the chuff and whir of traffic. I know. That's why I live in the Village, too, even if it's not in the same fancy neighborhood. That's why I walk the city at night.

So she's walking. She's drifting. This is a world-class beauty. You can tell by her stride. She has a dancer's long gait that makes her feet look like they are plucking rose petals off the ground with those white Nikes. And the faux leopard-skin coat that she got at an East Side retro store does little to hide the easy curves of her legs in those black leotards. With her long, dark hair pinned up under the green berét, her neck seems like a foot-long pedestal for the pale face of Audrey Hepburn.

If she roamed the Village like this by day, eventually the paparazzi, the autograph seekers, and the gawkers would be up in her face. She used to love the attention, but it got old. Now, she craves the anonymity of the night. She always knew she would be famous someday ... but not for this. Not because of the man she married. Bianca Jagger and Hillary Clinton can't tell her anything she hasn't already learned about living in a glass house with a modern Solomon. Those photos of her sunbathing in the buff on Fire Island that turned up in the *Inquirer* last summer were the final straws ... although she had to admit it made her smile to think a woman past fifty could look so good. Since then she has found her sun as much as possible in St. Barts. New York is only hers at night.

By now she's all but forgotten the latest fight with her husband. She has forgotten how much she misses her girls who are off at boarding school in Switzerland. Only one of the people she has passed on her walk to Washington Square and back knows her, the rest of the people simply let their gaze follow her up the street because she is a beautiful woman. Only when she almost disappears into the collage of lights and shadows, does he take up her trail.

Crossing back over Seventh Avenue on her way west along Christopher Street, she hears the click of heels behind her and thinks she sees someone following her in a long, red overcoat that lifts a little like wings in the wind. But the figure disappears into one of the bars near Sheridan Square. So she decides to extend her walk and cruise past the Lortel Theatre to see what's going up for the coming Christmas season. She's walking toward Hudson Street and one of her favorite places.

St. Lukes-in-the-Fields is a dark little country church with a plot of gardens right here in the Village. She never has had her own garden here—someone said it took generations of living in the neighborhood and having your name on a waiting list before you came up for a plot. But when her young daughters had gone to the little school beside the church in their early years, she often lingered along the path among the gardens to smell the ripening tomatoes and basil and to listen to the robins. It was a serene place to wait before walking the girls home after school, and she always felt vaguely like she had bathed when she left.

After the girls moved on to boarding school in Switzerland, she still came here, like tonight. It even seems safe after dark because people think the gate is locked, but it isn't. It is like a secret garden. She can sit down in the shadows with her back against a tree, inhale the scent of the last tomatoes of the season, and push the past thirty years of fame, wealth, drugs, lovers, booze, bad decisions, Butch, and torture out of her mind. She can forget about his fetish for teenage groupies. She can stop worrying about what the tabloids are saying about her now.

She can let go of her guilt over having left the raising of her girls largely to nannies and boarding schools. She can even forgive her mother for walking out during the summer of 1965 before she ran away to New York.

Sometimes, when her mind settles, she starts to remember the girl she was before this New York City glamour rock-and-roll charade. Then, one-by-one, the names and faces begin to surface. And she sees us as we once were—the crazy fishy boys who were so desperate to brush her teenage neck with our lips. She has a rule about never looking back, and she almost never breaks it except when she comes to the night garden of Saint Luke's-in-the-Fields to clear her mind.

She's taken her spot in the garden, drifting off to the past, when she hears the snap of a branch near the gate and a male voice saying, "Hey, look, it's the village slut!"

Before she can rise to her feet, someone collars her from behind. Then she sees a switchblade alongside her right eye. It smells of fresh semen as her abductor rubs the wet blade along her cheek, down to the edge of her mouth.

"So what the fuck you doin' all by yourself in a place like this?" The voice stinks of stale cigarettes and some kind of cheap wine. "Didn't anyone ever tell you a lot of really nasty shit happens here?"

She is on her knees, and he is standing behind her. She heaves and tries to drive her left elbow up into his groin, but he sidesteps and takes the blow in the thigh. Then she feels the knife at her throat.

"On your belly!"

She thinks she knows the voice, even though it sounds ragged and hoarse, and she tries to get a look at his face. She thinks that if she can look him in the eyes, she can stop him. But he pinches her left earlobe between his fingers then rips her hoop earring from the flesh and rams her face into the dirt.

"Please!" she cries with a mouth full of grass and dirt.

"Please your fuckin' self! Don't move or I'll cut your throat, bitch!"

She hears a truck growling through the gears somewhere out on Hudson Street, coming uptown. The driver pounces the horn in traffic as she feels the knife scrape along under her chin and slide down to the middle of her throat. And she wonders if he has already cut her. She wants to rise up and scream to test her windpipe, but she lies still on her belly feeling the weight of his elbow driving into the small of her back.

'God help me,' she thinks.

"Let's see your hot little hiney," he says.

Then she feels the knife leave her throat for a second to slit the waistline of her tights and panties. Her thighs freeze as he pulls the torn clothes down around her ankles. Her knees knock against each other.

"Come on, please. You don't really want to do this," she pleads. Her fingers tear at each other against her belly. She keeps her eyes closed tight.

"It's not me, you faggot whore bitch," he says. I'd throw your sorry ass in the river. It's Herman, bitch. He loves you. He doesn't take no for an answer!"

Now she knows that voice and she cannot believe that he is the one who has come for her. Then she hears the truck horn again, sounding closer—probably at the Leroy Street intersection by now.

His cold arm girdles her bare waist, and he pulls his chest against her shoulder blades. She feels his hot mouth on the back of her neck, chewing the muscle at her hairline. And once again she tries to turn her face to him.

'If I kiss him, maybe he will stop,' she thinks.

"Herman wants it," he whispers in her right ear. "And he knows you want it too. You *do* want it, don't you? You love it. You always loved Herman. You used to wrap him in your hands, between your legs. He's hot for you, bitch. You've made him into a fuckin' hot rod. You want to be Herman's faggot whore, don't you? Don't you?"

He cackles to himself. She can feel his cold, coarse fingers rubbing across her back and legs, smelling the smoke of his breath. His beard grates against her left shoulder. A leg slides over hers.

The truck moans again. Just a block away. Engine chuffing. She pictures the cab swaying as it rumbles over the road construction at Barrow Street.

Now his heavy panting begins. She feels sweat or blood against her face and legs, the searing pain. God, fingers tearing and probing her rectum. Knife blade thrusting right up inside her nose.

"Come on, say it—you want to be Herman's faggot whore."

She'll say anything, but she can't get the words out.

Something slashes over her back like a cold whip or a lightning strike. An arm tightens around her waist. He's trying to ride her.

"You want to fuck? Say it. Fuck me!"

She tries again to say it, tries to buy herself some time to think, to plan her escape. But the air is leaving her lungs and she can't stop it. No words are coming. Her legs are ripping apart at their roots. Spine burning. Eyes opening. Knife dripping cherry red right alongside her nose. Truck rumbling past.

The cold whip slashes across her back again. She stretches for the truck in her mind. Trying to ride with it out from under the howling, the thrusting, the burning, and the lightning. The truck's brakes screech like a ferry whistle.

I imagine this was all that she remembered. Not her famous husband, not her beautiful daughters, not the lips of all the fishy boys who have loved her … not even the smell of those gardens or the taste of Cape Cod's ashes in her mouth. That truck's screech was all she had left when he suddenly rolled her onto her back and rammed a locust marlinspike through her chest with the sound of a table knife piercing a pumpkin.

2

Once, a long time ago, I was one of those fishy boys so desperate to taste the flesh of her salty neck. Even back then she was a phenomenon, more than just a sexy kid who grew up in a four-room flat over a fisherman's bar on the armpit of Cape Cod. She was Neptune de Oliveira's daughter, Celestina. Tina the Tease. The only child of a Cape Cod legend, who was the issue of the last of the old-time whalers. A hero who had finally come home from the sea stooped and gray, to keep bar and to father the closest thing Woods Hole ever had to a goddess.

That's who we buried four days ago in a chrome coffin. Tina, not Noelle Werlin. Not some fantasy queen of rock and roll. Neptune's daughter is the one who is lying down there on the churchyard hill next to the bones of the whaling captains, the Indians, and the gray-gowned Quaker ladies.

Zal called me in New York seven days ago about coming to Tina's funeral. I never thought I'd be catching up with my childhood buddy at a funeral. And who could have guessed that Zal would grow up to be Father Anthony Zalarelli, the rector at Our Lady of the Blessed Sacrament in Woods Hole. When we were growing up, he was hell on wheels.

He said he thought I ought to get out to the Cape for Tina's service. He didn't give me a lot of priestly guilt, he just said he needed me. He told me some people's lives may depend on my coming. When an old friend tells you something like that, you respond, even if you've been steering clear of the place like the plague for decades. And you know you owe this to Tina. You know that after all these years you have to finally say "so long." So I told my editor that I had a personal emergency and to get someone else on my sports column for a few days. And personally I'm at liberty, so to speak, since my wife Sukey packed up and moved out last winter.

My flight from La Guardia to Hyannis passes by in slow motion. The truth is that I keep imagining the murder. It's like watching a scene from a movie over and over again. Tina's murder is all over the TV and papers. If you're a beauty and married to a rock and roll legend like Butch Werlin when somebody murders you, you've got crowds of people to cry for you, your husband, and your teenage daughters. And the world tunes in when the *Today Show* and *Good Morning America* serve up details of how a morning dog walker found Tina's luscious body—nearly nude—with Z's carved all over her back like lightning bolts. All after just a few hours after her devoted husband turned up tweaked-out on high-grade nose candy at an East Village grunge club … with a pair of underage twins on his arms. Almost instantly Butch is in detox under suicide watch and about 70 million people think he killed her because Tina, Noelle, told him she wanted out … with the girls, the houses in St. Barts and Fire Island, and 50 percent of his Pepsi and Calvin Klein deals.

Zal meets me at the Hyannis airport just before dusk. He's not your typical priest. He reminds me of Richard Gere. It's the face, the salt-and-pepper hair, and that pampered look Gere had in *Pretty Woman*. And Zal drives that Saab like it's an Indy car so he has us from the airport to Woods Hole in twenty-five minutes flat. We don't go to the rectory or my parents' house where I'm staying. We drive out on the road to Nobska Lighthouse.

Vineyard Sound looks just as swollen and black as I

remember it in all those other Octobers of my dreams. When Zal gets to Woods Hole he turns down toward the Steamship Authority docks and the Eel Pond drawbridge where the fishermen's bars still look the way they did when we were underage kids drinking. In the dark, the old port seems pretty much the way it did when Zal and I left for college. But he says I wouldn't recognize the place at the height of summer when it's packed with vacationers visiting the aquarium, touring the science labs, and catching ferries for the islands.

The name Woods Hole gives you no clue to our town's character. The town has no class identity like Osterville where a lot of the Boston blue bloods live, golf, and go yachting together. Today, the Hole doesn't even seem to have a clear ethnic or racial soul. The railroad left back in the spring of 1965 when I was a junior in high school. Sam Cahoon's fish pier and market closed the next year. And now almost all of the old draggermen are retired or drowned. Most of the fish boats have gone to New Bedford. These days, people just think of Woods Hole as the place with the oceanographic institutions, or the place you catch the ferry to the Vineyard. A jumping off place, a suburb of Falmouth.

But here's the truth. Forty years ago plenty of second-generation Portuguese and Italian immigrants—even a few of us Irish—fished on day boats out of this port and raised families in the little houses clustered north of Eel Pond. These same houses that I hear the summer folk are now buying for more than a half a million. When I was a kid, my uncles and my father all worked on the draggers. They told me we had some of the best banks and holes for yellowtail, scup, and striper fishing in the world right out there in Vineyard Sound between the Elizabeth Islands and the Vineyard. You could get rich on the fish out there. "Catching fish is a holy obligation," they said. "Not a job."

But I don't think when we were young that my friends and I had the same ties to the water as our parents or grandparents had. They were real fishermen like my old man, Skipper Wade; we were just fishers' kids. We had dreams of a different kind of life from working on boats, raising a family, and going to Mass on Saturday night. Woods Hole was a great place to grow up when we were little, but when we were teenagers there was a war brewing in Southeast Asia and in our souls. Or maybe it was just all about sex. Or maybe something I can't even put a finger on. Who knows? But whatever lit the fire in our bellies, we thought we had to turn this little water town upside down … or get the hell out of here like Tina.

When we circle back toward the village, Zal swerves off the road into a dark parking lot. A second later, the engine dies. Zal reaches down to the floor between his legs and produces two cans of Miller from a bag. He cracks one open and hands it to me. Then he opens one for himself.

"So how are you doing, Bagger?" he asks.

Bagger. Shit. I haven't heard that name since we were teenagers. Bagger, Bags, the fucking crazy Bagman. He just isn't me anymore. He is like some kid I knew once in a nightmare … and who could just as well stay buried. I thought Zal knew me well enough to let the past alone. We're adults now, right? But I guess it's still not easy for us to act our age around each other for long. So how am I doing?

"Fair to shitty."

I give it to him straight. Things were kind of rocky for a while after Sukey moved out last year. I curled up with a bottle of Stoli for a few months … until a stomach ulcer went pop and landed me in the hospital. That was a turning point. When I got out, I started hitting the gym hard. Boxing again, well actually, just working out on the bags, jumping rope, and running.

Three hours a day, rain or shine. Did a 10-K race a few weeks ago in less than thirty-seven minutes. Sticking to the occasional beer or two. That's all. I get by. I started dating a bit. Nothing serious. The assistant travel editor. We're friends. She's more like a sister, but we don't need to get into that. So was Sukey, to tell the truth. You can't really blame her for walking out. With work and sports, I never have much time for romance. Maybe I am one of those guys women just can't stand.

"I know some people who would beg to differ, Bags."

"Like …"

"Neptune's daughter."

He nods out the window to a shadowy building across the street. Neptune's Bar stands waiting for the next wave of migrants to arrive off a ferryboat. Neon beer signs glow from a couple small windows. I can feel the faint pulse of the bass from the jukebox, and I remember the days when Tina had dragged me to her parents' apartment over the bar. After all these years, I still have Tina—and maybe the rest of this town—under my skin. Zal and I finish our six-pack in silence.

At my parents' house, in my old bed in the room that my mother has not changed since I left for college, there is a 5 x 7 color picture of Tina among a dozen black-and-white year-book photos of my friends that I had tucked between the mirror and its frame on my dresser. In her picture, Tina's long, dark hair hangs in a sheet over her left shoulder and falls below her heart. Her skin has the silvery paleness of milk that seems out of place with her arched brows, enormous brown eyes, and the red lips of a mouth that look too big for her fine face. Back in the days when this picture was taken, everybody, including Tina, thought she was a ringer for Cher. You can see that Tina was playing with the Cher look in this picture with her low-cut, gold peasant blouse, enormous hoop ear-rings, and a smile that says, "I dare you."

In the bottom right corner of the picture, Tina had written an inscription, "Keep the faith, Bagman! Love and roses from NYC. Your new Noelle. Dancing up a storm. 1966."

She had sent the picture to me during the spring of my senior year in high school. It had come without any letter. Tina left for the city in July after eleventh grade, the summer her parents split up. She had told people she had some kind of summer scholarship for modern dance ... but she never came back to Woods Hole. Later, I found out that a lot of guys in town got one of those pictures. I guess she wanted us all to know that she had a new name and a new life. One of her old boyfriends said that the picture meant Tina hadn't really left us. She had just gone to a different dimension. He said part of her was always in Woods Hole, and maybe he was right.

3

Tina and I are walking the three miles home from school to Woods Hole along the old Cape Cod railroad tracks. It snowed about three inches during the day, but now a warm sea breeze is beginning to turn the snow to slush, the way it almost always does on the Cape even as the snow squalls continue to come and go. Tina's holding onto my waist with her thumb hitched through a belt loop on my pants. My arm curls inside her rabbit coat, feeling the easy curves of her hip. She's my girl now.

Today she sent me a note in history class: "My dad is working, and mom's gone to Hyannis. Come home with me today. I want to give you your Valentine's present." She signed the note with a clutch of X's and O's and soaked the whole affair in perfume.

After school we walked to Falmouth Village so I could stop at a market to buy her a rose. We have been going steady for a little over a month. Tina is so pretty and confident; she can have anyone. But she just kind of latched on to me at the all-night teen dance on New Year's Eve at Blessed Sacrament.

"I pick you, Bags. You're the one," she said as she asked me to dance during a Lady's Choice.

My jaw must have dropped as about a hundred questions began to fill my mind.

"Don't ask, don't bring up the past, I swear." she added. "Just dance with me. I need you."

By the time we reach the end of the rail line and the

wharves for the ferries to Nantucket and the Vineyard, my guts are twisting in anticipation for what's to come next in that apartment over the dark bar by the docks. Turning the corner around a break of trees with the bar coming into view, Tina suddenly stops. Standing on the corner in front of Neptune's Bar are two hazy figures—one kind of big and gorilla-looking, the other one smaller. Maybe men, but maybe kids. The street is a swirl of snow.

"Bastards!" Tina spits. "That asshole and his goon are following us. He thinks he owns me!"

Of course, this is nothing new. Guys are always following Tina around. She has this effect on males. And she leaves the proverbial trail of broken hearts in her wake.

"You better wait here for five minutes. Go around the block and come up the back steps to the kitchen."

Seconds later, she disappears behind a curtain of large snowflakes that are just beginning to fall.

I glance at my Timex. Already four o'clock. Up the road, I can see that a few streetlights have come on in Woods Hole Village, and as I squint my eyes against the snow I think I can just make out the silhouettes of two figures leaning against a parked car. But by the time I get to Tina's back steps, no one, not even those two guys waiting out front, can see me in the blizzard.

Neptune's Daughter is so unpredictable I don't know what to expect next. She might treat me to a show of her mother's collection from Frederick's of Hollywood or sit me down to a candlelight dinner with music by Johnny Mathis. During the course of going steady she has promised me both of these things, but who knows what she has in mind. Sometimes I get the feeling that she just kind of makes up her life as she goes along. "Play it as it lays, Bagman," she's always saying. Maybe that's why I like her; absolutely nothing seems to phase her. She also has a body that won't quit … and style. I could kiss off a season of football for such a girl.

By the time I climb the back steps to Tina's apartment the

snow is coming down so heavily that my hair is soaked. The foghorn at Nobska Lighthouse bleats with shrill urgency.

"Fast," she calls, the door creaking open and slamming behind me.

"Poor baby, you're freezing," she says as she hugs me. Her eyes dart around the kitchen, which is lit only by a red light glowing from the top of the stove.

"Here," grabbing a dishtowel from the back of a chair. "For your head."

Almost within the same motion she hands me a jelly glass full of dark liquid. "Drink, for your soul. It's blessed."

Setting my books down, I swallow something that tastes like a cross between the wine they serve at Mass and cough syrup.

"Mano-Manischewitz," she says imitating the radio commercial. "Jewish wine. Blessed by rabbis, did you know that? My mother says it's good for what ails you. What ails you, pretty boy?"

Taking the towel from my hand, Tina ruffles it with both hands over my scalp. Then hooking it behind my neck, she pulls me in for a kiss. Even after more than a month of this kind of playing around, Tina sometimes strikes me like a lightning bolt.

From the small living room drifts the sound of music. Bobby Freeman is singing, "Do You Want to Dance?"

Nothing seems more natural than to kick off my shoes, put my hands together against the small of my girl's back, and begin shuffling to the music.

A couple more songs come and go on the phonograph while we dance and finish two glasses of wine. Finally, we topple on the couch.

Instantly we are tugging at each other's belts and shirt-tails. In the time it takes Gene Chandler to sing "The Duke of Earl," I succeed in ripping holes in both of Tina's red stockings as I free them from the snaps on her girdle and pop a button while undoing her blouse. The zipper on my fly seems stuck at half-mast, and somehow the sleeve of my sweater tears open at the seam as Tina pulls it over my head. All of the change in my pocket is falling out onto the floor and I fear—though I'm not sure—that I just swallowed one of Tina's heart-shaped earrings.

"Stop!" she shouts, her voice sounding raw.

She pushes me off the couch and onto the floor, stripped to my Jockeys and feeling a draft on my chest and legs.

Tina sits up on the couch and looks around as if she has just come out of suspended animation. Her hair is swirled around her head in a bush. All she's wearing from the waist up is a pink scarf around her neck.

For a second she just stares vacantly at the clothes scattered across the floor. I think she's angry with me, and I wait for all hell to break loose.

"I forgot to give you your Valentine! Don't move."

Tina leaps up and sprints across the room. Her silvery girdle flashing as it streaks between shadows. A second later she disappears behind a door.

For a minute or two I sit on the floor where I've fallen. The winking lights on the bar's sign hanging outside the front window dapple the rug and my bare legs in pools of red and green, and I wonder how long I have to sit here feeling like a statue in a Christmas display before my erection will lie down and let me put some clothes on.

When I finally slip into my pants and shirt, a strange buzzing sound catches my attention—an annoying pitched whine. At first I think it's the refrigerator, but the sound seems to be coming from somewhere near me. Then I think it's the buzzing of electricity through the lights on the bar sign; but the sound is coming from lower down in the room—maybe under the couch, and it's beginning to make my ears ache. I have to stop it.

Down on my knees peering beside the corner of the couch,

I find the culprit under Tina's skirt. In our frenzy to disrobe we knocked a plastic Westclock off an end table. The clock shudders in its death throws as if its alarm has frozen "on." I yank the plug out of the wall. Shit. It's late. My parents are expecting me home right now. I have to get out of here. I picture Tina's ex-boyfriend and his buddy smoking outside. Just waiting for me.

Suddenly, a toilet flushes and I hear a door unlatch.

"Close your eyes," Tina commands.

I close my eyes and sit back on the couch with my shirt half buttoned. Then I open my eyes. Tina is standing in the middle of the room. Her hair is combed back like a black mane. She's wearing nothing but a burgundy v-neck sweater that ends a quarter of the way down her thighs.

Her hips bounce to a slow rhythm as she moves toward me.

Tina straddles my lap, rises on her knees, and kisses me. Her lips drip with Manischewitz. The heavy scent of Jade perfume stings my sinuses.

"Happy Valentine's Day." Her tongue probes my ear. "How do you like your present?"

Backing away from our embrace, she sits on my knees with her hands on her waist, shoulders back at attention, head cocked to the right, chin raised—modeling.

"I love this sweater. You'll be irresistible. Feel. It's cashmere."

I press my face against the soft sweater and the softer breasts.

"Come to bed, and take it off me."

Sliding to her feet, she takes my hand. I follow like a blind boy.

She's leading me down a short hallway past the doorways to the bathroom and a small room dominated by a canopy bed and stuffed animals. Then we enter a room that is so dark that all I can see from the wink of the red and green lights on the bar sign is a giant unmade bed and—beyond it—a makeup table with a large circular mirror. The place smells of cigarettes and a musty odor that reminds me faintly of my grandfather's garage where he had once kept a horse and buggy. This must be her parents' room.

We grab each other and fall onto the bed. I slip the cashmere over Tina's head and squirm out of everything but my shirt. During a long kiss that wanders all the way down my chest, Tina pulls me up on my haunches facing her and peels the shirt off my back.

Over her shoulder, I see us in the mirror above the vanity. We are hazy shapes, and the distortions of the light and the mirror make us seem strange. The breast I'm tracing with my fingers has none of the booby weight I have seen in *Playboy*; Tina's chest has the same easy curves as her neck and back. My own arms and legs look thin and shiny, reminding me of a picture my father had snapped of me when I was eight or nine after swimming at Tarpaulin Cove. When we embrace, I see two wrestlers locked and struggling for a take down.

"Holy Mary, Mother of God, forgive me," gasps Tina. She pants against my neck and fiddles with something on the floor. "Put this on."

I bury my face in her neck and hair. Her hand guides my fingers to the floor beside the bed into some kind of can filled with a thick greasy substance. I understand she wants me to slather my penis with it. We kiss again, roll supine, and plow each other with our knees … while I try to paint myself with the grease. Jesus, it looks like this is it—the dirty deed. Now. In an adult bed and everything. A clarinet moans on the phonograph.

"Hurry."

Tina's thighs feel stiff and trembling, and for a second I wonder if she really means what she says. But then I hear my body screaming to get on with it. I fumble with the grease, wondering where to wipe the excess. Something is wrong. Am I doing this right?

"Pleeeeaassse. Hurry. What if my mother …"

Suddenly Tina slides away. I open my eyes and see that

she is up on her knees and elbows in front of me, looking like some kind of beast with her sweet toosh almost in my face.

One arm reaches back for me, fingernails clawing at my neck and shoulders.

"Come on …" Her voice low and wild.

I put my arm around her waist, knowing she wants me to mount her like a dog. I curl over top of her back, feel for her, and try to enter a place I can barely imagine."

"Nooo!"

Tina grabs at my privates. I feel her nails cutting me. Her head is tucked between her arms. She forces her ass back against my loins. Her hand jams me against her anus.

"More!" She has my hand in the can again.

I smear us with grease. A ferryboat's horn bellows from the wharves. I think I smell smoke.

"Fuck me."

There's a tremendous push. From her, from us. Then her anus swallows me. The air rushes out of my lungs. Something snaps in my head.

"Don't hurt me!" I shout.

Tina bolts upright with a wide-eyed, vicious look on her face, "What the hell?"

I peer down. In my left hand lay the remains of a can of *Crisco*.

For maybe four or five seconds I just kind of look at this thing in my hand, and then something begins rising in my throat. I can't stop it. I lie back on the bed. My body collapses in silent sobs.

Over the sound of the phonograph, I hear the rumble of a ferry getting underway and bells ringing from a pinball machine downstairs in the bar.

"You're pathetic. You know that?" cuts Tina as she moves to the edge of the bed, puts her feet on the floor, and begins pushing the hair out of her eyes.

I don't know why, but suddenly I need to prove something

to her. I want to hurt her. My hands latch onto her collarbones. They are so thin and long; they feel like they could snap if I just closed my fingers around them a little tighter.

"Let go. You're pinching me."

I hang on, and touch my lips to the back of her neck. My mouth opens. She lets out a deep sigh.

"Bite me."

So ... she wants it too. Pain and destruction. My teeth are against her neck, and I start to suck the blood to the surface of the skin. I feel like I'm eating her, and as I feed I wonder what sick person has ever called this act a love bite. She starts to moan or cry. Then the door bangs open and footsteps start up Tina's front stairs. Both of us bolt upright. The footsteps stop. Tina grabs a clock on the nightstand and gasps. Six-twenty.

"Someone's coming."

Christ. I'm wicked late for dinner. My father is probably driving all over town looking for me.

"Fuck you, bitch," shouts a hoarse voice from the stairs.

Something hard smashes against the apartment door and shatters into pieces that ricochet around the hall. Tina's eyes are as big as half-dollars.

"Go, jesus, please just go. He'll do something awful! She's made him mad again."

"Fucking whore of a wife," screams her father.

More glass shatters against the door with the distinct pop you get from a Coke bottle, a beer, or something igniting. In what seems like one gesture I tug on my shirt, pants, coat, and scoop up my shoes. Ten seconds later I'm racing down the back stairs. The cold, new snow feels good against my bare feet ... until I realize that I have left behind two sweaters, three textbooks, and my watch alongside a Valentine's rose. Damn her. Damn me.

4

I've learned not to relish homecomings. It's not that Woods Hole is a bad place. It's not. In fact, if I were a visiting scientist or traveler passing through, the town with its boats, harbors, laboratories, quaint houses, and hip restaurants would probably charm my socks off. And maybe if I had never left, I'd still feel a connection to the people and places, a bond that is as basic and essential as the air I breathe. But for me, coming back after long periods of time away, it always seems as if the things I wish would stay the same in Woods Hole have changed, and the things I wish would change have remained the same. Whatever.

Zal picked me up from my parents and we again sat and shared a few beers. Then Zal drove us two blocks down Water Street and pulled up right in front of Blackbeard's. It's a bar in an old frame, gray-shingle fish house on stilts built out over Eel Pond. The red and gold Narragansett beer sign is still glowing in the window just like thirty years ago, even though the brewery has been out of business for decades. Instinctively, I look across the pond to see if I can spot my father's tidy little dragger at the dock on the far side. But all I see are bass boats and sailboats bobbing at their moorings. The old man had retired and sold the *Ellen B* a decade ago.

"What's this?" I ask Zal.

Zal slides out of the Saab and pulls on a black leather bomber. I'm still struck that in a million years you wouldn't think this guy is a priest unless you saw him in those white robes, waving incense.

"Auld lange syne, Bagger."

I follow Zal into Blackbeard's. Hardly anything's changed. Same bowling machine, same potato chip rack, same old Blackie behind the bar. Thirty years ago, Blackie looked like Walter Brennan, when seven-ounce drafts were five for a buck. He looks just the same. He wobbles down to the end of the bar by a tray of stuffed quahogs and thrusts out a hand of bone and boot leather.

"Billy Bagwell, you're the spittin' image of your grand-father," says Blackie with that bullfrog voice of his. "Got some men here like to see you."

Down the bar, in the gloom from the Christmas lights that have been twinkling around the bar since Blackie bought it in the fifties, sit the shadows of three guys I half recognize.

"Bottom's up, Bagman," says a balding, red-haired ape, spinning on his stool and thrusting pony glasses of draft in Zal's and my hands.

I know I am supposed to know this fat, smiling Irish face, but my mind is coming up empty when the giant claps an arm around me and pulls my body against his sumo wrestler's gut.

"Curly Sullivan," his voice chuffs. "I'm a cop now. I work for this chump, can you believe it?"

When Curly releases me from the hug, I find myself face-to-face with a black guy in a blue blazer and gray flannel pants. He has a tight, hard body and a smooth face like Denzel Washington. Except for the threads of gray in his hair, Reggie Jones looks almost exactly as he had when he and I shared the running back slot for the Clippers.

"Midnight's the fucking mayor of this joint," hoots Curly, and I take it that by "joint" he means the entire town of Falmouth, which includes about six villages like Woods Hole as well as Falmouth Center.

"I'm still doing the blocking for him."

"And he's still talking white-trash, dumb-honky bullshit like he never grew up. How you doin', Bags? My man's still working out; I can see that. Looking like the Marlboro man in those boots and jeans."

Reggie gives me a wink as we shake hands fist to fist.

"The bagman's always been the cowboy in the group," says a voice from behind Reggie's back. "One time he tried to fuckin' ride the bow of my bass boat like it was a goddamn bronco. You were one wild-ass piece of work, Bagger."

Sometime over the last thirty years, Rollo had shed his baby face and about thirty pounds of lard. Now he has the hollow-cheeked, dark-eyed look of a drinker. He wears a brown toupee and a tight, olive v-necked sweater that makes him seem like one of those guys who takes toll money on the turnpike. When he hugs me, his sweater stinks of mothballs. Even when I hear Rollo's voice, he seems like someone I have never really known, someone I never want to know.

Rollo grabs a fresh pitcher of beer from Blackie and motions us to seats around the table where we had our Thursday night blackjack games after evening football practice during high school. I had lost a pile of money in this place.

"To Tina," says Rollo raising his glass. "One of a kind. She loved us all in her own way. But she just never loved anything forever!"

"She broke a lot of hearts," sighs Curly.

"Amen," says Zal.

We drink a toast to the foxy Portagee kid who in her seasons made a lot of boys think they knew what it meant to be men. And left them feeling like seagull shit and wanting to smash things up.

"She fuck you, too, Reggie?" Rollo asks after we drain our glasses.

He gives a sloppy laugh.

Reggie flashes Rollo one of those 'Fuck you and your white-ass slut' looks, which means, 'I don't have to answer that!'

Then he rubs his eye sockets for several seconds like he is trying to shake a bad dream. In high school the white girls had been all over Reggie like stripers on an eel. A lot of girls called him "The Snake" for reasons that weren't hard to guess at. They knew, or had heard, what he kept coiled in his pants. You think Tina was any different? But those were different times, and the black ram tapped his white ewes behind closed doors, so to speak, on the dirt roads leading into the Sippiwissett woods. The Snake had his secrets; you could bet on it.

Finally, Reggie clears his throat and speaks.

"I'll get to the point, Bagger. There's something funny about the way Tina de Oliveira died. We've got a hunch that Butch Werlin didn't kill her. We think the killer's someone from around here … someone who grew up on the Cape. Someone with an old grudge to settle. And we don't think he's finished, if you get my meaning."

ψ ψ ψ ψ ψ

Since ninth grade, Tina has pretty much been a loner. She doesn't go to the movies at the Elizabeth Theater in Falmouth with girlfriends or on dates anymore, and she doesn't hang out in front of the Community Center or at the drawbridge with a lot of the other kids, not even on dance nights. But she makes guest appearances as if to mark her territory before moving out into her own dark world.

On this hot, spring night, the drawbridge—where most of us Woods Hole's teens hang out on weekend evenings—is filled with about a dozen girls in pleated skirts and guys in madras shirts and pegged chinos. Kids milling around, flirting, leaning against parked cars, and listening to the sweet sounds pouring from the radio in Rollo's faded-gray '48 Dodge.

"I love this song. Rollo, turn it up!" Tina calls from across the bridge, as the song "Being with You" plays across the air-waves.

During the past two years in Woods Hole, Tina's rep has developed a life of its own. Behind her back boys call her "Lady Godiva" after a popular song about a stripper, and the caddy girls in school call her "The PC," short for "The Pin Cushion" because she's had so many pricks stuck in her. And, as she has been since ninth grade, she remains the Shade Queen, Tina the Tease. She knows what we call her, and at least she pretends not to care. She even seems to enjoy adding new fuel to the fire that burns all around her. And this spring of our tenth-grade year, she's been setting off alarms all over the Upper Cape.

Before I even look, I know Tina is making her way across the bridge. The moans of pleasure tumbling out of Rollo's mouth, Curly's whistle, and Zal's "shit" are all I need to hear. Walking right up the middle of the street is Tina, taking slow, hip-swiveling playgirl steps, wearing a little lavender cotton dress with spaghetti shoulder straps. It looks like something she should be wearing to bed. No bra, no panty line. And her deep-red, low-heeled pumps make her legs seem about six feet long.

The smile on her face radiates pure self-absorbed pleasure, which seems to grow with each lick from her scoop of vanilla ice cream that she must have picked up at the frappe stand near the landing. And that smile is spreading to all of us like some kind of magic light. By the time she reaches us, we are all grinning. Even the other girls are smiling, the ones who bad-mouth her.

That's the thing about Tina that you can't ignore. She comes on like some kind of siren, but it isn't her sultriness alone that brings us to our knees. It's that smile, too. The way she tilts her head slightly, gives you a sideways glance, and cracks a cockeyed grin. Tina always smiles at you like she is recalling a delicious secret known just to the two of you. A secret in which she remembers you as daring, brave, clever, and—most of all—irresistible. In school we read *The Great Gatsby*, and I'll never forget reading about Gatsby's smile. A smile full of romantic readiness, an extraordinary capacity for hope. A smile that promises it sees you just the way you see yourself in your sunniest dreams. 'That's Tina's smile,' I thought. And so Tina is wed forever in my mind to Gatsby. Both larger than life, both magnificent imposters.

Walking right into the clutch of guys lounging around the outside of Rollo's Dodge, Tina gives Curly's belly a pat, slaps Zal on the butt, and then walks right up to me until we are almost nose to nose, the scent of Jade filling my head.

"Hey, cutie."

Rocking me with her smile, Tina's fingers run through the curls over my ear. Then twirling away, she moves over to plant a sloppy kiss on Rollo's cheek.

"Come on, stud!" her voice suddenly sounding desperate as she throws herself into the front seat of the Dodge and cranks the tunes. Seconds later the loving couple rumbles out of sight up Woods Hole Road, already locked together into a single twisted silhouette behind an enormous steering wheel.

"Rollo's gonna get some poon tang tonight," says Curly licking his lips.

"Tell me something new," I say.

Zal looks disgusted. "Let's go drown our sorrows," he says, flashing a pint bottle of Jim Beam he had stashed in the pocket of his cardigan.

The thought of drinking almost makes me ill. I lie and say I have to help my father mend his net on the Ellen B. I want nothing more than to go to the fish pier and climb aboard the old green, Eastern-rig dragger.

At this time of night, even the old black ladies who come down to the pier with their poles and bait buckets to fish for scup have gone home. The fish pier feels like the loneliest place in Woods Hole. Sometimes I just like sitting in the wheel house of the boat, listening to the whir of the wind, inhaling the scent of the bait from lobster boats, watching the foggy darkness settle over Devil's Foot Island, and thinking about nothing at all. I feel safe, like no one can touch me here. Besides, if I wait long enough, Tina will probably show up if she's running true to form. And something in me always needs to know she still has control over her night.

It's a little after nine o'clock when I see Rollo's Dodge veer onto the wharf and drop off Tina. Who knows what excuse she gave him for bringing her here tonight. Maybe she told him she didn't want to be dropped off in the center of the village where lots of prying eyes and wagging tongues could work up new versions of the saga of Tina the Tease. Whatever. Rollo played along. He's had his screwing for the night. His Tina fix. He feels like a god, so he lets her go to the fish pier and the night and me.

She walks down to the end of the pier, sits down on the edge, dangles her feet over the side, and casts broken clamshells dropped on the pier by the gulls into the harbor. Once or twice she looks back over her shoulder and stares at the wheelhouse of the *Ellen B*, as if she knows I am there and watching. Then she holds her head in her hands as if trying to press away the pain of a killer headache. Part of me wants to go to her and comfort her. But I don't. There is something so profound about her solitude and her pain. It has a weird kind of beauty that makes me just want to keep watching.

A half hour passes and another car comes rolling onto the wharf. It's the gold Plymouth Valiant that belongs to Reggie Jones, and it has its headlights off. As soon as Tina hears the car, her head perks up. The dark car drives right down to the end of the pier to her. She gets in without a word, closes the door silently, and rides away into the night again. This is a new twist. On other nights it has been different cars—cars of fishermen, cars of guys who are long gone from high school. And now Reggie. Whew. So Tina is crossing the color line. Or maybe not. Her old man has the mocha-colored skin common to a lot of Portagees whose roots go back to the Cape Verde Islands and Africa. But her mother is lily white. I haven't really thought about this before.

The first time I saw Tina going with guys like this to cheat on Rollo, I was almost petrified with fear for her. I wanted to pull the horn cord in the *Ellen B* and send Tina and her toys fleeing in shame. Good god, this is how girls get themselves killed.

Once I told her that I'd seen her leaving the fish pier in a strange car.

"We all do what we have to do, Bagger; play it as it lays." she said. "Please don't tell Rollo." She squeezed my hand the way she always does when she wants to thank you for something and can't find the words.

So … I keep watch out for her. These fish pier rendezvous of Tina's never last longer than a drive up the road to the Sippiwissett woods and back. Just long enough to drink a can of beer and give a blow job. When she comes back, she walks down the pier until she finds a water hose. She turns on the water, washes her face, and brushes her teeth with a toothbrush that she carries in a little rhinestone clutch purse. Sometimes she gives a little smile in the direction of the *Ellen B*. Then she walks home, a shadow among shadows, a click of heels on the wharf. Then I can go home too.

But tonight after leaving Reggie's car, she does something unusual. She stands at the head of the wharf holding her head again as if it is going to explode. And instead of washing up, she walks down to the rocky little beach beside the pier. I can't see her anymore, but I hear the scraping of a small boat on the rocks, then the creak of oars in thole pins. I move to the other side of the Ellen B for a better look. All I can see is the shadow of a dory pulling off across the harbor toward

Devil's Foot Island or one of the houseboats moored nearby.

'Stop,' I scream. But the shout is only in my mind, and maybe I am already too late to save her. Anyway, I follow her counsel. I play it as it lays.

I am a fool. And so is she. The evidence is as plain as the fat, cracked lip and black eye that Tina has when she returns to school that Thursday.

Ψ Ψ Ψ Ψ Ψ

"You're the man, Bagger. We think maybe you can help us find the killer before he does somebody else," says Curly.

I must have given that look Sukey used to call my *Twilight Zone* face. It creeps over me like shivers or guilt when something terrible has happened … even when I have no clue.

"Look, Bags, there's no easy way to say this," begins Zal. He puts his hand over the sleeve of my old, tweed sport coat and wraps his fingers gently around my forearm. "A long time ago back in school, a lot of rumors went around about all of us. Most of it exaggeration or pure fantasy. But anyway, you had some rough years, especially after eighth grade. You were caught up in a lot of crazy, violent stuff. Kids said a lot of ridiculous things back then. But there was a story going round that everybody believed like fact. We had all heard a story about how someone almost killed you one time when you were surf fishing down by Oyster Pond. You never said anything to anybody about it … but kids just thought that whatever happened to you had twisted up your insides for awhile and made you—well—wild."

"That's absurd. Almost killed? Fishing? No way. Everybody was wild back then. That's just how it was. Don't you remember? We did crazy things."

"Right. But for you it was something different."

Rollo seemed to be stifling a smug little smile as he refilled my beer glass. The little prick. Like he had been some kind of angel when we were kids.

"This is important, Bagger. Just have some beer and think about it," coaxes Curly. "Look, you think I give a fart in a jar about what's happened to Tina after the shit she pulled on me back in high school. Crazy, lyin', sorry-ass wench. Hell no. Good riddance to bad garbage."

Like hell he didn't care. I can't remember what grade it was, but Tina had stood Curly up on prom night. Just sort of disappeared on the night he came to pick her up. I can picture it ... Curly standing on the street outside Neptune's Bar for half the night, holding a $30 corsage, and watching the ferryboats come and go from the Vineyard in the fog. Classic Tina. Just classic.

"Bags, see this ain't about Tina exactly; we got us a real problem here. And it ain't over if you want my best guess. Other people are going to get hurt. We need you. See, Rollo came to me with this story about how someone supposedly killed his dog—with a marlinspike—on a hunting trip you all made to Nomans. Zal was there, but he can't really help us with the details. Rollo says you were the only one except Smitty to have seen everything, and—you know—Smitty got it in Nam."

I drank my beer. It's weird. I had forgotten that Smitty had been killed in Vietnam.

"What's this all have to do with how Tina died?"

"We don't know for sure," says Reggie.

"Take your time." Zal squeezes my arm again. "We've got nowhere to go."

Rollo pours us all another beer and orders a pitcher from Blackie. Then he seems to eye me with that smug little secret smile again. He pushes his beer glass back and forth between his fingers like a hockey puck. A stony silence settles over the table. Curly makes a ritual of lighting his panatela. Zal lounges back in his chair with his legs stretched out straight and his hands folded in his lap; he stares intently at his knees. Reggie leans on the table with both elbows and props his chin in his hands. His left thumb and index finger tug at his upper lip.

Finally, Zal speaks. "I always wondered what happened between you and Freddy Farnham that night at the drive-in, Bags. I heard the rumors, but I never asked. I guess I didn't want to know if you were the one that beat on him and sliced him up."

"To tell the truth, I pretty much believed Danny Sider," coughs Curly. "Danny told everyone you jacked up Freddy, and he deserved it. But I never held it against you. I know we're supposed to be tolerant of gays and all, but maybe it's my upbringing or the church that makes me feel sick when I think about what they do with people's bodies. If Freddy touched you, that's something else. No respect. A guy does that kind of thing, he gets it back in the face. In spades. No offense, Midnight. I figure those old cops like Bullet Bob thought the same way, that's how come nobody ever made a case of it, you know? Like you did what you had to do, Bags."

"Tina said you did it," says Rollo. "Right after Freddy went to the hospital, she told me that anything to do with sex made you all crazy inside. But, hey, who was she to talk? Hell if I ever even connected the story about all of those marks they say you carved on Freddy's back with what you said happened to my dog. Or how Tina just got her ass staked out with a marlinspike in New York City. Never crossed my mind. Didn't even think about it until Curly and I were talkin' in here a few nights ago after we heard about Tina's murder."

Suddenly, I think I see what's going on, why all these guys who aren't much more than ghosts from somebody else's past have turned out at Blackbeard's to welcome me home and coax a couple of stories out of me. Freaking Rollo has fingered me, and now the rest of the posse is lining up behind him to make me the fall guy for their own sins.

"You bastards are setting me up. You brought me here to try

lynching me for Tina's death and all that old-time shit. Well screw you, and thanks for the vote of confidence!"

"Whoa, man!" Reggie grabs me by the left biceps and holds me in my seat as I try to squirm to my feet. "You got it all wrong, Bags. Chill! Just mellow out. We're only trying to separate fact from fiction."

Zal fixes his eyes on mine and speaks.

"Maybe there's no connection, Bags, but those old stories put you at the scene of two attacks—Freddy's and Rollo's dog. And you have to admit there's a certain odd similarity to what happened to Tina in New York. When Curly came to me with a lot of questions about you, what you were up to in New York and those old rumors, I told him we had to give you a chance to tell your side of things before we took any of this information anywhere outside Woods Hole."

"You know, I'm not the only one here that lives with a cloud over his head when it comes to Tina and a lot of other stuff, Zal."

He blushes and stares at his hands in his lap.

"Things were plain crazy back then for all of us," says Curly.

"You can say that, again," sighs Reggie. "I remember one time a bunch of us got into some wild shit after football practice in eleventh grade."

Rollo pours us another round of drafts. Curly heaves a mean belch as Reggie begins his story that I guess is intended to break the ice. I remember that story too.

ψ ψ ψ ψ ψ

I have football fever like I have never had it before. This is our junior season at Falmouth's Lawrence High School, and over the summer I put on weight and muscle working on Skipper Wade's boat, dragging the Sound for scup from four in the morning to four in the evening. The work felt good. And while

I figure I am a ways from making the starting roster, I sense that I'll see action as a ballcarrier for the Clippers. It looks like Reggie Jones and I will trade off at the left halfback position.

Stripping out of my football pads after practice and heading for the showers at the other end of the locker room, the tiles start to echo with the words and melody of "He's so Fine."

This is not somebody blasting a transistor radio; this is real singing … and it sounds silky.

First, one tenor coos, "He's so fine …"

Then several voices cut in with the backup, "Doo lang, doo lang, doo lang."

"Wish he were mine."

"Doo lang, doo lang, doo lang."

Turning the corner on a row of lockers, I find a group of a dozen or more guys clustered in a circle. Some still wearing shoulder pads and jocks; others standing naked and wet, dangling towels; a third group wearing towels wrapped around their hips. Each swinging his eyes my way as the tenor sings, "That handsome boy over there; the one with the wavy hair …"

Fifteen feet away in front of the entrance to the showers, the singer stands sighting me down the length of a long black arm. With a towel wrapped around his head the way Tina does when she has just washed her hair, Reggie Jones stops me in my tracks.

Laughter is breaking out as Reggie crosses the circle toward me, with a stripper's bump and grind.

Three other black teammates in towel skirts sway together and click their fingers, "Doo lang, doo lang, doo lang."

"You know I'm really gonna do it," Reggie sings, backing me against a brace of lockers. His hips shimmy. His lips pout.

Hoots and shouts roar in my ears.

I feel my cheeks catch fire, but I'm laughing.

Reggie's funny … and almost close enough to kiss me.

He breaks into a smile, cocks an eyebrow, and leers at his audience as he sings, "You know I'm gonna make him—"

Wham. A locker slams behind me with a crash. Reggie's song stops like someone has thrown a switch on his voice. His eyes are bugging out, and he steps back a few paces. A wet towel snaps out and stings him twice on the belly.

"Hey!" he squeals, staring at the welts already beginning to rise. "Hey, man, what you think …"

"Take your faggot booolshit back down to niggertown," orders the pock-marked, pink body brushing past me into the middle of the circle. Chicky Boyle is swaying there in his sweat-soaked gym shorts like an immense hairless monkey. Without his thick glasses on, he squints so hard his lips curl back exposing the roots of his chipped front teeth. Chicky shakes a fist at Reggie.

"He was just foolin' around, Chicky," someone says.

"Be cool, honky chump," warns one of the black backup singers.

"It's okay. Reggie was just having a little fun," I say.

Chicky turns on me and gives me a look that says, 'Shut the fuck up.'

His chief suck-up, a squirt named Danny Sider, lets out a goofy laugh.

"Watch your mouth with that 'faggot, niggertown' shit, Chicky." Reggie points and shakes two fingers at Chicky, a frozen glaze settling into his eyes.

"Honky, camel-riding, goat-fucking, son-of-a-bitch," Reggie says to the crowd that is growing, and he smiles the smile of a little guy who can make a giant squirm.

For several seconds nobody says anything, then Chicky shifts his weight on his legs as if getting ready to spring.

"Bobby Kennedy is the greatest man alive today," says Chicky in a voice that has grown reverential and drops a register. "But he can't know we got pansy-ass, lying niggers like this one … or he wouldn't put up with all this Martin-Luther-

King-freedom-march booolshit."

The crowd grumbles. Chicky is really on the edge now. By bringing up Martin Luther King and the Labor Day march on Washington, he has tweaked everyone in the locker room. None of us are neutral regarding the racist stench, spewing across the country from places like Birmingham and Selma.

"Mr. Robert Kennedy don't know he got Irish cousins like Chicky putting the boots to Old Lady Seeley's nanny-goats down in the Sippiwissett woods!"

Chicky's mouth drops open. He looks ready to shit himself silly.

I almost laugh. Reggie says the craziest shit. He has a way of dreaming up the most humiliating images.

Across the circle stand Zal and Curly. They catch my eye, smile, and clinch their fists.

'Be ready,' says Zal's faint smile. 'Fight.'

Meanwhile, Reggie lays on more, "Some of us seen you bare-assed down there in the cattails. Crawling around on your knees with your cock plugged in … whispering shit into the flea-bitten ears of some shaggy, uncouth mother-fucking—"

"You're dead, Reggie!"

Before the phrase is out, Chicky sails across the fifteen feet of clear concrete floor and holds Reggie's neck in both hands.

A second later, three black guys cling to Chicky's back like dogs on a bear.

I press my back up against a set of lockers and watch the fur fly. More than a dozen players dive into the struggle … punching, kicking, yelling. The air fills with flying towels, pads, and helmets.

Suddenly from between two rows of lockers I see Danny Sider emerge, racing to Chicky's aid with a baseball bat he's picked out of someone's locker. I'm not thinking. It isn't some kind of moral decision against using weapons in a fight. Hell, I've used worse than a bat. This is something else. Like some kind of instinct that steams out of my belly and drives me forward on rails. I put my head down, charge, and tackle the little tool around the waist. We both groan with the hit. My face smashes against his hip blade, and I taste blood in my mouth. But I get him before he ever sees me coming, and the two of us slam onto the floor and slide into a wall just as a whistle sounds.

"Back off," barks Coach Bolino. Usually our coach looks bent and hobbling, a man near the end of his career. But now he seems to tower. Six-four. Two-forty. Shoulders thrusting back. A two-foot-long paddle—riddled with air holes—swinging from his hand.

"Chicky, you're first. And do *spare* us the pain of having to listen to anything more from your scum-bag mouth for the rest of the season. Up against the wall!"

While Chicky takes a half-dozen swats across his naked ass, the rest of us wait our turns. Reggie shrugs his shoulders and rolls his eyes at me like 'What the fuck?'

Ψ Ψ Ψ Ψ Ψ

"Did I miss the point?" Curly burps, after listening to Reggie's version of the story. It snaps me out of my own memory. "What the hell does a fight after football practice have to do with Tina's murder, Midnight?"

Reggie takes a deep breath and a swig of his beer.

"I don't know, Curly, maybe nothing. What the fuck do you think, Sherlock?"

Zal clears his throat, "We were all part of the general insanity back then. Bags doesn't need to feel alone in all of this. It was like some sickness we had. We thrived on violence. Pounding something until we saw blood—football, fights, even with each other."

Well, Zal has that part of the story right.

Ψ Ψ Ψ Ψ Ψ

On Friday we're going up against our rivals from Barnstable. Everyone in the high school is feeling electrified, and I am definitely with them. Each day of the week is planned with some new event to stir us up—pep-rallies, the Class Follies, a sock hop, and Bonfire Night. I know that if I have to pick one game to prove I can play football, this is the one. The more I run my pass patterns and practice adding timing and finesse to the plays when I block or carry the ball, the less people like Tina or even Zal seem to get tangled up in my mind. Game time.

When the final horn sounds I can barely remember the game. Reggie gives me a big hug, the backfield coach shakes my hand, and I hear the sound of Tina chanting my name from the stands.

Zal plays defense, and he had a great game too. He kept coming from his linebacker's position to torment the Barnstable's ballcarriers on almost every play. He's strong and fast. But what really unsettles me is the thoroughness with which he attacks his opponents. His tackles never stop until the man is lying like a lamb mauled by a wolf.

And I wonder if that lamb will soon be me, now that the season is ending. A few days ago, Zal's ceaseless teasing pissed me off so much that—perhaps stupidly—I challenged him to go one-on-one with me in the boxing ring. It seemed like a good idea at the time; I wanted Zal to back off, and I was feeling pretty cocky about everything I had learned during the last year of sparring with a pair of boxers named Daryl and Mugs.

But watching Zal tearing up the Barnstable ballcarriers made me think again. I wonder if Zal can be as vicious in the boxing ring as he is on the football field.

It's Saturday morning after the game, and I wake to the sound of Zal's voice outside my window.

"Up and at 'em, Bagman. The Gorgeous One is here to

measure the size of your balls!"

The next thing I hear is Zal entering through the side door without knocking.

"Good morning, Zal," my mother calls from the kitchen. This was her way of interjecting a little courtesy into Zal's casual familiarity with her house.

"Nice game, Mr. Zalarelli," calls my father from the breakfast table. He never goes out fishing on days after our games, probably because he hangs out at Neptune's with a bunch of the other fish boat captains from the time the game ends until closing.

"How about that Bagger? What a stud he was on the old gridiron yesterday."

My god, an honest compliment from Zal. I had to be dreaming.

"We are PROUD of our son," says my mother. "And glad that neither of you boys got hurt."

"Oh, that comes today. Your son challenged me to a little boxing match. I'm going to send him home in a body bag. Right, Bagman?"

Zal barges into my room and lays a wet-willie in my ear before I can even sit up in my bed or cover my head with a pillow.

"Fuck off!"

"Hey!" grumbles my father. "Watch you mouth."

"Sorry," Zal says as he takes aim on my right shoulder and drills it with three sturdy jabs. I'm still not out of bed. My body is suffering from some kind of hangover. Yesterday had been enough banging against boys for a while; I wanted to be with a girl.

"It's just a question of whose got more ..." Zal pauses, reconsidering his choice of words. "Grit—a question of whose got grit. Bagger thinks he does. We'll see. Where are the gloves, Palooka?"

"We need to find Daryl and borrow a couple pairs. But he's

probably not home today. I think he's going to Brockton for a bout."

"Your kid's backing out on me," Zal calls to my parents. "I think he's afraid. I think he's some kind of ... faggot."

"Your ass is grass," I say as I spring from my bed, stuffing a pillow in Zal's face, and slamming him against the sliding closet door. It snaps off its track, and the two of us fall down as it gives way.

"Goddamn it! Will you two deck monkeys go to a gym somewhere? And fix whatever it is you broke now!"

My mother pokes her head into my room. I have Zal pinned to the ground on his back and I'm pounding his chest with punches.

"You boys better clear out. The Skipper is ready to blow!"

Two minutes later I'm dressed and out the door. I hate leaving home like this with my parents in a fuss. One of these days I have to make peace with them. I promise myself that as soon as we get this boxing business over, I'll try to patch things up with mom and dad. Hell, I'll skip school and help Skipper Wade on the *Ellen B*. Jesus, I have a lot of things and people tugging at me.

"Snap out of it, Bagman; have you been listening to me or what?" Zal hangs up the phone in the booth near the Eel Pond drawbridge.

"Hell no," I didn't even remember the walk here to the bridge ... let alone who he was calling on the phone.

"Look, Captain Video, your buddies Mugs and Daryl said they will be working out at the high school gym today. I told them we would meet them there in an hour or so to borrow the gloves. So ... you ready to kiss a little cowhide?"

"You might be surprised."

For some reason, I'm not feeling as worried about this match as I had been last night; even though Zal has kicked my butt every time we have resorted to fists or wrestling to settle our differences. Whatever is going to happen will happen. Sure, Zal is one hell of an athlete, but he has never really trained at boxing. He'll make mistakes and his cockiness is something I can exploit. If I fight smart and don't let him tag me, I have a chance.

On our walk east from Woods Hole along the railroad tracks to the high school in Falmouth Village, Zal stops sniping at me. At first, I think he's retreating into himself to try and focus his mind on our coming fight, but suddenly he starts making small talk about yesterday's game and some of our teammates' performances: Reggie gets our nod as the MVP (though Zal says I am "right up there") and Chicky Boyle stands out with some amazing number of tackles—like twenty-eight. And Curly Sullivan broke some guy's arm.

"He's a sick cowboy," grunts Zal. "Curly thinks football's really important—like it's life; he doesn't ever stop and realize that football's just a game. Just a way to pass the time ... and maybe a way to figure out a little bit about who you are. Just a goddamn game."

I'm surprised by what Zal is telling me. In all of the years I have known him, he rarely lets me see behind his sarcasm, teasing, and competitiveness. Now he's getting philosophical about the limits and values of games?

"So you really don't give a shit about football?"

Zal shrugs, "Yeah, but football, boxing, table tennis ... I don't know. Adults always give you this crap about how sports are rehearsals for the real world, but maybe that's a lot of bull. Like football will prepare us for going to Vietnam, huh? And what the hell has football ever taught Curly or Reggie or you or me about dealing with girls? You think all there is to love is running plays and keeping score? Ask any girl, ask Tina, if she agrees with that, Bagman!"

As he says all this, I think I hear an odd—almost pan-icky—note in Zal's voice … and suddenly I have an idea.

"Are you in love?"

Zal's eyes flash. I have gotten too close.

"Give me a fucking break, will you?" spitting on the ground just missing my shoe. "But don't worry, Bagger. You aren't going to have many more chances to say stupid shit. You're going to be dead in about ten minutes."

We change into our t-shirts, shorts, and sneakers and start warming up with a little jogging, rope exercises, and a couple of rounds at the speed bag. Mugs hands us cups to protect our groins, and Daryl tapes our hands so we won't break our thumbs and fingers. Then they lace on the gloves. Grabbing our football mouthpieces from our lockers, we put on the protective headgear and jog to the ring. It isn't really a box-ing ring at all—just a square taped off on the gym floor with some gymnastic mats placed around the perimeter to add some definition.

"Three rounds, two-minutes each," Daryl shouts.

He's the referee; Mugs will keep the time. Daryl's my cor-ner man; Mugs is Zal's. No holding, no blows to the kidneys, no punching below the belt. If a fighter stays down for the count of ten the bout is over.

"Okay, mouth pieces in, shake hands, go to your corners, and come out fighting," Daryl directs.

It's always a funny feeling going into your corner, throw-ing a couple of punches against the palms of the corner man, then dancing back into the ring. When you go into the cor-ner the gym always seems dark and the air feels like syrup; when you turn around and go back out—skipping, gloves up on guard—the ring looks so bright you can hardly see and the air smells like pure oxygen. I can hear nothing but the murmur of the blower in the heating system. No crowd.

Just Zal and me … and two witnesses. We circle clockwise. Each of us is left handed, and this rotation will give our lefts the advantage of the momentum from our circling. Our eyes lock on each other … each waiting for the other to show himself, to engage. It seems like we've been circling for a long time. Who's impatient; who's holding back? We paw at each other a couple times, but these are just playful jabs to stretch out our arms and to test the other fighter's concentration.

"Watch for the frustration to rise in his eyes," Daryl told me before the match. "Wait 'til he is mad with adrenaline and starts plotting an offensive … then sting him and turn him on the defensive before he's mentally ready. Open up his guard and try to work on his eyes. Fuck up his vision."

So I circle and watch, and I see the fire of frustration starting to burn in Zal's eyes. It isn't the fire of anger, but more like the look of someone who is on the verge of snatching up a chicken and snapping its neck.

Chicken. The image is sticking in my mind, and I know that if I let it sit there just one more second, Zal will see it and break my neck. So I do the only thing I can do to keep myself in the game, I charge.

I can't believe it. I've caught Zal just at the moment he's settling back on his heels the way some fighters do when they think their adversary will never attack. As I come on him with three rapid rights, he counters with a wicked left hook that bites my ear, and a right that slides off the top of my head without slowing my drive or rattling my brains.

Mistake. Now he's open and I'm inside. If my left can just pack the wallop of one of Daryl's punches, I'll drop Zal right here with an upper cut to the jaw. But no such luck. The best I can do is throw my left hook into his nose then catch him again between the eyes with the right while he's still blind from the flash of the gloves.

Blood is shooting everywhere. In an instant it blots out

Zal's face and splatters all over both our shirts and makes a slick on my gloves. Shit. I remember Zal used to have nasty nosebleeds in elementary school. For a moment I wonder why I have opened this old wound on my friend, and I drop my guard. I don't even see the punch that knocks me the whole way across the ring.

"Time," calls Mugs. "End round one."

Zal stands in the middle of the ring and uses his forearm to apply direct pressure to his nose. He spits his mouthpiece into the palm of his free glove.

"Just a game, Bagman," he says. His eyes still have that bright curious look that proposes, 'Let's see what happens next.'

In my corner, Daryl dabs at the corner of my eye with a wet towel. My eye doesn't hurt, but I can feel it beginning to swell at the spot where Zal landed the last punch.

"You had him; why did you stop?" asks Daryl.

I start to explain about Zal's nosebleeds, but Daryl cuts me off.

"That's his problem. Your problem is to disarm your opponent before he kills you. The guy's a thug. He's bigger than you, and now that he's wounded he's going to be mean. You feel what that last punch did to you? You know what happens if he connects with a couple of those? We scrape you off the floor. Go for the nose. It's just a piece of skin. Just blood. But if he can't breathe or see right, you might survive."

"Round Two!"

I throw a combination of punches against Daryl's open palms, and spin around to face Zal. He has gauze or a bit of a rag hanging from one of his nostrils, and he is charging at me almost as if he's moving in for a tackle. I try to side step him, but somehow I trip. Mugs laughs. Daryl starts the count. Zal hovers over me pounding his gloves together.

"Get up, asshole!" he growls through his mouthpiece. "You're dead."

As soon as my knee rises off the floor, Zal comes after me again. He doesn't bother trying to loosen me up with some jabs; he just begins throwing one hook after another. Left, right, left, right—like that. All I can do is put my gloves up in front of my head and try to back-pedal enough to ease the force of his punches.

'Let him waste energy; let his breathing get heavy. He can't keep this up forever. Ride it out,' I tell myself when I put more than an arm's length between the two of us.

Sometimes this is what I do when I'm sparring with Daryl and he gets in a blood-thirsty mood—just hang in there and take it. But not like a punching bag. I need a focused, rational defense. I have to watch Zal's eyes and chin and shoulders as they signal each punch … then catch it with one of my gloves and slide my head and body out of reach so that the punch explodes short.

The gloves slap with rhythm. My forearms start to ache from cushioning the blows and my mouth is dry.

Usually, Daryl's frenzies last fifteen or twenty punches, but Zal has thrown about thirty, and he still keeps coming. His breathing is heavy, but it isn't wild. It sounds like a steam train gaining speed. At this rate he can go on until I blink or trip or a punch slips by one of my gloves. Then he'll drive me out of the ring or waste me.

'Break his momentum—throw the switch—reroute the train,' I tell myself. 'Duck right!'

I plant my left foot as I do in football to reverse field, drop my head to waist level, and kick off toward the right. Zal's right hook sails over my head, and his left jars my left shoulder only slightly as he struggles to pivot and find his clockwise momentum rocking his equilibrium.

Then I rise on my toes and strike a straight left to his nose. Zal hits the floor. My punch carries him beyond the edge of his balance.

"Time!" calls Mugs.

"Fuck time!" says Zal as he spits out his mouthpiece, throws it out of the ring, and jumps to his feet. "Last round—come on, Bags—you ready, you Tina Toy? You faggot whore?"

I hear something snap like a noise from a branch breaking in a dream. Then I hit Zal four times as hard as I can right between the eyes. His nose rag flies. Blood splatters. I swing again as hard as I can. I smell smoke and I picture the flash of a knife blade. I want to kill the fucker.

Zal blocks me with his right forearm, and the hit makes my hand seem to buckle inside the glove as if I have hit a steel bar. Then I feel his other fist bury itself in my belly and the air goes out of my mouth with a whoosh. My legs shake and the ceiling begins to spin. But as I fall I throw both of my arms around his waist and pull him down with me. The blood from his shirt feels sticky and hot.

"Stop. Quit. Give it the fuck up!" screams Daryl. His arms clap around me in a full-nelson and pull me off Zal. Mugs throws a choke hold around Zal's neck and presses the towel against his nose.

"Jesus christ. What's wrong with you?" screams Mugs at me.

"I'll kill him." I feel my teeth grit as I try to break Daryl's hold and shout at the same time. Daryl tightens his hold on me, it is as if he has my neck in a vice. I close my eyes and open them. Zal and Mugs have disappeared, and Daryl is peeling me out of the boxing gloves and unwrapping the tape.

He looks me in the eyes with a sad, James Dean look on his face.

"I only have one thing to say," he begins. "You gotta stay away from this sport until you learn to deal with your temper. I don't know what it is, but you got a monkey on your back and you gotta get it off. Sooner or later you're gonna kill somebody … or they're gonna kill you. Hear?"

I nod. Daryl's right. But maybe he doesn't understand

everything. Maybe I needed this fight with Zal. Maybe it has been coming for a long time.

Zal is in the shower room when I get there. His eyes are closed and his arms hang from the shower nozzle, the water massaging his up-turned face.

"You okay?" I ask.

"Hurts like hell."

"Sorry. I felt like I was fighting for my life in there."

"Yeah, well you did a pretty damn good job. I never knew you were that good ... or that tough. You actually had me scared."

"You really pissed me off."

"I guess."

"You can't say shit like that to me, Zal."

"Like what?"

"Like half the crap that comes out of your mouth."

Zal doesn't respond. The showers make the sound of rain.

"Look," says Zal at last. "I'm sorry, Bags. I mean it. Is there something I don't know about—something weird? You want to talk about something? Does this shit have anything to do with Tina? Is that wench fucking with you again, man? I'd like to see someone give that cunt a taste of her own medicine."

How can I respond? How can I tell my best friend—or anyone—about this stuff with Tina or all these crazy images that just sort of pop into my head and make me crazy enough to kill? The snap of a branch, the smell of smoke, and all the rest.

"Just let it go," I say.

"Yeah, well YOU do that. Fuck Tina. Just fuck her if she's what's been eating you. She's got hers coming. I mean really. Let it go, man."

"Well, you too. And leave Tina out of this. It's not like you're Mr. Goddamn Clean in the Tina department."

I want to let all of it go, all right. Just like Zal says. The fight. The competition with him. Freaking Tina. And a lot of other stuff.

"Truce?" he asks.

"Truce."

"Good. Now will you please pass the soap. I have a rendez-vous tonight, and I don't want to smell like a gym."

We are alone. You can hear the sound of the blowers in the heating system.

Ψ Ψ Ψ Ψ Ψ

I don't know why but my mind seems stuck in the sixties, and memories keep parading past. It is like I have lost touch with these guys and the table at Blackbeard's. Does this kind of thing ever happen to other people? I mean do they ever just sort of go off into a zone for a few seconds and relive big chunks of random time from the past in excruciating detail? Like the character Billy Pilgrim who comes unstuck in time in Kurt Vonnegut's novel *Slaughterhouse Five?* In real time this whole thing only takes a minute or so … but inside my head, hours—even days—go by. Bizarre. I don't even understand the first bit of it. And I don't see how any of this stuff has any bearing on Tina's murder. Now, more than thirty years after all that crazy Bagman business. I feel a thick and sticky mass rising in my throat.

"You don't look so good, Bags," says Curly.

Smoke. Something snaps.

"Piss off. Get me out of here, Zal."

"Man, you sure can't drink any more," grumbles Rollo.

"Yo, Bags, what's the big deal? We're just talking about ancient history," adds Reggie.

"Then why don't you guys just let it fucking be?"

"BECAUSE … WE'RE … TRYING … TO FIND … TINA'S KILLER," enunciates Curly. "BECAUSE HE'S DONE THIS KIND OF THING BEFORE … AND

ANYBODY WITH THIS KIND OF ANGER IS GONNA DO IT AGAIN. JESUS, DON'T YOU THINK WE OWE HER SOMETHING?"

"Fuck her," I say. As Zal used to say, "She had hers coming. You get what you deserve, you know?" I can't believe I let Zal persuade me to come back to Woods Hole. Once upon a time I felt badgered and strip-searched in this place, and now it is happening all over again.

"This hunt for the killer is just some kind of leftover Vietnam obsession with violence that you guys still haven't outgrown. News flash: the Manson murders are ancient history. So is the fucking Mei Lai massacre. And you can stop pointing the finger at me; any of you bastards could have done Tina! Just listen to how the bunch of you are still talking about her … like she's still got you by your willies. You think I don't remember all the crap that went down between each of you and Tina? You think I forget that each one of you was a freaking Tina Toy?"

There it is. That's the expression, isn't it? The thing Zal said in our boxing match. Tina Toy. It had been like a brand back in high school. The kind of thing you said when you really wanted to squeeze a guy by his 'nads. Like cocksucker. The words twist in my chest, and I grab my jacket and head for the door.

"You're wrong," calls Curly.

"Don't kid yourself you sorry prick. You got Tina under the skin just like the rest of us," slurs Rollo.

"Let him go; he doesn't know jack shit," cautions Reggie.

"Think again," says Zal.

And then we are out the door, inhaling the diesel fumes of the ferry waiting at the wharf for the last run to the Vineyard.

"I'm sorry. I wish I could have kept you out of this," says Zal when we are in his car. "But some things are just too big to …"

He doesn't finish the sentence. Instead Zal pauses while the engine of the Saab catches. Then he adds, "You want to talk?"

"Fuck Tina. And fuck you, too!"

5

I'm in the mood to rip somebody's head off when Zal finally drops me at my parents' house after my little welcome-home party at Blackbeard's. Thank god the little two-story cottage is dark and my folks are asleep. I'm not ready to see them. I feel half-drunk, nauseated, and pissed that these guys think I have something to do with Tina's death. And Rollo. Man, there is one person I can do without. Really, screw him! Bringing up that old stuff about Tina and his fucking dog! Screw the whole bunch! Even Zal. All I want to do is to slip silently into my dark room in Skipper Wade's house and sleep for about a thousand years. But sleep isn't coming easily. My mind won't shut down.

ψ ψ ψ ψ ψ

All summer I have been feeling like a bottle ready to burst. I've been spending a part of almost every evening with my neighbor Becky King, sitting on the porch steps of her house, talking the way teenagers do when it's hot and there's little else to do except listen to the moan of ferryboats in the harbor. But nothing has come out of all this time together, except the chance to touch Becky's hand on the nights she's volunteered to give me dance lessons. She says she doesn't want me to look like a fool when some girl asks me out onto the floor for a Lady's Choice at the Saturday night dances we have at the Community Center or the church.

This evening in mid-August she's coaching me on the 'switch and twirl' to the beat of Maurice Williams' "Stay." Maybe it's just the overwhelming smell of honeysuckle in the front yard, or the red and violet sky of the sun as it sets over Buzzards Bay to the west, but I don't think I'm imagining that Becky is holding my hand longer and tighter as we dance. And, perhaps, it's just an accident the way our thighs keep brushing together, but it feels like something is beginning to change between Becky and me.

I start to think that I may have a chance to be something other than the boy-next-door. Then Zal and Rollo come gliding up in front of Becky's house in Rollo's Dodge.

"Gettin' any, Bagger? You pussy-whipped sack of dog shit!"

Zal snickers, Moe of the Three Stooges. I can tell by the sweat on his cheeks that he and Rollo have probably just spent the last two hours guzzling quarts of beer along with a lot of the older kids at a place we called "The Knob" at the entrance to Quissett Harbor.

Rollo poses at the wheel of his Dodge with both hands gripping the enormous steering wheel tightly. He has a smirk on his face as if he can't decide whether he is trying to look like A. J. Foyt at the start of the Daytona 500, or like Alfred E. Newman about to be sick on an amusement park ride.

Becky stops dancing and puts her hands on her hips in a way that says she is less than impressed with my friends. She pushes her long, blonde hair away from her green eyes and glares lightning at Zal until he curls the right side of his upper lip and snarls.

But Becky doesn't even blink. She looks down at Zal in a way that reminds me of nothing so much as the big blue statue of the Virgin Mary in the sanctuary of Blessed Sacrament.

"I feel sorry for you, Tony Zalarelli," she says in her soft Cape accent. "What makes you so mean?"

She is unbelievable. I feel like proposing marriage right

here and now. Becky King, the girl Zal and Rollo have dismissed as "the tightest toosh in the majorette corps" and the "most out-of-it broad south of Boston," has just reduced Zal to a charity case.

"Aw, buzz off! Let's go suck down some brews, Bagger ... if you're man enough." Zal's words challenge, though his voice lacks the usual tang of rebellion. And all of us see the way his hand shakes as he tries to light a cigarette.

Suddenly Zal seems something less than the ultimate male I usually picture. His TV-idol face looks pained as if some kind of invisible knife has just ripped across his forehead, leaving a moist glaze on his black eyes. His bulky linebacker's body slouches into the Dodge's dusty seat like a sack of flour. For a second, I remember Zal as the roly-poly new arrival in third grade who became my friend—the one whose laughing eyes, good manners, and brains have won the hearts of classmates and teachers. Zal doesn't look like the kind of guy who can bully me into anything. And tonight I have to make my own decision about going with the guys.

I stand there like a man of clay. I don't know whether to go or stay.

Becky reaches out and grabs me by the crooks of my elbows. Her fingernails pinch.

"Go on. Get out of here," she says ... and her voice raises a bit with each word. "You're just too wild. All of you are just too crazy!"

It doesn't take a genius to figure out that Becky is telling me I have just blown it with her. Her lower lip quivers, and I turn my back and let the emptiness suck me down the walk into Rollo's car.

We're sitting in Blackbeard's. Only broken old fishermen, high school boys, lonely homosexuals, and small-time book-ies ever venture into Blackie's. That's why we like the place;

and that's why Blackie never worries about serving under-age drinkers.

"Nobody with any self-respect goes near Blackbeard's," my father told me once.

I knock back a dollar's worth of drafts before I say a word to anyone. Only after the beer can I put my chin in my hand and tune in to what Zal's telling Rollo.

"My old lady's un-fucking-real," he spits. "Last night she said she was going to ground me for a month because I didn't do the dishes. It was Charla and Mona's turn; she knows that. But that doesn't matter. It's like she's been on my case full-time ever since the old man split on her. Sometimes I just wish they'd shoot each other and get it over with ... but my father has this Italian sense of duty that won't quit. He keeps showing up at the house, and it's like a fuckin' combat zone."

"Christ, don't talk to me tonight about combat zones. Look at this." Rollo pulls a hand-tooled wallet from his hip pocket and peels it open on the bar.

"It came today," he says pointing to a Selective Service card in the cellophane card holder.

Everyone at the bar crowds in to see.

"Shit, 1-A," says someone. "Good-bye Cape Cod; hello Vietnam!"

"You're dead meat," lisps a queer newspaperman from the end of the bar. "We're gonna get our asses kicked over there."

"Shut up, Lem!" says a half-dozen voices in unison.

"Why doesn't someone beat on that cocksucker for a while," slurs an ancient fisherman.

Nobody picks up the challenge; most of us are too busy looking at Rollo. He is nearly in tears. At this moment, his fine brown hair and childish face make him look exactly like Beaver Cleaver.

"It's all fucking over," he keeps repeating as he stares at the picture of the girl he says he was going to marry—Tina de Oliveira—opposite the draft card in his wallet. "The god-damn draft's got me by the balls."

The cliché hits me as if it were the first time I've ever heard it, and I begin coughing in sympathy when Zal speaks up.

"Hey, Rollo, Bagger will take care of your little baby Tina while you're away; won't you, Bagman?" Zal's teasing, and I know it is his way of getting Rollo's mind off self-pity, but I wish he would leave me out of his stupid, little plan.

"Yeah, Rollo, just the other day your old friend Mr. Bagwell here told me he wouldn't mind slipping Tina a little of the old in-and-out just for old time's sake."

It's true; Tina still has her claws in me … even though we've both taken up with other people after that Valentine's Day. But hell, she turns the whole high school on, right? It is a kind of primal longing for Tina that we feel. We are all Tina Toys. Some guys get all bent out of shape over her; they pick fights and things. Sometimes you want to kiss her right down to her toes. Sometimes you want to just kill her. Or she can kill you. The girl is a force of nature.

Rollo, man, he has just about the worst case of Tina I know. So I want to kill Zal for ratting to Rollo about this thing I still have for Tina. You can't trust anybody when it comes to the subject of Neptune's daughter. It was really dumb for me to say anything to freaking Zal in the first place … even something as vague as that she still has a hold on me. Now Zal or God is going to make me squirm for it.

Somewhere in the back of my head, I hear Becky's voice echoing "You're too wild; you're all too crazy." I feel a little ashamed, and I want to blame Tina. I wish we could get back to the way things were before Tina walked into our lives. Back to the days when the guys and I sailed my Beetle Cat out to the Weepeckets and slept huddled out of the wind with our campfire recessed in a ring of boulders on the biggest island. That was before Rollo talked about anything except his hunting knife collection, before Zal started on his diet of cheap-ass beer and sarcasm, before I started picking fights with everything that moved.

"Don't even think about it, 'Brother Bags,' or I'll kill you," growls Rollo. His blue eyes have a pale, piggy glare in them that scares me. Already a high school graduate, Rollo always makes me a little uneasy. There is something kind of odd about him that I can't put my finger on. Something that makes me think him capable of serious mischief. So now I'm ready to grovel for him, and I prepare to ask God to strike me dead if I ever so much as go near Tina again. But before I can open my mouth, Andy Smith walks through the doorway from the street and claps Rollo and me on the shoulders.

"Ike and Mike, I presume," he laughs. "Give these Sea Scouts a beer ... and Zal, too. The meeting of Troop 195—veterans' division—will now come to order."

Holy shit. After all these years Smitty still remembers we used to have Sea Scout meetings on Tuesday nights. It gives everyone a chuckle. A Sea Scout meeting at Blackbeard's.

"Those were the days," says Smitty.

Someone sighs in response.

"I'm ready," announces Smitty. "Let's put to sea again."

If Rollo or Zal or I were to say anything so sappy, the other two would have to laugh him down as some sort of case of arrested development. But Smitty can get away with talking about Sea Scouts in a wharf rat bar and have the rest of us take him seriously.

Although he is just a year older than Zal and me, and a year younger than Rollo, Smitty looks like a guy who has left childhood behind. He is a golden boy without the ego to match. He has the grace of a panther, but varsity athletics have never interested him. Every girl in school would kill for a date with him but, except for a mad month with Tina back in ninth grade, Smitty has remained loyal to his girl Lily, year after year. In a dark madras shirt, worn with the tail out of his tight chinos, and polished Italian boots, Smitty dresses in a way that makes you think he likes looking good not just for vanity, but because it is an act of respect for those of us who have to gaze on him.

During Sea Scouts, Smitty never got in to the merit badge collecting that had won Rollo and me our Eagles, nor had he been the studly leader we had in Zal before he quit the troop. Smitty was the kid you wanted to build your fire, splice your lines, furl your sails, or put up a tent. He did things right. He enjoyed attending to the little routines of the water and the wilderness, and that is what made him an exceptional seaman. Smitty was the kid who could find you striper or oysters on the shores of the Sound or deer and fox in the woods. "He thinks like he was born in the salt marsh," said our scout-master, and we all knew what he meant.

So when Smitty says he knows the perfect place for an adventure, we all jump on the idea like it is the best thing that has happened to us since Neptune de Oliveira sired his lovely, faithless daughter.

I don't know whose idea it was to take rifles and make this a rabbit hunting expedition, but with guns in hand and beer in mind, we head out for our adventure on a deserted island called Nomans, four miles south across the water from what they used to call Gay Head on the Vineyard, before the Indians changed the name back to their native word *Aquinnah*. The U.S. government had once used the island for aerial bombing practice during WWII. Since then Nomans has been off limits to the public, supposedly it's strewn with unexploded ordinance. A lonely and dangerous place with rolling hills of tall sea grass and sassafras thickets. a place that calls to young men and boys bored with the predictability of life in a Cape Cod village.

Smitty and Rollo have been rabbit hunting here before, and they say it is better than going to the shooting gallery at the Barnstable County Fair. You go to Nomans from Woods Hole by taking a boat southwest about ten miles down Vineyard Sound until you pass Aquinnah. Then the low, circular island rises out of the sea before you, and you end in a place where boulders form a lagoon on Nomans' north shore. Legend has it that once a wharf had stood on this site, and a hamlet of fisher folks and sheep farmers had grown up around it. But nothing remains but a few foundations and some cellar holes.

Rollo says he heard that back in the days of King Philip's War in the 1600s, hostile Wampanoag had forced the settlers to leave. Somebody's children had been scalped here, he thought. The graves are supposed to be somewhere near the lagoon.

It sounds like a lot of Rollo's usual creepy bullshit to me, but I'm game for any excuse to get away from Becky. I can't face her yet. Plus hanging around the house depresses me. This heat and humidity have brought a flare-up in my mother's dermatitis that almost drives her crazy with the itching. If I stay home, I'd have to watch my mother parade around coated with great Uncle Sean's ointment smeared all over her body like green slime. With my father gone for two weeks on a scalloping trip offshore aboard my uncle's boat, my mother has grown more and more odd … to the point where she has begun sleeping on the lower bunk in my room.

I feel sorry for her because of the dermatitis and Skipper Wade being out dragging on Georges Banks, but when she moves into my room, well, that just seems too weird. Maybe she guessed what I was feeling because she consented to my trip with the boys without any clear idea of where I was going. She even baked my favorite oatmeal cookies for me to take along for the guys. I felt guilty.

Smitty's parents thought he was staying at Rollo's, and Zal didn't even tell his mother he was going away. He ducked out a window with his gun and a sleeping bag while she was talking on the telephone. And Rollo? Rollo is eighteen. He does what he wants. His parents can't stop him, and he never bothers to tell them his plans.

I've grown used to this kind of disregard and deception. Especially with Zal. For the past couple of years, starting shortly after his own close encounter with Tina, he's led his life like some kind of exile. I don't think he counts on much except his own ability to lead ... and, maybe, my devotion to follow. Getting no support at home, he has learned to under-write his social budget by taking a cut from the money kids offer him to buy them beer. With his dark skin and heavy beard, Zal looks plenty old enough to buy booze. Besides, he has an accomplice working on the inside, so to speak.

Before heading out, we pull up around noon outside the Harbor General Goods and Package Store that Neptune de Oliveira runs in the building next to his bar. Zal goes in to make the buy. Pretty much the normal state of affairs for this summer, the only difference is that we usually buy a couple of quarts of Narragansett or Rolling Rock when we go drinking. This time Zal wants to get some Colt 45 malt liquor. Four six-packs of tall boys. We feel fired up.

Usually one of these buys takes about two minutes, so after sitting for fifteen minutes with the Dodge parked in the mid-day sun in front of Neptune's packy, Rollo, Smitty, and I are beginning to get a little nervous. To make things worse, Rollo's half-assed hunting dog, a nervous black lab bitch he calls Wanger, is shedding and drooling all over me. God, I can do without this creature. Where is Zal? Has he gotten into some kind of jam with a fisherman, Neptune, or—worst of all—an undercover agent from the State Alcohol Control Board? Such things have been known to happen.

"We're sitting ducks," says Rollo. "Any one of a hundred people can spot us here; they'll figure out we're making a buy and call the cops!"

As if on cue, a police cruiser rounds the corner and closes

in on us. Sliding alongside the Dodge, it stops. The cop in the cowboy hat is my neighbor, "Bullet Bob" Bidell. I try to make myself blend in with the back seat and say a prayer that Zal doesn't come sashaying out the door with an armload of Colt 45.

"What's doin', boys?"

"We're waitin' for my father," lies Rollo.

"Don't make it too long," says the cop. "There's no parking here."

He rolls on … perhaps half convinced by the lie. Rollo's dad has been known to set up camp in a back room of Neptune's where some of the fishermen keep a pretty steady poker game going. But we know Bullet Bob will circle back after his patrol of the four-block strip of businesses and wharves on Water Street.

"Shit, we've got about five minutes to get Zal out of there," moans Rollo.

Smitty takes control.

"Listen, Bagger, hustle your ass in there. Buy some potato chips or something and tell Zal to get the hell out here. Got it?"

He doesn't have to ask twice. At this point I'll do anything to get away from Rollo's mutt.

"Hey, look who's here. It's the Bagman."

A female voice announces my entrance before I fully cross the threshold. The voice tinkles with laughter, and even before my eyes have adjusted to the lack of light inside, I know the speaker can only be Tina. She stands before me tending the meat counter and register in the small general store and packy. Her dark hair falls in waves over her shoulders and frames a face that looks pale as silver except for the bright lipstick. God, she looks like a wet dream in that white cotton tank top and cutoff jeans.

Zal must be thinking the same thing and remembering his own bad old days with Tina. He leans toward her in such a way that every word she breathes seems to draw him farther over the butcher case toward her lips. An empty bottle of Pabst stands by his elbow, and Tina is fetching another from the beer cooler and opening it for Zal.

I can't believe Tina is actually serving Zal beer in the store. Shit, selling beer on the sly to minors is one thing, but this is just plain nuts. What the hell is wrong with Tina? Man, does Rollo have a wack girlfriend. But I guess this is no news to him; the poor son-of-a-bitch just craves her like everyone else I guess. And next to Zal stand a couple of other guys from the football team with beers of their own, smiling at Tina like cats who have swallowed canaries. You have to wonder what is going through Tina's mind.

Every time I think there is nothing that Tina can do to surprise me, she comes up with something new. Damn. What the hell won't she do for male attention? Her old man will kick her ass from here to Nantucket if he finds out what she's up to, running her secret little pub from behind the smoked salami and chicken salad. I have a vision of Bullet Bob walking in the door and busting all of us for drinking, and I know I have to do something fast.

Thank god the store is empty except for us teenagers. I drop any idea of asking for a bag of chips and blurt out the news about the cop. Just the mention of cops these days can boost Zal to high-speed flight. His last year has included several close escapes from the law, one ending in a hearing for brawling at the Falmouth Drive-In.

Without as much as a nod to our teammates—or a good-bye to Tina—Zal whirls away from the meat case, scoops two paper bags full of malt liquor from the floor near his feet, and hits the door in a dash for the car. I give chase.

Over my shoulder I hear Tina laughing, "Hang loose, Bags."

'Drop dead,' I think.

"Be cool." Her voice follows us out the door.

'You bet your sweet ass,' I think as a cloud of dust bursts from the back seat upholstery when both Zal and I hit the seat from opposite doors. The engine coughs alive, and Rollo does his best to coax the old tank down the road to the east side of Eel Pond. As we roll down the street, Rollo's freaking dog jams a hind foot into my crotch for purchase.

Rollo lets loose a piercing rebel yell.

"Let the good times roll," cries Smitty.

I watch out the back window for Bullet Bob. We are in it now, and we aren't even drunk yet.

6

By the time the Middle Ground shoal is abeam, Rollo has his old McKenzie bass boat humming along close to twenty knots. For the first time in weeks the air seems cool against my skin. The sun splashes the waves on the Vineyard Sound with a silver light that rushes across the foredeck of the bass boat like shooting stars. Wanger is straddling my lap again. I try to push her away, but she holds her ground like a statue and pokes her face out around the windscreen. Her nostrils flare with the smell of fresh-cut hay from the farm on Naushon Island to the northwest. Ropes of dog drool splatter on my shirt.

A weird mood grips me, and as Rollo slows to check out a bunch of schoolie blues that the terns are working, I shove the lab off my lap, burst from the cockpit and mount the bow. The bass boat has this thick stem-head; I straddle it between my legs and grip the toe rails for balance.

"Charge!" I shout and Rollo guns the Ford inboard.

"Hold on, Bagger, you horny son-of-a-bitch," screams Zal. I hear a note of worry in his voice, but fear hasn't even crossed my mind. Not now, not yet. I'll show those guys; the Bagman can ride out anything. Rock and roll, mothers!

The boat takes off against the flood tide and southwest wind like a mad shark. Spray rains against my face, but it can't stop me from watching the blur of white caps rushing at me. Sheets of water claw at me, but I duck and dodge the worst of them. It is like one of those dreams you have of flying through a tight canyon.

Then we hit a rogue wave. The boat slows with such force that I feel cheated out of what I has hoping would be the sensation of blasting through some kind of waterfall with rockets on my back. As the boat lurches to a stop … I just release the stem-head between my legs and let momentum catapult me in a somersault through a geyser of water and onto my back in the middle of Vineyard Sound. When I surface, my friends are staring down at me from the cockpit of the boat, pale-faced and mouths agape.

"You crazy bastard; I could have killed you," shouts Rollo.

"Fuckin' A."

I don't care. Something has switched off in my brain. For a moment, I knew the thrill of total, uncontrolled flight. I was the man shot from a canon.

As it turns out, the rogue wave and Rollo's sudden stop to keep from hitting me brought a wall of water aboard the boat and stalled the engine. Only after paddling for a half hour and drying out the distributor, did we get the engine fired up and running well enough to carry us the remaining seven miles to Nomans and the lagoon.

It seems as if each of these last seven miles has passed with a comment from Rollo that blames my birth on my mother's sexual adventures with dead donkeys and the like. He says I have ruined his boat. He may be right, so I just put up with his heat as best I can and stare out to sea as the boat bucks and backfires toward Nomans.

When we finally beach the bass boat in the lagoon, I scuttle out of earshot of Rollo as fast as I can. Screw him and his dog and his girlfriend Tina the Tease.

A deep tide pool at the head of the lagoon draws me toward it. Here the water backs up behind boulders bigger than the boat and makes a pond so deep and clear that you can see stripers weaving over the sandy bottom eight feet beneath the surface.

Clearly, men have been here before because basketball-sized rocks fill in the crevices between the big boulders and form a dam across the pool—except for a flume where water from the ebb tide leaps between two boulders and shoots an arch of green froth downstream with the force of a fire hose. With my back to the jet, the water has the strength to levitate my shoulders when I try to lean back to plug the hole in the dam. Even though the temperature of the water is well below the seventy degrees we have at the beach back in Falmouth, the way the stream roars around me makes my skin feel electrified. So I close my eyes and try to relax and strike a balance between gravity and water power.

The sound of laughter makes me open my eyes, and I see Smitty beside me with his back leaning into the flume with his hair slicking forward over his face in a dark web.

"Christ," he says. "Jesus christ. Beat this, I'm a sperm!"

With that he raises his arms over his head like a diver and lets the rushing water blast him down stream into the lagoon where the water settles itself again. In a second, I raise my arms and follow. I close my eyes and my ears with the sound of a churning water stinging my sinuses. I'm laughing underwater. When I surface I hear Smitty laughing too. For a few minutes we float on our backs and spray geysers of seawater into the sky. Finally, we drag ourselves up on a hot smooth boulder near the edge of the lagoon, strip out of our clothes, and lie belly down to bake dry in the sun.

When I wake I can already feel the chill of sunburn on my butt. The cracks of three or four rifle shots ring in the distance. Smitty sits up beside me.

"What the hell's going on," I ask.

"Blood letting," says Smitty. "Behold, man is in the forest, Bambi."

"Zal and Rollo?"

"No doubt. Fucking ruined this incredible dream I was

having," Smitty moans. He stares down at an ungodly erection between his legs. It is the look of a boy who has just discovered that his body has grown a second head while he was sleeping.

"Jesus. Goddamn, jesus christ," he keeps saying. "I think I was just about to get it on with Tina D. What a piece!"

Awh shit. Why does he have to bring her up again? I turn my head away and try to concentrate on the ripples fish are making as they feed on the flies droning over the lagoon.

A lone gull is filling the late afternoon with his cry. I listen to it as if my life depends on it and begin counting the stripers as they rise to feed on the bait fish. Already I wish I was somewhere else, and we still have all night to go.

"Look at the fucking faggots," Zal's hard voice cuts off the gull's song as striper number nine breaks the surface. "Look at the blowboys, Rollo."

"Eat shit, Zalarelli," I hear Smitty say. "The only faggot here is the one that dripped down your mother's leg."

"Jump back, Rollo; we've got a tough guy here."

I look up toward the sound of Zal's voice and see him standing bare-chested on the grassy bank. He has a can of Colt 45 in one hand and a fat, dead rabbit hanging by its feet from the other. Blood drips from its mouth. Wanger sniffs at it. Rollo is standing beside Zal, rifle across his chest in both hands; his bare belly looks waxy and bloated against the deep tan of his lower arms and the cherry stalk of the .22.

"Get 'em up," smirks Rollo. "You dumb fuck." He fires a shot into the lagoon at my left. "And, jesus christ, will you assholes put on some pants."

He cocks and fires his rifle again. The round splashes near Smitty's bare feet. He skips into the air involuntarily. I jump into my cutoff shorts. Zal snickers.

"Hands up, I mean it," Rollo continues and fires his rifle again. "Over here, douche bags."

He motions us off the rock and ashore with the gun in

one hand while he takes a long swill from Zal's beer with the other.

"Okay, whatever you say, Rollo, but can we cut the fucking army games?" asks Smitty. "I could use a beer."

"Not yet," laughs Rollo. "You have to be initiated."

"You're gonna eat dead rabbit pellets, Bagman," teases Zal.

'Bullshit,' I think. Zal's jokes are getting really old. I want to be back on Becky's porch dancing the slop … but I guess that is no longer an option. The best thing to do is play along until I find my chance to get even. That's how it always is with us. The hell with it.

Rollo's hand swipes across my face as I climb up the bank ashore. But it isn't a slap. Instead, he slashes my left cheek with two fingers as if he is applying makeup at high speed. My face feels sticky and wet; Rollo's fingers drip with the blood from Zal's rabbit … as they stroke my right cheek. Then Rollo turns on Smitty. Seconds later the four of us stand face to face, smearing each other's cheeks, arms, and chests with blood from the rabbit Zal has gutted with one of Rollo's hunting knives.

Then, suddenly, a chill rushes over me, and I feel my arms turn to goose flesh. Smitty and Rollo twitch as a gust of wind strikes us. A cloud blots out the sun, and the sky to the north sounds with the rumble of thunder.

"Clear the fuck out," shouts Zal as if we're walking into an ambush.

He wheels toward the bass boat floating at anchor just off the beach as a lightning bolt strikes the ridge of the island and rain hits the lagoon with the force of a depth charge. The rest of us follow … all four of us tumble into the cuddy cabin of the boat with the slap of wet skin against skin and the groan of floorboards and lifesaving cushions.

The rain makes a steady drum on the deck overhead, and the daylight fades into the cobalt that blurs everything long before sunset on a stormy evening. But we hardly notice.

We suck down three cans of Colt 45 apiece, fill the air with smoke from a pack of Philly Panatelas, and belch at each other.

"Why don't you just go out and stand in the rain, Rollo," teases Zal. "May as well get used to it. They say it rains all the time in Vietnam, you old piece of bung fodder."

Rollo groans. Then he pops out of the hatch and launches himself into the drizzle. "I've got to drain the lizard."

"Take the Bagman with you. You guys can have a pissing contest to see who gets to sniff Tina's undies next."

Screw Zal. The bastard is out of control. Jesus, get me out of here.

I climb out of the hatch and follow Rollo to the transom of the boat. Zal slams the hatch cover behind us.

The rain has let up, but it is still enough to soften the rabbit blood on our skin and send veins of pink lacing down our cheeks, chests, and arms.

"Are we having fun yet, Bags?" asks Rollo as we stand side-by-side arching our urine into the lagoon.

"I feel like shit," I say honestly. "I feel like I want to kill something."

"I know whatcha mean. Sometimes you just feel so screwed, you wanna bite off a few heads."

"This draft thing really sucks, huh?"

"Naw, I don't know. I don't give a shit about the army. I like guns. It's Tina. It's just gonna be all fucking over with us. She ain't gonna wait. You know that. Hot bitch."

"Piss on her."

"Yeah, you can say that. Maybe you don't love her. I do. And that's the whole fucking truth. I'm dog shit without her."

I think about dog shit and Tina and about fifteen things I hope Rollo—or anybody else—will never find out about his girlfriend and me. Tina and me; it has always been sick business, and it isn't heading anywhere good. Then I think about today and how I've blown it with Becky. I figure I understand

something about dog shit. What the hell. At least Rollo has
Tina now. We can all be dead tomorrow.

"So you're dog shit, man. Everybody's dog shit."

"Right," says Rollo. "You're an astute son-of-a-bitch, Bags,
when you're wasted. Why don't you just shut the fuck up?"

With the back of his hand, Rollo wipes away the traces of
the rabbit blood dripping from his chin and flicks them on
me before he starts slogging around the cockpit picking up
anything he can find on the sole like old bait fish, clamshells,
and beer cans and fires them off into the dark water.

"Fuck you and Tina and the goddamn army, just fuck
you all!" Rollo spits ... then he mutters, almost to himself,
"Sometimes I just wish someone would kill us all and get it
over with."

For a few moments I stand at the stern of the boat and
stare off at the dark island in the rain. I see Wanger scamper-
ing around on shore amid the beach plums and poison ivy,
trailing something. She is soaked and coated with mud and
burrs. What a mess. You have to wish a dog like that will just
go get herself lost somewhere.

The next thing I know, I see Becky's sad green eyes and
remember how completely I have blown it with her. Then I
picture Tina the way she looked in her tank top and cutoffs
at the packy. And I have a boner. God, I wish I was back in
Woods Hole instead of on this god-forsaken boat.

When Rollo and I get back into the boat's cuddy it is totally
dark. Zal and Smitty are sitting on a narrow wooden berth
with the voice of the WCOD crackling from the speaker of a
transistor radio. Zal is snapping the bolt on his rifle open and
closed. Smitty is roasting hot dogs on one of Rollo's hunting
knives over a buddy burner set up in the middle of the cabin
floor.

"Holy hell, you guys are going to burn down my goddamn
boat," Rollo begins as I follow him into the cuddy.

But before he can really work into a shrill complaint,

Smitty hands both Rollo and me hot dogs rolled in slices of Wonderbread and lathered with French's mustard.

"Christ," grunts Rollo with his mouth full. "Jesus christ, this is good."

"Fuckin' A."

"Ah, the old fillet of tube steak," Smitty sighs with satisfaction.

"Donkey dick delight. The Bagman's favorite. Here, Bags, have another."

I feel Zal forcing something warm and sticky in my left ear. A goddamn hot dog. Jesus christ! I strike out in the direction of the hot dog with my left elbow raised shoulder high. I swing fast and hard to break something. To kill. The way you do when you've got the ball, you're busting through the line, and they're on you like wolves. Growling, tearing at you with their claws. And you taste the copper in your own blood when you bite your tongue as your elbow connects with something hard as death. Then you feel a sharp pain race up your arm to drive a knife into the base of your skull, and you hear something crack.

I can't see what I've hit, but I both hope and fear it is Zal or Rollo's nose. For years these crazy bastards have annoyed me by sticking everything from spitballs to grape jelly in my ears.

"Temper temper, Bagman," coos Zal in this sarcastic falsetto voice he has. "Hey, Rollo, Bagger's trying to destroy your boat. Look!"

You can see a spider web of cracks spreading from the plywood veneer that covers the boat's fuse box. Rollo looks at me as if he is ready to strangle me.

"Let it go," says Smitty. This was an order. "Eat!"

Outside the rain stops. A half-moon appears high above the eastern ridge on Nomans and bathes the sea between our lagoon and the Vineyard with a ribbon of silver. We peel back the hatch, climb into the open cockpit, and pull the boat up to the beach. Under the voice of Mary Wells singing "You Beat Me to the Punch" from the radio, I can hear the drops falling from bushes ashore. The frogs begin their chorus, and the night smells like a bed of mussels.

In the beam of the boat's searchlight, we gather driftwood and Smitty builds a campfire that blazes with the help of a canteen of gasoline siphoned from the boat. Zal fetches the last two six-packs from the ice chest on the boat.

Colts pop open. We drag sleeping bags to the edge of the fire and stake out our territory, just as we have done dozens of times in our Sea Scout days. Smitty squats on his bag to windward where he can stir the fire. Rollo lies next to him, props up on an elbow, and feeds the fire from time to time with his other arm. Wanger curls up against his knees. It is the first time the creature has calmed down all day. Next to them Zal sits hugging his knees and rocks with his beer can clutched with both hands right under his chin. Closer to the downwind side of the blaze, I lie on my belly trying to keep my face below the rising smoke and watch the salty drift-wood blister and burst in the heart of the fire. It seems like a perfect night, and we are just a bunch of good buddies on a camping trip. I have no way out.

7

With a start, I wake up in one of the bass boat's berths with Rollo's hunting knife in my hand, feeling like I've been on a long strange voyage of some sort. Somebody is shaking me.

"Bagman, come on, wake up, man. We gotta go." Smitty has his hands in my armpits and pulls me upright. My mouth tastes like rotting flesh.

I hear the crack of a .22 ... and the whiz of a round as it cuts through the tall grass ashore and ricochets off the rocks on the beach. Flying bits of rock and sand ping onto the deck of the boat. Now that the tide is out, the boat is completely beached.

"That's just a warning. You fucking Tina Toys better get the hell out of the boat unless you want me to blow you a new asshole!" a voice laughs. It is a stupid animal laugh like something out of a dream.

Two more shots crease over our heads. Each seems to come from a slightly different direction.

"What's goin' on?"

"What the fuck do you think?"

"Rollo and Zal are playing Lone Ranger and Tonto again." Smitty spits.

"I dunno. I just woke up. They weren't by the fire, and I found you in the boat. But I'm telling you, if this is another one of their goddamn stunts, I'm gonna kick some ass. This cowboy shit just gets old. Let's get the hell out of this boat before someone gets hurt."

Smitty eases himself onto the rail of the shadowy side of the bass boat, waiting a second, then slithers over onto the wet sand and seaweed of the beach.

Three more shots crack, and the bullets whiz over the boat.

"Stay in the shadows," Smitty says faintly. He begins an alligator crawl to the bow of the boat's silhouette cast by the glow of the campfire. I roll to the ground and follow.

One round, then two more, crack into the fire sending out a spray of sparks.

"Run for your lives, you fuckin' faggots," cackles a voice. Is it Rollo's? I'm not sure.

"They're up on the ridge. In the tall grass. We gotta get up under the lip of the sand dunes where they can't see us," says Smitty.

We lie at the very edge of the boat's shadow. The nearest cover is the stand of sassafras. It's about twenty yards away near the high dunes on the far side of the beach. Between it and us lies the flame-lit sand surrounding the burning logs.

Another volley splatters the fire.

"You dweebs got 'til the count of five to come out of there with your hands up." It doesn't sound much like Rollo's voice this time … or Zal's. But those clowns both have a collection of fake voices they can drag out for any occasion. It isn't Rollo's annoying Dracula imitation, yet I know I've heard this voice before; I just can't place it. I guess I'm still drunk.

"Now." Smitty's hand lobs a palmful of sand over his shoulder. It hits the deck of the bass boat like a hailstorm. Almost immediately, I hear the shooters crank off more shots—one of which zaps the boat. Smitty grabs me by the sleeve of my football jersey and sprints toward the sassafras.

Shots erupt in the sand behind us. We dive into the bushes, hit, roll, and keep on scrambling toward the dunes that lie another twenty yards through thick brush. Bullets smack into the leaves overhead. One of the shooters lets out a rebel yell.

In the dark, Smitty and I tumble into a tidal gully. We lie in a bed of rocks and the shadow of a steep bank cut by winter storms.

"You dumb shits!"

Now that's Rollo shouting.

"You left me with the boat, the guns, and the ammo. Really, stupid. You don't know crap about war."

He begins honking the horn of the boat in triumph. Bastard. Smitty and I lie with our backs in the mud bank. We try to catch our breath.

"Oh, christ." Smitty wipes the sassafras leaves and sand off his face with the back of his hand.

His voice catches in his throat like a sob, "Oh, christ. Look. Look at the dog."

In the moonlight reflecting from the gully, I see the lab's body as it lies on an island of turf. She can't be more than fifteen feet away, and you can see the dog is dead. Wanger lies on her side with blood spilling like tar all over sea grass around her.

"Come on," urges Smitty.

We crawl to the dog—why, I'm not for sure. I guess we can't quite believe our eyes. But close-up you can smell the blood that oozes from around a wooden stake, a fisherman's marlinspike, driven almost to its hilt into the left side of Wanger's rib cage. Trails of exposed and bleeding flesh zigzag across the lab's back like Z's.

"Oh, man. Someone has carved up Wanger like a tree. What the fuck?"

Smitty has the look of someone who has just swallowed a mouthful of sour milk. I picture the marlinspike driving through Wanger's chest. I imagine the snapping of ribs. And a knife slicing a trail of Z's over the hot, hard back. Then I heave … maybe five or six times. Then the cat calls start again and Smitty drags me back to the shelter of the creek's high bank.

"Come on, fuckers! Come on you old you pussy-whipped peckerheads." The voice is Zal's, and it cackles from somewhere in the high grass of the island's upland meadows. Is he shouting at us or someone else? At Rollo?

A shot cracks from somewhere near the beach. Jesus. What is going on? I can't figure it out. Is Zal shooting at Rollo; has Rollo been shooting at us? What the hell? Has this draft card stuff and Tina and way too much Colt 45 just totally pushed Rollo over the edge? Or is it me who is off the charts?

Several shots crack out from behind the boat.

I squint through the brush and see a barrel flash … then I see Rollo rise out of the shadows. He springs aboard his boat, slams open the cuddy hatch, and grabs a web belt containing an ammo pouch with several boxes of cartridges. A second later he dives into the shadow of the dunes on the far side of the beached boat as bullets start whizzing in the direction of the boat. Rollo fires back.

"You can run, but you can't hide," calls Rollo. His voice seems farther from Smitty and me now, and I get the feeling that Rollo has circled away from the beach into the dunes. I can hear feet scrambling through the brush coming closer.

"Take your best shot," crows Zal. A flashlight ruptures the darkness. Perhaps one hundred feet beyond the glow of the campfire, Zal's face looks like a Halloween spook with the beam of light pointing up from beneath his beard.

Shots erupt from the plateau just above our heads and—I can't explain it—but suddenly nothing seems real anymore. It is almost as if I have passed out from the Colt … but not quite because I'm aware of some things. The air seems to glow like a pale metallic curtain, and in my mind a tape keeps playing, "Somebody's going to die. Somebody's going to get killed."

Now it seems like there are more than just Rollo and Zal shooting. There are others in the game. We are at war on some far away beach with a name like Da Nang.

I sometimes get the experience of being frozen with panic

in my dreams—the feeling that my arms and legs cannot rouse themselves to fight or flee in a moment of crisis. It feels that way now.

I feel Smitty putting his hand on the back of my head and pushing me closer to the steep mud bank. Storm seas have carved out a hollow beneath the spartina that overgrows the edge of the stream's gully. Smitty pushes me into this hollow under the lip of brush and earth. Almost instantly I am deep in a burrow and I am alone. I can't touch or feel or hear Smitty anymore. It is like he has just vanished. I am a caterpillar tucked in a cocoon and lost in fantasies of flight.

In my dream or my stupor or my terror, or whatever it is, I fly through the night on swift, dark wings, and dive to rip at a carcass, swallowing great globs of flesh, and plowing the earth with a soft wet phallus.

Then a volley of shots sounds—so many so fast that it makes me think of an ambush scene in *The Guns of Navarone*. The earth shakes overhead. Pieces of dirt rain into my hair following the sound of breaking branches and the clatter of rocks as a body falls into the tidal gully.

"Shit. Goddamnit," a voice groans.

"Fuckin' idiot, bitch Tina Toy."

Where have I heard this voice—or was it two—before? From some distance up the gully—near where I have left Wanger's body—comes the scuffle of feet slipping among the rocks. They are scrambling away from me.

Then Smitty is shaking me.

"Let go."

I feel like I am coming out of a dream. My hands have seized on protruding roots under the bank and refuse to release them. I feel Smitty's hands on top of mine, his thumbs prying between my palms and the roots. He exhales—hot and moist on my neck.

"What happened? What do we do?"

"Our Father ..." Smitty begins. "Who art in Heaven."

"Hallowed be Thy name," I follow.

"Thy Kingdom come."

"Thy will be done."

"On Earth as it is in Heaven."

Something like an electric shock ripples through me. It is so weird. Like God really exists or something! I can feel Smitty inching out of our burrow with me in his arms.

"Give us this day," he whispers.

"Our daily bread."

"And forgive us our trespasses."

"As we forgive those who ..."

Overhead the spartina crackles, and dirt hits me in the face. I stare up. Against the background of the moonshine, I see a shadow standing over us, his rifle hanging in our faces ... before he plunges onto the ground beside us. Zal. Bullets slap sporadically into the gully and ricochet among the rocks as we crouch in the shelter of the bank.

"What the hell?" asks Smitty. "Has Rollo gone mad?"

"I was asleep by the campfire and woke up to the sound of a dog whimpering real loud and sad from somewhere. Then someone started shooting into the fire and shouting a lot of crap about Tina," Zal quickly explains before running for cover in the high grass, leaving his gun behind.

"Rollo?" I call out.

"I haven't seen him," Zal yells back.

"So ... here we fucking are!"

"Christ on a crutch!" growls Smitty.

"Wanger's dead," I say. "What next?"

Under the cracking of more gunfire I think I hear an outboard engine sputter alive somewhere way off down the island. Then someone shouts like a voice from my fading dream, "Stay away from Tina or you're gonna die mother fuckers!"

"Who was that? Did you hear that?"

"Huh?"

"That boat. The shouting?"

"What?"

"Forget it," I say. Maybe I'm just imagining things.

For just a second, things grow so quiet you can hear the ocean swells hit the beach on the other side of the island with a rhythmic hush.

"This has got something to do with Tina," I say.

"You can take that up with Rollo," says Smitty, nodding in the direction of the campfire on the beach.

Rollo lumbers up to us. He puts his gun down and begins shouting.

"Where the hell's Wanger; where the hell's my dog?"

With the ammo belt slung over his shoulder and his belly filling his dirty t-shirt like a sack of corn, Rollo reminds me of pictures I have seen of Pancho Villa. The night has taken on the color of milky ink as a moist ground fog settles over the island and the water.

I seize Zal's gun and stand up.

"She's gone," I say. I have the gun pointed at him.

He makes no move toward his weapon on the ground. If he does, I swear I might blow him away. I've had enough of being his target for one day. Forever, really. Sometimes you just reach your limit with a person.

"She ran off again?" He shakes his head like he is coming out of some kind of daze. He lurches toward the gully and me where I saw his dog staked out with something like lightning bolts carved across her back.

"No, man, she's dead."

"Don't bullshit me, Bags. I'm tired of all this crap. I don't want to hear any more shit from you or anybody else about the fucking draft or Tina. Not even about my goddamn dog. So don't be dickin' with me. I know you hate Wanger. What the hell'd you do to her?"

I wait for Smitty or Zal to say something, but they stand back on the high ground, looking like a pair of zombies in the fog.

"What's this?" growls Rollo bending over and fishing through the grass slick with Wanger's blood. "Oh, jesus …"

He picks up something and thrusts it toward my face. Wanger's green web collar cut clean with a knife. But the dog's body is gone. It just vanished as if I dreamed her there. I can see Rollo's face swelling as tears boil in his eyes.

"Someone carved her all up, man. Sliced Z's all over her back and drove a fucking marlinspike …. Shit! For all I know, you did it. Freakin' crazy drunk. Shooting up the night like goddamn Billy the Kid."

"You fuckin' faggot whore," he explodes. "You think I don't know about you and Tina, and now you've killed …"

I don't hear the rest. I taste the blood and smell the rank odor of Wanger's fear as Rollo rubs his dog's sticky collar in my face. Then a branch snaps. I smell smoke. And I am on him.

I throw Rollo to the ground, pinning his body chest-down under me, gouging his back with my elbows, and driving my knees into his crotch. I hold him by the hair and pound his face into the sand as he shriek like a gut-shot rabbit. Smitty and Zal have to nearly strangle me before they can drag me off Rollo.

For a long time the four of us lie in the bloody grass on the island panting. After a while, I feel Zal's arms loosen his bear hug on me. He sighs, asking if I'm ready "to cool it, to truce it up? Come on, aren't we all friends?"

I cry. I can't help myself. And once I have begun, I can't stop. What if Rollo has been right? Maybe I did still have my secrets with Tina? And what if I have killed his dog? The beast made me crazy. What if I just didn't remember it because I've been too damn wasted? But where has the body gone? What could I have done with it? And when? Jesus, what can I say? It is like somebody has cut my throat, and I lie here in the blood, drunk and caught in Zal's arms. Pathetic.

"Come on, Bags," I hear Rollo say after what seems hours.

"Forget it. No hard feelings, okay. There was someone else on this island tonight, I swear. Fuckin' raiders. Right? Somebody's been messing with us. I don't blame you." He speaks as if he is making up a story that he doesn't really believe, but he can live with … for the moment.

It's coming on sunrise. We head back to the fire and Zal stokes the flames. I bury myself in a sleeping bag. On the edge of the ring of light cast by the fire, Rollo paces back and forth swinging a hunting knife up in sharp lunges as if he's gutting a tom cod. Smitty opens a large can of baked beans with his pocketknife and lowers the can into the center of the heat, stirring the beans with a twig. After awhile he smothers the beans in mustard and passes the can around. We take turns raising it to our lips and mucking the beans into our mouths with the twig. The smoke, the steaming beans, and the mustard percolate through my sinuses like a warm veil rising over my mind. For a long time nobody speaks.

Finally, Rollo breaks the silence.

"I'm gonna tell everybody that Wanger took off after a rabbit and just never came back. But fucking things just don't add up. Either one of us did it to that dog, or it was raiders. It's fuckin' bad. Someone was messing with me royal tonight. And I'll find out who it was if it takes me a hundred years. I'm gonna get fuckin' even, trust me! Everybody hear that?!"

Smitty groans, "I don't want to talk about any of it. Put it behind you. It was a mistake. This whole trip has been a mistake. I should have known that we're too old to play Sea Scouts. Guns and booze? What the hell was I thinking. We should have never come here. Some wicked ugly shit has hit the fan, and I don't think any of us is really ready to deal. So this night never happened. Nothing happened, okay? Nobody says shit."

"Zal?"

"I didn't see a thing. I don't know anything about a dead dog."

"Bags?"

I picture Wanger with that marlinspike in her chest and for some reason I see Tina again the way she looked behind the counter at the packy—her dark hair, the cotton tank top, and cutoff jeans, oozing the scent of Jade. Then I see the empty spot where the dog had bled to death. I can't make sense of it, and I can't figure out if I have been more than a witness. There are just these dark spots in my memory.

"No body, no death," I say at last.

Smitty raises Rollo's rifle from the sand, ejects the live rounds from the chamber, and removes the clip.

"There's a dance at the Community Center tonight."

"Yeah," sighs Rollo.

I know what he means. Tina will be there.

"Let the good times roll," says Zal. It sounds like a prayer.

8

You can forget about sleeping late in a fisherman's house—even a *retired* fisherman's house. My mother's rattling around in the kitchen for coffee and eggs starts before sunrise while Skipper Wade sings freaking opera in the shower. I pull a pillow over my head and try to drown out the noise and the coming of day. I don't know what time I finally fell asleep. Too many memories have been rising from the dead in my mind.

By eight o'clock there is no more chance of sleep, and my mouth tastes like dried smoke. When I stumble out of my bedroom door on my way to the bathroom, I walk right into a hug from both my parents and an invitation to help them and other parishioners at Blessed Sacrament decorate the church with flowers for Tina's funeral. My father says hundreds of flower arrangements have been arriving at the church from mourners all over the world.

My parents' invitation is one I would prefer to pass up. Unlike Zal, who was drawn back to the faith, I have drifted away from the church. Sukey wasn't religious, so during the years of our marriage I don't think we stepped into a church unless it was some kind of tourist attraction in Europe or Mexico. I can't remember the last time I have been inside Blessed Sacrament. Its statues of bleeding Jesus seems like another nightmare from my high school days.

But the church has become their life since my father sold his boat and my mother retired from teaching. So I feel that lending them a hand lugging flowers might be something I can do to help them and show my thanks. Besides this isn't really like going to church. It is more like a chance to say good-bye to Tina. It isn't something I want to do; it is an obligation.

I must be on my second or third trip of lugging six-foot wreaths and orchid bouquets to the sanctuary from the field or recreation room when I catch sight of a woman in the dim light. She stands beneath a stained-glass window of the Virgin, removing purple gladiolas from a vase and spreading them along the windowsill. The red, gold, and blue light filtering through the window makes a silhouette of her face. The high forehead, ski-jump nose, apple cheeks, pouting lips, and prominent chin look more than familiar. I drop the wreath I'm carrying to the hardwood floor and stare.

The noise from the wreath startles her, and she turns her face in the light to see who has intruded on her solitude. Before she raises her hand to make a visor against the sunlight, I see her face full on—the snowy skin, the pink lips, and those green, green eyes. Her hair is slightly shorter and a darker blonde now, but it is Becky.

"Oh my god," she sighs.

A second later she has me locked in her arms, and we are laughing like kids.

She takes my hand and whispers, "Come with me." Then, after a pause while she holds me at arms' length and smiles, she says, "I can't believe I'm seeing you. I just can't believe it. Especially here. I can't imagine you ever coming in this church again."

I hold tight to her hand, follow her through the sanctuary, and begin to explain that I have come to Woods Hole for the funeral. But before I get much beyond telling her about my divorce, Becky draws me into another long hug.

"I can't believe it," she keeps saying over and over again as we climb to the balcony. "I'm just so happy to see you."

"You're an angel," I say. It sounds stupid, but the words fly out of my mouth.

Becky hugs me again, and then asks me to help her gather up flowers to decorate the balcony railing. I am glad for something concrete to do. My hands tremble, and I feel speechless. I'm sure Becky senses my uneasiness—she was always able read my moods—so she makes small talk for relief.

A half-hour passes while we sit lingering in the privacy of the balcony, and Becky talks. She brings me up to date on her family. She and her husband Terry divorced nine years ago. He had begun living for blue fishing, duck hunting season, and poker parties, and she had found she wanted a career in psychology. So they had split. Now she is an associate professor of adolescent psychology at the University of Massachusetts at Dartmouth and the single parent of her fifteen-year-old son Brandon. Becky says her life has turned out different but richer than she ever expected after her marriage broke up. The church has been good for her. It keeps her from feeling lonely. That and her parents are reasons to keep living in town. I try to keep the positive energy going.

"Motherhood must be the best."

She shrugs, smiles.

"Yes and no. Brandon can be a handful. Being a teenager these days isn't easy."

"Was it ever?"

"You had a rough time," she says. "You worried me."

Becky shakes her head the way she did thirty years ago when I disappointed her. A chill passes through me, and I feel like my bowels are about to let go.

"Are you okay?"

"I'll get over it," I shrug. "I kind of had a long, hard night at Blackbeard's last night with Zal."

Jesus, it is like we are kids again. Here I am telling Becky about all the crazy stuff going on in my life. I tell her about how Zal called and asked me to come home for Tina's funeral. And I tell Becky all of this nonsense Zal and the others have been dreaming up about how I am the key to finding some local madman who has been killing with marlinspikes and carving Zs all over victims for thirty years.

When I tell her the last part about the local killer, Becky digs her fingers into my wrist. She says she has been having some funny feelings that someone she knew killed Tina.

I shrug, "Well you guys live here; you may be right, but dragging me into this is just a waste of everybody's time."

"How can you be so sure? How can you just close off the options? Maybe they're right. Maybe you really know something. You live in New York; she died in New York. Maybe way down inside you've buried something, some clue. Maybe that's what made you so crazy back in high school. Something was ripping up the Bagger in those days. Maybe it really is connected to Tina's death."

God, now Becky is starting on me, too.

"I don't see any connection at all, and I'd rather not talk about it if you don't mind!"

I must have given her a withering look because she turns her eyes away toward one of the stained glass windows and is fidgeting with a wreath of white roses in her hands.

"Okay," she says after taking a deep breath. "But maybe you could come over to my place tonight. I could make dinner, and we could talk … about other things."

I tell her I already have plans.

"To go drinking with the boys again?"

I shrug.

She shakes her head and laughs a scratchy little laugh. "Still the same Bagman; still blowing me off."

"Sorry."

But what I really want to say is, "Back the fuck off!"

9

Within two minutes of leaving Becky at Blessed Sacrament, I know I have screwed up. Going drinking with the boys again? Am I crazy? Do I want another interrogation, another hangover, another night of humiliation as Curly, Reggie, Zal, and Rollo parade the ghost of the Bagman and all of his screwups before my eyes again. No way! And as far as Tina's killer is concerned, what does anybody really know? We all have, had, our reasons to wish Tina dead. I mean, we were all Tina Toys. But you know what? Right now I don't really care about Neptune's daughter, our dead Cinderella. You can't touch her anymore, or try to make things different. And I have unfinished business with another long lost girl of my dreams. Who is still alive.

It is mid afternoon when I find Becky's number in the phone book and give her a call. She's not there, but I leave a message. I say that I want to apologize for my temper, for my insensitivity. I want to see her. Can I take her out to dinner?

She doesn't return my call. So I call again … and again until she picks up.

"I don't think this is such a great idea," she says. "I don't want to relive the past."

"Trust me, neither do I. But today when we talked, I … I don't know, Becky, I guess I just want to see you. I wish I could have a present with you, not just a past."

"You're not going to ditch me again for the guys?"

"No chance."

"We have to get out of this town."

"That's what I was thinking."

"It's going to cost you big time!"

"Your wish is my desire."

"The Black Dog."

"On the Vineyard?"

"Where else?"

"We're taking the ferry?"

"I have a boat."

"I didn't know you ..."

"Messed around in boats?"

"Yeah."

"You never took the time to ask."

This isn't the first time Becky has surprised me. Especially before a date.

ψ ψ ψ ψ ψ

Shit definitely happens. Pre-season football has begun, and exhaustion and concern for physical survival on the gridiron has all but buried the empty feeling I get when I think about Becky. As underclassmen, Zal and I know we have something to prove to the coaches and the seniors who carried the team to a championship the year before. During the early morning and late-afternoon practices, we pump each other up to kick ass, make it hurt, and hustle. Side-by-side in the conditioning drills we psyche one another into a teeth-gritting frenzy. In the blocking and tackling exercises we dare each other to take on the biggest and meanest of the superstars—pursuing and hitting no matter how many lumps we take.

"Never quit. Never!" says Zal as we walk home late one morning after two hours of hitting drills in the ninety-degree heat. "Show 'em you can take the pain. That's the secret."

"No shit from anybody," I spit. "Nothin' any of those ass-holes can do to put the hurt on us. We're animals!" I like this kind of talk. It gives me a way to make my fat lip and sprained ankles badges of courage.

"Mean mother f …"

The squeal of bicycle brakes at our backs interrupts Zal's testimonial to our balls.

"My god, what happened to you guys?" The voice is Becky's, and now she and her bicycle are alongside me as I hobble down Woods Hole Road in the shade of the maples and oaks. It is the first time I have seen her since the night before the hunting trip to Nomans. With her yellow gingham top, pink short-shorts, and hair streaming down her back in a ponytail, she looks more like a blonde Natalie Wood in *Splendor in the Grass* than a girl who has just spent the last two hours sweating through majorette drills in the high school gym.

At first, Becky leans on her handlebars and tightens her eyebrows and lips into an expression of pain as her eyes move from my swollen lip to Zal's face, but then her hand rises to cover her mouth and nose as a giggle bursts forth.

"You look like Flute Snoot, Zal," she chuckles. Flute Snoot is a kid in our math class who has a nose resembling a cucumber.

Zal throws his head back on his shoulders and offers us a full profile of his nose taped over with gauze that looks as if the trainers have fashioned him a breathing apparatus out of a Kotex pad.

"Broken," he says after a long pause. His eyes give Becky a dewy look.

Becky is still covering her own face in embarrassment.

"He got it inspecting Coach Bolino's rectum," I say.

"Oh, don't be so infantile!" she bursts. "The poor guy. It must really hurt."

Zal raises his hand to the left side of his face and shoots me the finger from an angle out of Becky's sight.

"Fuck you, Zal," I fire back before thinking about how little tolerance Becky has for profanity.

"REALLY, you EAT with that mouth?" Becky turns on me.

Zal smiles smugly in my direction ... then covers his face with both hands for a couple of seconds and sucks in a deep breath ... as if the pain is almost too much. Bullshit.

Then Becky does something I couldn't have expected in a thousand years: she sweeps off her bike like some kind of Florence Nightingale and wraps Zal in a hug.

"I'm gonna give you just what the doctor ordered, Zal. A little TLC. You're coming with me to the movies tonight. They're bringing back Shirley McClain in *Irma la Duce* ... with Jack Lemmon. He's soooo funny!"

I could faint. What has gotten into this girl? She wants Crazy Zal to go to a movie with her? Is this an honest to goodness date? Has she forgotten Zal's reputation as a whore monger?

"Ellen and I are going to the movies."

'What about me? How can she forget me,' I think.

"You can come too," Becky nods to me as she drops her grip on Zal and remounts her bike. "Just watch your language for a change. Grow up, Billy. I think Ellen has a crush on you."

Ellen? Me? Zal nudges me with his elbow as if to signal that I have just gotten amazingly lucky.

"Call me in an hour," her voice drifts over her shoulder as she peddles away ... ponytail swaying down her back.

"We're in like Flynn, Bagman!" Zal elbows me again. "Nice girls, Bagman. A whole new experience. We must live right!"

An hour later when we call Becky from my house, I still can't believe this is happening. At seven o'clock Zal and I will meet Becky and Ellen Servis at Becky's. We'll get a ride to the Elizabeth Cinema on Main Street in Falmouth with Becky's sister Arlene and her boyfriend Butch. This is a big deal. Nobody from Woods Hole goes all the way to the

Elizabeth unless you have a serious date, unless you are trying to impress somebody. Most nights we just go out to The Knob in Quissett or the eighteenth tee at the Woods Hole Golf Club, drink quarts of Narry, and try to score with who ever shows up in a bra.

"You know you make me want to SHOUT …" Zal sings at the top of his lungs as I relay the news from Becky on the other end of the phone. He has the big cabinet radio in my parents' living room cranked up to full volume as WCOD belts out the Isley Brothers' rock 'n roll war cry.

"Keep your hands clappin. Shout! Keep your hands clappin. Shout!" Zal wails. His hands rise over his head and double claps every time his voice and the song reach the word "shout." His face rises toward the ceiling and his eyes squint shut in ecstasy. The nose bandage flashes among the shadows. Simultaneously, Zal's feet do a kind of pony prance as he zigzags across the living room carpet.

Suddenly, the music ceases.

"Look, Martha, it's a raging hormone!" Skipper Wade stands with his hand on the volume knob of the radio. My mother, pausing beside him, stares at Zal as if someone has just called her attention to a cockroach the size of her husband's fish boat. Apparently, my parents stepped into the living room through the front door during Zal's performance. With their arms hugging grocery bags, they look like Fred McMurray and June Allison in some fifties movie depicting middle-class bliss.

"Maid Martha," Zal gives a deep cavalier bow. "Admiral," he snickers as his baritone voice lingers over the nicknames he has given my parents.

My father's free hand releases the volume knob and tightens into a fist. Zal backs away toward the kitchen … then skips out the side door of our house.

"Pick you up at six, Tina Toy," he coos in falsetto just before the screen door slaps shut.

"Keep a cool tool, Bagman, and don't let your meat loaf!"

I can hear him laugh in giddy amusement.

"I'm gonna kill that kid …" grumbles my father, handing me a sack of about thirty cans of Friskies cat food.

"I'm sure it's just a phase," sighs my mother, always the philosopher. "This, too, shall pass."

"These guys have dicks for brains," Skipper Wade says with the seriousness of a brain surgeon looking at an x ray of Zal's skull.

I can picture it—my father in surgeon's pajamas holding up a two-by-three negative of Zal's head (flute snoot and all) filled with fat, shadowy dongs. And, involuntarily, I begin to laugh.

"Shape up, mister!" my father points a finger at me.

I retreat to my room.

If past experience is any kind of predictor, I will be grounded for about the next week because of Zal's and my little show. But when I face off over baked scrod and peas with my parents, and raise the subject of going to the movies tonight with Becky and Ellen, my parents are all for it. Skipper Wade even offers me $5. What's got him so revved up is that Becky and Ellen are regulars in his Sunday school class for teenagers.

My parents seem happier about this impending event than I am. In fact, I'm not really sure I even want to go—especially if I have to watch Becky making a fool of herself worrying over Zal as he does his imitation of the wounded gladiator. What is going on in Becky's mind? Just a few weeks ago Zal repulsed her. But noooooo, not now.

And what is all this about Ellen Servis having a crush on me? We barely speak except at church. I like her, okay, but the girl scares me. She is a couple of inches taller than me—a cheerleader with the same thin frame and fresh-scrubbed prettiness of her older sister who works as a stewardess for American. She is the kind of girl our women teachers love. Ellen earns A's, is class secretary, and sings in the church choir.

What do you do on a date with someone like that? What do you say? How do you dress?

"Start with a shower and a shave," counsels my father when he finds me in my room banging a pencil to the rhythm of WCOD.

Right—a shower. But a shave? That is once a week—before Mass.

"Shave, Billy Boy," adds my mother. "Girls like soft faces. Have some pride in yourself."

Saying that, she enters my room and begins digging through my closet. I flee. And when I come back from shaving—and showering until the water goes cold—I have just about decided that I will wear a pair of tight black pegged pants, my pointed Italian boots, and a white long-sleeve shirt with a tab collar. Ricky Nelson dresses this way. But returning to my room, I find that my mother has laid out a whole set of clothes for me on my top bunk. God, it is the stuff she bought in Hyannis for my birthday—a short-sleeve madras shirt with a button-down collar, baggy khaki slacks—with cuffs—, and penny loafers. Penny loafers!

"It's the collegiate look. All the older kids are wearing it," assures my mother when I give her a look that asks whether she has been living on Mars.

"You're going with Becky," argues the Maid Martha as if this information changes everything in my life.

She has a point. Maybe I need to change for Becky; maybe Ellen likes this stuff, too. What do I know about nice girls?

"You look sharp, buddy," judges my father when he sees me decked out.

"He looks like a geek, Admiral. He's got dicks for brains!" Zal mimics my father as he peers in through the front-door screen. "Let's beat it!"

I shrug at my parents—gotta go—and leave. Over my shoulder I can hear their voices talking low and earnestly. The words I catch are Becky's and my names.

Walking down the sidewalk toward Becky's, I notice Zal's nose bandage has disappeared, and we has on nearly identical clothes. I begin wondering if someone has dressed him too, then a voice from the street interrupts.

"Jesus christ, you guys look like the Marx Brothers!"

Butch da Silva, a not-so-recent high school graduate and boyfriend to Becky's older sister Arlene—our ride—points a long arm at Zal and me as he watches us stroll into view. He leans against the polished maroon fender of his '63 Chevy Super Sport. Except for the car, he looks like an image snatched right out of *Rebel Without A Cause*.

"I'm really disappointed in you guys," Butch continues without dropping his arm or moving anything but his lips. "Oh girls, girls. Come look at what the Easter Bunny brought you. Twin fruitcakes!"

High up on the front porch that juts out from Becky's house like the bridge on a ship, our dates rise off a glider swing to see the twin fruitcakes for themselves.

At first, I barely recognize Becky and Ellen. Their cutoff blue jeans, rolled into cuffs just above creamy knees, look like they have been painted on the girls' loins. Even from thirty feet away I think I can see the vertical crease between the roots of each girl's legs. With her tight pink halter top exposing acres of bare belly and the buds of her breasts, Becky's deep purple lipstick and bangs teased into a fluffy fringe over her eyes complete the girl-of-the-streets look.

Ellen shows her belly, too … beneath a red and white boat neck jersey that slips off one of her shoulders and hides so little of her torso that from down here on the sidewalk I can see the black lace of her bra. Ruby lipstick, mascara, and pixy-cut, frosted hair makes Ellen look like the woman who sells tickets at the adult movie theater in Boston's Combat Zone where Zal and I took in *Fanny Hill*. Her legs look eight feet long.

"Holy shit!" whispers Zal.

"Stop staring; it's rude, Bagman," Becky commands as she descends the stairs from the porch—her legs moving oh so slowly, and her feet touching the ground so softly that she seems to be stretching for stepping stones in a stream. Half way down the steps she stops and turns back to Ellen behind her. For a second they bend face-to-face and whisper. I hear the tinkle of laughter, and then the girls squeeze each other's hands. Zal and I stand shoulder-to-shoulder alongside the Super Sport as if waiting for someone to explain to us how to get into a car. Something is really wrong here.

"Maybe we ought to put these dweebs in the trunk," proposes Butch to Arlene as she catches up with the younger girls. "Then these babydolls will have a chance of picking up some real men!"

"Eat it, Butch!" Zal growls through his teeth. His eyes flash at our driver. I see Arlene, Becky, and Ellen watch with fascination as Zal pulls a pack of Camels out of his shirt pocket, lights a cigarette, takes a deep drag, and blows smoke in Butch's face. Everybody understands that Zal will wipe the street with Butch sometime soon if the thin, older boy doesn't back off.

"Now, that's my man," smiles Butch as he sidesteps the cloud of smoke. "Give me some skin!"

He and Zal slap hands like a pair of street thieves.

"Get your women in the back. That means you too, Bagman."

I raise my left hand to my eye as if to scratch it and give Butch the finger, but he doesn't see it. Becky does.

"You're impossible," She shoves me into the backseat between Ellen and her. Arlene scoots in next to Butch, and Zal slides into the shotgun seat—still smoking. Then we are off with Butch banging the Hurst Shifter through four gears and leaving a trail of smoking rubber as he swings away from the village streets onto the Woods Hole Road to Falmouth.

Martha and the Vandellas launch into "Heatwave." Arlene

cranks the volume on the Super Sport's speakers and the females all burst into song. Becky and Ellen sway as they sing and rock me between their shoulders. The scent of perfume rolls through my nose. Sweat runs down my chest.

'These are nice girls,' I tell myself. 'We are not dealing with Tina here. Don't lose your cool!'

But by the time we approach the movie theater I have an erection that seems to spring from the same place where a song is swelling in my guts in harmony to the radio— "Shop Around," by Smokey Robinson and the Miracles. Becky and Ellen sing in full throat … pressing me between their thighs. I have never seen Becky so loose, and I don't know whether I like her this way. I guess I don't know whether I like the way I have begun to respond to her and Ellen either—spreading my legs so I can better feel the girls swaying to the music.

Things get even more complicated in the theater. As soon as we enter the dimly-lit auditorium, Arlene and Butch vanish into their own corner of darkness … leaving Becky and Ellen to guide us into the back row. First me, then Ellen, Becky, and—finally—Zal. It doesn't take a genius to figure out that this is a set up for a make-out session. But usually it is the boys who couple up and place themselves between the girls in order to assure that the girls won't distract each other from the mission at hand. Now, here we have Becky and Ellen taking charge, separating Zal and me as if we are a couple of bimbos.

Almost as soon as we sit down and the credits begin rolling, I see Becky reach over and hold Zal's hand then drag it onto the skin at the cuff of her shorts. At the same time, I feel Ellen slinking into her chair and begin nuzzling the back of her head against my shoulder. Then I feel her moist breath on my neck and my arm rises and wraps around her with a will of its own.

"Are you afraid of something?" she whispers.

I realize that these are the first words to pass between just the two of us all night.

"I feel kind of blown away; I mean this isn't like church where …"

Her hand brushes over my lips to cut me off.

"Good," she smiles up at me. Her blue eyes dance like eyes do when a girl knows she has the looks, talent, and class to get away with anything.

"You're cute," she adds and then takes a long swallow as if gathering courage. "And I want to know what makes you wild."

Jesus. There it is. Everything is falling into place—Becky's coming-on to Zal, the girl's clothes, the singing, the rock and roll of flesh in the car, these seats … this entire night. Becky and Ellen are slumming. They are curious about bad boys.

Suddenly, I feel really stupid. Zal has probably figured this out hours ago. He probably put on those dorky collegiate clothes just to cover his bets with Becky. She knows all too well his reputation for trouble, but tonight he's given her the illusion of safety. And even if Zal has misjudged Becky's invitation—even if he has let himself believe for a couple of hours that this untouchable, nice girl has mysteriously taken a fall for him—he has no doubt freed himself of such delusions when he saw the girls parading off Becky's porch … and when he heard Butch da Silva calling us fruitcakes. Butch must have known from the outset that Arlene's little sister and her fellow beauty queen wanted to upset their perfect worlds with a walk on the wild side. And Zal knew how things stood soon enough to keep himself from looking like a fool. That cool-guy crap with the Camel smoke gave Becky just what she wanted when she wanted it—the Crazy Zal act.

Now he has his arm around her back with his hand spreading across her ribs along the lower seam of her halter top. I can't believe how Becky leans into his clutch. She is letting Zal have a feel.

The son-of-a-bitch catches me watching and bats his eyelashes at me.

I am such a pud! A pud for dressing like some kind of collegiate clown that I will never be. A pud for believing Becky and Ellen could have ever taken Zal and me seriously as human beings. A pud for sitting here doing nothing but growing jealous of Zal and Becky … and angry at these girls who charge the darkness with their perfume and their bare, warm skin.

On the theater screen, the camera leads us through the streets of a Paris market district to the neighborhood where Irma la Duce works as a prostitute. To the tinkle of concertina music, the camera surveys the faces and figures of the whores as they lean in doorways offering the bodies of Asia, Africa, and Europe to anyone with three hundred francs. When the camera pauses on Shirley McLain in a short, tight dress, Becky and Ellen jostle each other's knees in excitement. They recognize the look. The teased, dark hair and bright green stockings remind Becky and Ellen of Neptune's daughter.

"That's Tina, that's absolutely the Tina look," gushes Becky.

"K-I-N-K-Y," Ellen spells. "Ummm humm."

"Too much for the Bagman to handle. That's why she dumped him," informs Zal.

"Right, Zal!" says Ellen with thick sarcasm in her voice. The fingers of her right hand trace the inseam near the knee of my trousers.

I try to find the words, but before I can, Ellen speaks again, "My god, she's such a slut!"

We all know who she means. Tina. The hooker on the screen wears a pair of white, heart-shaped sunglasses just like those Tina had come to school in for just about the entire winter when we were in ninth grade.

"Maybe Tina ought to charge for it too," giggles Ellen.

Then she puts her lips to my ear.

"Tina pulled a train, didn't she?" Ellen whispers.

'Christ,' I think.

"How does a girl …"

I have no intention of talking about Tina—or a night almost two years ago in the cemetery—and shake my head so violently that I think I make Ellen bite her tongue. She jerks back into her own seat, pulls her knees up to her face, and hugs them. Her eyes close.

"Asshole." She gets to her feet and beats a path out of our row.

"Yeah, Bagman you ASSHOLE," Zal adds.

Becky shoots me a squinting look that says, 'You hurt my girlfriend, fool!'

But all of that barely matters. I have gone glassy-eyed with a buzzing in my brain. Christ, if Ellen has heard about me and Tina in the cemetery, what else has she heard about me?

"You like sloe gin and Coke?" Ellen nudges me out of my funk when she settles back into the seat next to me with a Coke from the refreshment stand. Her free hand produces a pint of sloe gin from her shoulder bag. She hands me a paper cup of Coke with a toss of the head that means she wants me to suck off a couple of mouthfuls so she can add the booze.

When I've done my duty, Ellen stirs a third of the bottle into her Coke and takes a long gulp. Her eyes close and she smiles.

"Just like cherry Coke," she purrs … "only it makes me crazy."

"Be nice!" she adds and gives me a cockeyed smile over the rim of the cup.

I take a drink and try to shake the images of that night at the cemetery from my mind.

Ellen swills again. Liquid spills down her chin and leaves a trail of dark spots on her shorts.

"No worries," she giggles, flicking the drops from her lap. "Here's to no worries!"

She raises the cup in a toast and drinks again.

"Like … to hell with Coach Bolino," I volunteer, trying to cast off one of my own demons.

"Like … to hell with the Virgin Mary!" Ellen laughs.

"And math teachers," I add.

And MY MOTHER, FUCK MY MOTHER, my oh so proper MOTHER," Ellen spits. She presses her forehead against mine as if she plans to scheme up some devilment with me.

"You eat with that mouth?" I tease, dredging up Becky's line.

"And more." Ellen presses her lips to mine and rams her tongue against the back of my mouth. It is a kiss that is so bold, so full of death … so caught up in a girl's own fantasies … that I wonder whether at that moment Ellen has even the vaguest notion that she is on the verge of smothering another human being.

Next her tongue is in my left ear.

"Tell me about Tina," she gasps.

I feel something thick and sticky rising in my chest.

"I heard you were there when …"

I cut off Ellen's words with a kiss. But not a kiss of passion. It is a kiss to stop this conversation from going any further. It is a kiss to distract Ellen while I lift the cup of Coke and sloe gin from her hand and pour it on the floor. I don't want to talk about this shit … or think about it either. Ellen has no idea what she is prying into. A branch snaps in my head. A knife flashes, and I hear a boat horn howling in the fog.

"Oh shit," I stutter.

"What? Are you okay?" asks Ellen. "Your hands are all clammy, and you're sweating like a pig."

She lifts her head off my shoulder and rubs my hand over the belly of my madras shirt to show me what she means. It is soaked, and the dye is running in streaks over the waist of my khaki pants.

On the movie screen Shirley McLain is seducing Jack

Lemmon. It seems like a harmless scene—comic and tender. But as I try to watch it, my stomach begins to heave. The taste of sloe gin and Coke rises into the back of my mouth as I catch a glimpse of Becky's back. She half-straddles Zal's knee. His hand disappears beneath the waistband of her shorts right at the hollow spot where her hip blade curves into her belly. Her face buries itself in his neck.

"What's the matter?" prompts Ellen.

I put my hand over my mouth and dash for the men's room.

When I finish heaving—and clean myself off—I call Skipper Wade. I ask if he can come and give me a ride home. I think maybe I have the flu.

10

I meet Becky at a boat slip behind the MBL labs on Eel Pond at five that evening. The sun has almost set to the west over Buzzards Bay. It's been a warm Indian summer day, but now with night coming on you can feel a sharp chill in the air. Not the kind of chill that stops the fishermen from going out on Vineyard Sound to drag for the squid that schools up around the ledges. But a coolness that makes you think twice about going on a boat ride four miles over to Vineyard Haven just for the fun of it.

But all thoughts about the cold trip fade away when I see Becky standing at the consul of her twenty-two-foot white Mako outboard with her shoulder-length hair tied back tight on her head and the collar of a burgundy field jacket pulled up around her neck against the breeze. Remember how Meryl Streep looked in *The River Wild?* That's Becky. She's like Streep; she's into her fifties, but in those jeans, baggy, gray fisherman's sweater, and the field jacket, you could never guess her age. Her looks seem to have locked in place well over a dozen years ago. Those green eyes flare with the light of the setting sun. The engine on the boat is muttering and putting out a thin blue fog of exhaust on the surface of the pond.

"You're late," she growls. But the big smile on her face shows that she is teasing.

"I had to buy wine. If I remember right, the Black Dog doesn't have a liquor license."

I flash her the bag I'm carrying that contains two bottles of Australian Merlot.

Becky hears the clink of the bottles and arches an eyebrow at me as if to pose a question. Suddenly, I feel foolish. Why did I buy *two* bottles? Kind of overkill with a date who probably won't even drink a whole glass.

"Cast off my bow lines."

I stow the wine in a seat locker and just about sprint forward, glad as hell to have something to do besides standing there in Skipper Wade's old, yellow winter slicker feeling like a man carved out of a banana. We sure are getting off to a terrific start.

Becky has the Mako doing thirty by the time she skirts Great Ledge and swings the bows southeast across black water that seems to just suck up the light from a continent of stars overhead. There is no moon at all yet, just a slight veil of clouds over the eastern rim of the horizon. The wind has fallen off to a whisper, but the force of the Mako racing into the speckled darkness blows our eyes shut unless we huddle together behind the windscreen. West Chop light winks out of the dark from its bluff on the Vineyard. Becky turns toward the light like a deer blinded in headlights and presses the throttle to the wall. The Mako, which has been rapping over the waves, now begins to launch itself off the tops and go airborne for a second or two at a time. Even with our legs spread wide and our knees bent to absorb the shock, the pounding of the Mako sends explosions up my spine. I feel on the edge of catapulting off into the sea, and instinctively I grab the frame of the windscreen with one hand and Becky's waist with the other for support.

"Got your attention now, sailor?" she smiles.

"Like a monkey on a chain."

"In my dreams."

"What?"

Becky twists her head around to look at me over her

shoulder. It is an odd look, and with the wind whipping a few strands of her hair across her face, I can't read it. For a second, I have the idea that she is asking for a kiss. But then the moment passes, and I feel like I am being judged with clinical skepticism.

"What did you say?" I shout again over the whine of the outboard.

"Don't talk. Let's just enjoy the ride. And don't you dare let go of me!"

Her torso presses back into the circle of my arm. Her back against my chest and my thighs. The Mako flies across the inky Sound toward West Chop and the lights of Vineyard Haven. The engine sounds like a distant whisper, and I find myself remembering for the first time in years how I used to love boats and the water ... how I used to love Becky.

Ψ Ψ Ψ Ψ Ψ

After the horror show at Nomans, I just plain feel like bad company. And I try to keep my distance from everyone, particularly girls—Tina, of course, but Becky too. I know she is still disappointed with me for bagging her to have a night with the boys. And I feel just plain dumb about my choice. When she passes me in the hall during class changes at school, I notice how she gives me this nervous little wave of her hand from her hip and a sad smile before her eyes dart away. I don't know what to do ... I just keep walking.

It's late-September and everything seems to be crumbling around me. Not only have flashbacks of smoke, knives, and boat horns been hitting me like sniper fire all day, but earlier in the day I got thrown out of English class for not having kept up with the reading in *David Copperfield*. And now, after our pre-game practice, I check the posted list of players dressing for tonight's game against Nantucket and find my name has been erased from the list of running backs.

I bump into the backfield coach as we turn in our dirty towels and practice gear to the equipment manager. He pulls me aside.

"Something's bothering you," he begins. "You can play the game, kid. But lately it's like you're in Neverland. Or you do something mean and out of line—like today with Zalarelli. I can't trust you out there anymore. Now, what's it going to take to get you back with the program?"

He's a good guy, and I know he really wants to help. But the weird stuff running around in my brain about Tina and gunfights and Becky are not the kind of things I can ever imagine telling my football coach … so I give him a raft of excuses. I'm not getting enough sleep with my morning newspaper route, homework, and football. Each takes its toll. Just let me get some rest … then I can focus. I will get back in the groove.

"You bet you will, pal," he gives me a hard slap to the shoulder and retreats to the coaches' room.

I can leave the locker room by a door that leads straight out to the street, but like the other guys on the team, I like to exit toward the stadium … particularly if the band is playing and the majorette corps is strutting up and down the field.

Tonight the band and majorettes are there, putting the final touches on their half-time routine. Like five or six other players, I stop to watch and listen. The music is the Tornadoes' "Telstar."

Dress rehearsal— kids marching in formation wearing maroon and white uniforms. The scene reminds me of my days as a toddler when my grandfather used to bring me here to watch the band.

'Maybe this will clear out my head,' I think and climb up in the stands to watch and be alone.

As the song gathers momentum, the band and majorettes march down the field in the shape of a rocket. Then at the fifty-yard-line the trumpeters in the nose fan out while thirty majorettes come strutting and twirling their batons out of the nose of the spacecraft. They gather in the spiked-ball shape of a Telstar satellite and begin to slowly wheel downfield.

I think I have finally picked out Becky from the crowd of twirlers, then the bleachers creak beside me.

"I ought to kick your ass, Bagman," Zal says as he plops beside me and jars my right bicep with a pair of jabs.

"What the hell were you doing out there today? Game day—helmets, shorts, and t-shirts. No hitting. But you spazzed out. What the christ did you do, give me a karate chop? My neck feels like dog food."

"Look. Sorry, okay? What's the big deal?"

I know I'm being defensive, but I can't help myself. I just want to sit here and let the marching and the music smooth the kinks out of my mind. I don't feel like I really need another reminder of what a screw-up I am. But yeah, I did give Zal a karate chop to the neck during our no-hitting practice an hour ago. I was running a play as a mock Nantucket ballcarrier against our team's defense when Zal moved in from linebacker. He was suppose to tag me with two hands to simulate a tackle—like touch football—but he had come charging at me in a tackler's crouch, feet drumming the turf, laughing because he knows he has me. Then, suddenly, I slashed my hand at his throat out of instinct and dropped him flat.

"Man, you're a mess!"

I barely hear Zal. The satellite of majorettes has spun through the goal posts at the climax of "Telstar," and now the band has launched into "The Stripper." Trombones slur. Snare drums rap out a beat. And the majorette corps sashays right down to midfield in front of us with a bump and grind routine that seems straight from the stage of the Gilded Cage in Boston's Combat Zone.

At the very left end of the majorette's chorus line, dances Becky. I watch her as she sights down the line to keep the row of girls in creamy tunics straight. She clutches her partner's waist in one arm and pumps her baton to the beat of the music in the other. Her hips sway in rhythm with twenty-nine other girls. Thighs and calves kick the air. Knees flash in the sun.

"It's none of my business, but I think you need to talk ... to her," Zal says.

"Right," I say being sarcastic.

"You're all cramped up inside, Bagman."

"Like you really know?"

He shrugs.

"I've been there. Come on, you know that. All the shit going on between my parents. My drinking, the fights."

"What's that make you—Dear Abby?"

I really wish Zal will leave so I can just listen to the music and watch the show.

"That's not the point, okay? Look, my old man's sending me to Father Marley. We talk about shit, you know. I'm trying to get my life together. I don't want to fuck up forever."

What fish gurry!

"You mean you're giving up drinking on school nights?"

"Will you goddamn listen a minute." For a second he grabs the chest of my shirt in his hand and holds it up under my chin.

"Just ... for once ... listen!"

Right! Crazy Zal shooting the shit with Father Marley, getting his life together. I mean, I know things change, but ... really.

Zal let go of me, his black eyes turning away to stare out at the majorettes still strutting. It is the part of the song where the brass section goes blast, pause, blast, pause ... and you imagine a burlesque stripper peeling off a net stocking or a shawl. The majorettes don't have shawls, but they have maroon-and-white pleated shoulder capes, and they give a pretty convincing interpretation of a striptease as they slide their capes off their shoulders, swing them before their bare thighs, and fling them toward the boys gathered to watch.

Zal clears his throat, "All I'm trying to say is that it helps—talking to someone. You know that? You and Becky used to be tight."

Zal is making my head spin. He sounds like a Sunday school teacher.

"She doesn't want to hear it from me now!"

"That's bullshit. Just a chickenshit excuse. Since when did you become such a coward?"

Zal stands up with a grunt, saying he's tired of the Dear Abby thing. Suddenly, he throws a headlock around my skull.

"Wish me luck in the game?" he asks turning my head until I am close enough to smell the cinnamon gum on his breath. Zal has won a starting position in the defensive backfield, and I guess I am proud for him.

"Yes, jesus christ, turn me lose, you homo!"

He laughs and rubs the top of my head with the knuckles of his fist before he breaks the hold and turns away.

"Kick ass!" I shout as he saunters down through the bleachers.

He looks back and yells something, but I can't hear him over the band winding through the final refrain.

"What?" I shout.

Zal steps out onto the playing field, halfway between the majorettes and me.

"YOU ... TALK ... TO ... HER," Zal yells. As he speaks he waves his arm first toward me, then toward Becky.

I can see her head turn and watch.

"YOU ... TALK ... TO ... HIM." Zal swings his pointing arm from Becky back to me. Then he gives a little bow and jogs out of the stadium.

The idiot! How embarrassing. Now I can never face Becky.

The best thing I can do is to get out of this stadium as fast as I can. But before I can clamber off the bleachers, the music ends; the band and majorettes break ranks. Musicians and twirlers block my path to the exit. In the midst of them—

poking my chest with a baton—stands Becky. The wind is catching her hair and raising it off her back. Her face glows from an afternoon spent in the sun.

"What was that all about?"

"Zal is crazy."

She lowers the baton to her side and speaks again, "Did he say we should talk?"

"Yeah, well, what's …"

I stare at my feet.

"Will you walk me home?"

"Why?" I don't know what makes me say this; my heart is screaming 'yes.'

Becky's green eyes well with tears.

"All of a sudden you hate me …"

I shake my head no and turn to look out at the empty playing field. My words catch in my throat.

"Just walk," she says. "Just walk with me, please. We used to do it for hours. Remember?"

The other kids have vanished and left us alone.

"I'll carry your stuff."

Becky passes me her baton, cape, and a stack of books she has stashed on the sidelines. We walk out of the stadium and start toward Woods Hole—both of us staring at the ground and kicking up the maple leaves that have come down with the first frost last night. It is about a three-mile walk along the railroad tracks, but I swear neither of us said a word for the first mile and a half.

Finally, I try to make small talk.

"You guys look pretty sharp. I mean that Stripper number will knock the socks of all those Knights of Columbus guys who come to the games."

"So will the team. If you guys are as tough on Nantucket as you are on each other, you could go undefeated. I saw the way you laid Zal out today. I guess you're ready."

God, it makes me feel sick that Becky was watching our

practice and witnessed what I did to Zal. I wonder whether she understands so little of the game that she doesn't know she's seen me deliver a major cheap shot. But I don't want to get into it so I give her the bottom line.

"I'm not dressing."

For some seconds Becky is quiet—the way she used to get when she felt clumsy for bringing up something that hurt me.

"You can't expect to dress for varsity. Not many eleventh-graders do."

"Zal is."

"Forget Zal. You can't compare yourself."

"Why not?" I ask. Something perverse makes me challenge Becky. I want to see her squirm.

"The guy's a bear."

"So …"

"You're not. You're … you're like half of what I remember best about childhood."

"You mean I'm a boy," I snap. "I'm a boy so I can't dress for high school games yet. But you can. Right? Then you're not a girl anymore; you're a woman and you want to flaunt it?"

"Please," she moans. "Can we change the subject? I can't help how I look. Isn't it okay to be good at something … even if it's just twirling a baton? You know how many years I have dreamed of being out there with the majorettes. When we were little kids you practiced with me. You played the clarinet, Gary Pervis had his trumpet, and we'd march all over Mrs. Talrico's yard. Now, why do you want to make me feel old and dirty about it?"

I shrug.

"Hey, if the shoe fits …"

Becky reaches out and grabs all of her books and gear that I have been cradling in my right arm.

"I can't stand this. You've gotten so mean and moody. Why are you always so angry with me? What's happened to us? You were like my brother and now …"

We have reached the steps to Becky's front porch. She drops all of her things on the ground and sinks to a seat on the bottom step. Her long white hands cover her face.

I can't stand looking at her knowing I've brought on her tears again. As I stand there like some useless sentry, something inside of me slowly bursts … and I begin to babble. I apologize. I tell her I know I have been acting like a jerk. I say that there are things running through my mind confusing me. Things I can't even find the words to talk about. Things from the past and things from now. She has to know how much I miss being with her—how much I miss those hours and days and years when I was her brother, but now … .

Becky raises her face and looks into my eyes as if she is trying to read something.

"Come on." She nods at her front door. "No one's home."

A sad sort of laugh breaks from her lips.

The air seems to vibrate with diamonds, and as I look beyond the door Becky has opened, I get this strange feeling that I am peering into a chapel. In all the years that I have known Becky, I have never before been invited in here. The house is the hermitage of Becky's aged grandmother, her daughters, and her daughters' daughters. The man of the house, Becky's father Butler, always seems away on scallop fishing trips.

The living room beyond the door of this boxy frame dwelling from the 1920s glows with the sun's crimson light filtering through dark curtains and shades by the front-porch roof. It smells of lavender and cherry pie. Large, yellowed portrait photos of men in beards and women up to their necks in lace pose against the violet walls. Brass floor lamps that look like they may have once burned oil stand like pillars in the corners. A purple over-stuffed couch rests with its back to the front windows, a quilt of some kind lies over the back. Across the room sits a pair of faded, red recliner-rockers with a sewing cabinet between. Under the candles on the mantle, and in front of the bricked-off fireplace, stands an immense mahogany cabinet with a TV built into one side and a record player in the other.

"Go ahead and pick some 45s," Becky advises after she has led me in and arranged her gear at the foot of the steps leading up to her bedroom. "I'll get us something to drink."

I find the brass rack holding about fifty 45 disks on top of the record player. As I thumb through the songs by Elvis, Connie Francis, Brenda Lee, and Pat Boone I realize that this collection of oldies belongs to Becky's sister Arlene. All of the songs remind me of days when I'd stay home sick from grade school, listening to the radio.

"Oh," says Becky sneaking up on me. "Try these. They're not exactly new, but they're mine."

She points to a stack of disks already primed to go in the top of the record changer. Then she flicks a couple of knobs. The speaker crackles and a record flops onto the turntable.

The Everly Brothers sing "Cathy's Clown."

"Cheers," says Becky handing me a blue, rubber tumbler and raising a toast.

We each take a sip—good old strawberry Kool-Aid just like we've been drinking together for ten years. Then we settle at separate ends of the couch. Becky kicks off her white majorette boots and stretches her feet across my knees and giggles.

"Remember when we were kids; we used to rub each other's feet because the older kids said it was magic?"

I smile at the memory.

"Maybe we could use some of that magic now."

I don't say a word—I am afraid to let a noise come out of my mouth for fear of spoiling things. So I simply reach down and draw Becky's feet into my lap and slowly roll the athletic socks from her feet. It has been years since I last did this, and I almost forgot the grassy smell of my friend's feet and the feel of her soft, flat insteps. But now, that smell and the touch of my thumbs kneading the soles of her feet bring back a snapshot from the summer evenings years ago when Becky and I had spread out under the lilac bushes in her sideyard, rubbed each other's feet, and searched the sky for Venus and Mars and the Big Dipper.

I close my eyes, rub, and listen as Becky breathes deeply. The Marcels sing "Blue Moon." After a while I feel Becky pull off my sneakers and socks. Her thumbs press into my arches, and pain spikes right up through my neck. But then she begins on my toes, taking them one at a time between her fingers and straightening them out. A wet fire rising out of every pore in my body.

"Uuuuummmmmm," says Becky giving in to the music and my hands. "Who needs to talk?"

Her bare legs slide alongside mine as if she is stretching them to the length of every muscle fiber. When I open my eyes for a second, I see she has her head flung back on the arm of the couch with her face tangled in her thick blonde hair. In the deepening shadows her head looks small and impossibly far away; her body in its majorette's tunic appears the very image of Becky as she looked in her ballet tutu for the fourth grade Christmas pageant. From somewhere in the distance comes the low drone of a bumblebee's wings caught between a curtain and the windowpane, searching for a way out. I close my eyes again.

"This is really dangerous," says Becky.

"Trust me."

I really have very little idea of what I am saying or promising. Becky's breathing, the soft music of a clarinet instrumental on the phonograph, the bee, and the dark has me in a place where I have never been before.

Eventually, the buzzing of the bumblebee brings me back to reality. It is not just an ordinary whirring of a bee but an annoying chatter like something that has disturbed me somewhere before. Behind the couch, the insect dives and climbs between the curtain and the windowpanes. Once it whines so near I bat the air with my hand … then it drones into the distance.

"Hey … were we asleep? The phonograph stopped."

Becky's voice sounds dreamy. Her hands run roughly up my left calf to the knee.

"OOOOOOH," she sighs, stretching. "How delicious!"

I open my eyes. The room is almost dark. At the far end of the couch Becky looks like little more than a shadow swinging my feet off her lap and onto the floor. She sits up, and hitches down the couch until her hips and shoulders press against mine. Then she props her elbows on her knees and holds her head in her hands. Her hair hangs over her face in a veil.

"I wish …" she begins and then stops.

I think I know what she is thinking. Like me, maybe she wishes this moment could go on forever. I imagine us both dead in this purple room smelling of cherry pie, lavender, Kool-Aid, and grassy feet until all time stands still.

'Kiss her,' I think. 'Just put your arms around her and bring her face up to yours. Kiss her—not because you are alone in the dark, or she stirs you with her womanliness; this is not like that afternoon above the bar with Tina. Kiss Becky because she is always kind and gentle and your friend. Now or never! Kiss her before someone dies here.'

So I do.

Our lips brush, and Becky's arms reach behind my back.

'Yes,' I think. 'Yes, oh god, at last!'

But then I see her eyes—green and wide and filling with water. Her whole body begins to tighten and tremble as she squeezes me, pressing her head on my shoulder, and looking out through the curtains.

"No. Please don't ruin things. We can't—you're my brother."

"I'm sorry," I say. It seems like I am always apologizing to her … and I mean it. I feel sorry for causing her pain; but what the hell is she saying? I want to tell her that I am NOT her brother—that I love her.

"That's an excuse," I blurt.

"No. You ARE my brother." She squeezes me harder. "Don't destroy us. Pleeeeeease! I don't know what I would do if I didn't have you."

She begins to sob, and between the sobs she says a lot of things I'm not sure I understand. There is this guy Terry in the senior class; he is thoughtful and responsible and not hung up about proving he is a man. He wants her to go steady.

"But still he'll never know me—not like you do."

She pauses and swallows hard.

"You're—I don't know—like the tomboy in me. And maybe I'm a little bit of you in a funny way."

She says we take care of each other. She remembers silly things like how I rolled Gary Pervis in a pile of fresh dog turds for shaking a jar of red ants down her back.

And what about the times I took her along with me to the Barnstable County Fair—when I could have gone with the boys? We rode the Tilt-A-Whirl and the Octopus, and she squeezed my arm so hard you could see the fingerprints for a week. What about the ghost hunts at church camp ... or the time I sliced open my chin doing gymnastics on her porch rail? We went to the emergency room together at Falmouth Hospital and had it fixed up—just the two of us.

Becky's sobbing has moderated into occasional sniffling. She breaks the hug. Now, she's sitting facing me on the couch with her legs crossed Indian-style. Meanwhile, I feel like every neuron has been blasted from my head in the last few minutes. All I can do is stare down at my left hand that's clasped between her two as they lie on her knee.

Becky talks about the secrets we have. Nobody knows except her about how I almost ran away from home after Tina dumped me. Nobody else knows how she had cried about having to wear glasses and being Arlene's ugly, little sister. How could she ever forget the times I've seen her being sad and alone—the times when I quit playing army or ball with the boys and made her come out and play Duchess.

"Look at me," she pleads. "Only YOU know how boys terrify me, and how I hate the way they look at me now. I always wanted to be pretty, but I don't want to be a toosh—somebody's piece. I'd die if that happened to you and me. I don't want to be like Tina or any of those other girls that just sort of lose themselves over you for a while."

Becky puts her hands on my shoulders and shakes me gently.

"Do you understand? I can't stand losing you to another girl. I don't know how I'd live if you ever used me for sex. I'd lose my mind. You might as well just kill me. And where would you go if you wanted someone to listen and try to understand; who would you talk to?"

Slowly my brain begins to function and two thoughts cross my mind. First, I will do anything she says if she just keeps holding me in the contact lens of those green eyes. Second, maybe she's right. Romance—as I have known it with Tina and others—would rip us apart. Kill us.

Then my mind does a flip-flop, and I think if Becky were my girl how things would be different. How it wouldn't be just a feast of flesh. What would stop Becky and me from being like my parents or hers or Smitty and Lily … or Arlene and Butch?

This last couple enters my mind when I follow Becky's eyes as they shift from my face to the front door where Arlene and Butch have suddenly appeared without a noise.

"Oh christ," I mutter.

"Look at the lovebirds," teases Butch.

"What a little wench YOU'RE becoming," says Arlene to her sister. "You're not supposed to have boys in here."

"Arlene! You have no idea …"

The older sister shrugs, "Save it for mom and dad. I'm sure they will be more than a little interested to hear how you came to be curled up on the …"

"I better go." I stand up.

"Good thinking, man," winks Butch. "Beat the heat!"

"The sooner the better," adds Arlene.

Suddenly, there is just this huge shit storm in my head, and I run right out the door.

"Billy!" calls Becky.

I don't know what she wants to say. I don't look back … or even try to listen. I just can't. I want to rip all of them to pieces.

11

Becky docks the boat at the wharf in front of the Black Dog. We find a table with a view of the harbor from the enclosed porch of the legendary sailors' tavern, and I open one of the bottles of Merlot. We are long past our salads and cutting into a couple of seared tuna steaks, when Becky snaps me out of whatever warm fog it is that I've drifted into.

"Tell me things," she says pointing her fork at me and almost dragging me across the table to her with those huge, green eyes. You're the writer. You're the storyteller. Tell me things."

"I'm a sports columnist. You want me to tell you why I'm gonna bet on Baltimore for the Super Bowl?"

She shakes her head no.

"You know what I mean. Tell me about us."

Jesus, the bill always comes with women, doesn't it? You play; you pay.

"I don't know …"

"Yes you do. Thirty years ago you just got up and ran out of my life one afternoon. We were in my living room. On the couch. We were rubbing each other's bare feet. It was September. I was head over heels in love with you … and scared to death of what I felt. I wanted you to sweep me off my feet and protect me, save me from my caution and a world that was closing in on me from all sides. But I was so afraid of you and of getting hurt. You were so wild. So unpredictable. So kind and understanding one minute, so rude and violent the next. I remember babbling on about not kissing you because you were my brother. But you know what? All I wanted you to do was kiss me again until I shut up and my mind went numb. I wanted to make love with you. But then my sister showed up with Butch. And you literally ran out the door. No good-bye. No nothing. As if you had somewhere else you just had to be."

"That's not quite how I remember it."

Damn, what is the point of getting into this? I thought we had both agreed that we didn't want to muck around in ancient history.

"How do you remember it?"

"I tried to kiss you, and you made me feel like I was wrong and dirty."

"I'm so, so sorry," she says. Her hands leap to her cheeks as if she is trying to stop her head from exploding. "I was so confused. But I was crazy for you. And then you just took off. And you never came back. Do you have any idea how many times I've replayed that scene in my head? Sometimes I think I spent the rest of high school wondering where you went that day and why you didn't come back. Ever. Was it because you went to Tina's? I used to think that you and Tina had a thing going that you never let anybody else know about. I used to think you two were secret lovers. And now, I guess because she's dead, all this old stuff is coming up for me again. Am I crazy ... or did you go to Tina's that day?"

I take a long, slow sip of wine and then stare at Becky. I can still see the sixteen-year-old majorette in the face of the woman across the table from me.

"You have no idea," I begin.

ψ ψ ψ ψ ψ

I start to run ... and maybe I am crying some. I have the feeling that I have to get away from our neighborhood as fast as

I can. At first I head around Eel Pond and start toward Zal's house. I think that seeing him may give me an ally, and I have this vague hope that some of his self-confidence might rub off on me.

The houses along here are on my morning paper route, and the yards are full of fishermen's kids and wives—people I know well—raking leaves. They all look at me expectantly, as if my presence has something to do with delivering or collecting for their papers. But I am just running—running to stretch my legs, running to clear my head ... I don't want these people looking at me; I don't want to have to explain my running to this audience of the cheerful. So I let gravity pull me away—before I reach Zal's—across Water Street toward Great Harbor, the ferry wharves, and Neptune's Bar.

By the time I hit the harbor, my skin feels on fire even though it is already after four o'clock in the afternoon and a crisp day. I pull off my shirt and a stiff southwest wind blows the sweat into lines across my chest. My stride lengthens, and I hurtle toward the water and Neptune's.

At one point, I pass Rollo, Smitty, and Lily in Rollo's Dodge chugging up the street. But my eyes are so full of sweat that I don't recognize my friends shouting, laughing, and flipping middle fingers in my direction until they are behind me.

I don't know what I am looking for or hoping for. Then I spy a bright red Plymouth convertible with its top down, parked among the drinkers' rusting Chevy's and pickup trucks in front of Neptune's. A new car ... with Curly Sullivan sitting on the hood and Tina leaning against the street-side door flashing thigh to passers-by as she cocks a knee out from under the pleats of her short skirt. From fifty yards away I can see that Tina has on Curly's football letter-sweater. Jesus, the girl is incredible. Is there a guy she won't flirt with? Has she dumped Rollo?! Or is she just looking for a few kicks on the side again? This time with Curly. Damn!

"Yo, Bagman," shouts Curly when he sees me. "Where the fuck ya goin'?"

I don't know what to say, and I suddenly veer away across the street.

"How the hell would he know?" laughs Tina. She has a knack for reading my moods. "His whole life's an accident."

I wave—screw you, slut, and Crisco too—and keep running. The tempo of my breathing has grown even. My legs feel strong enough to run until dark.

"Come back here and look at my studly new wheels, you crazy son-of-a- …"

Curly keeps shouting after me, but the words drown beneath the rustle of the leaves around my head as I turn off the street and start down a path along the railroad tracks that run east to Falmouth. I have run a mile or more along the tracks when suddenly I feel the black soil giving way underneath one of my sneakers. Then as I pitch forward, my other foot catches on a root, and the next thing I know my shoulder hits the turf and I'm tumbling down a steep slope thick with maple trees, prickers, and poison ivy.

Ψ Ψ Ψ Ψ Ψ

"So you didn't hook up with Tina," asks Becky.

"No," I say. And that is the truth. Not then. Not there. "But what are you getting at?"

Becky takes a deep breath.

"I know it wasn't just me who hurt you; the place a person goes to lick his wounds says a lot about what beat him up. Find that place, and you'll find something important. Maybe not Tina's murderer, but something that you've been trying to bury for a lot of years, Billy."

"You're crazy."

Becky gives me a long look. The corners of her mouth have a sad droop to them.

"I'm a shrink."

"Does that make you God … or just a wannabee guardian angel?" The words are out of my mouth before I can stop them.

"That wasn't nice."

"I don't get over some things all that easily."

"I can see that."

"So I'm still a little pissed."

"At me?"

"Yeah."

"Because I wouldn't kiss you?"

I shrug. I can't find the words.

Becky's hands fly to her cheeks again.

"I said I was sorry. I feel terrible about what happened that afternoon. If I could, I'd do just about anything to change it. But I can't. And I can't own all of your misery and anger. Maybe this is all about me and you, and maybe it isn't. Maybe it's about Tina, too. Or things you never talked about. But how can I know? You don't share. You never did."

"That's my business."

"I wish you would put down your glass of wine long enough to listen to yourself. You're all locked up."

"Why?"

"That's what I want to know."

My stomach begins twisting in knots. Wine rises in my throat, and I feel like something is choking me.

"Stop. Just Stop!"

Suddenly the restaurant seems as quiet as a tomb. People at other tables turn to look at Becky and me.

"I've made a terrible mistake," she says softly. Then she stands up and heads for the door.

Before Becky steps outside, I see her rummaging around the coat rack. Then she swears.

"Goddamnit. My coat's gone!"

12

Fifteen minutes after Becky left me at the Black Dog, I find her sitting on the end of a dock that belongs to a boatyard called Gannon & Benjamin. She has her knees pulled up under her chin and she is hugging them.

"You look cold."

"I couldn't find my jacket. I think someone stole it. Can you believe that?"

"I heard you swear about it. I looked everywhere after you left. I wanted to find it for you. I thought it was the least I could do. I thought maybe you were just so angry with me, you couldn't find it. But I looked. I even described your coat to the waitresses. We all looked. But none of us could find it."

"The word is 'disappointed.'"

"What?"

"I'm disappointed with you … and myself. Not angry. I'm saving my anger for the thief that lifted my coat."

"I'm sorry. About your coat. And I'm really sorry about me. I've been a bit of a mess lately."

"Lately?"

"All right. For about thirty years."

"At least."

"So I'm sorry. I'm sorry I went off on you back in the Dog."

I sit down beside her on the dock, take off Skipper Wade's foul weather jacket, and wrap it over her shoulders. For a long time neither of us speak. We just stare out at the shadows of two, one hundred-foot schooners riding to their moorings in the harbor as if it is a century ago. There is a clinking of chains, the screeching of metal doors, and the grumbling of engines as a ferry gets underway at the terminal.

"Do you have any of that wine left?" she asks.

I nod. There is a bottle of Merlot stuffed in my slicker pocket.

"Come on then."

Becky gets to her feet and leads me up the dock to where a black schooner of more than sixty feet lies tied alongside. The name on the transom is *When & If*. Weird name for a boat.

"It's okay," she says as she climbs aboard. "I know the owners."

"Let's go."

She walks aft on the deck, pushes open a hatch on a deck-house back by the steering wheel, and climbs inside. I follow. In the little deckhouse it is at least ten degrees warmer. But you can still see the town and the harbor through the windows almost as if you are on deck. There is a navigation table and a lot of electronics gear on one side of this little cabin, and a berth on the other side. It must be where the captain or mate sleeps, separate from the guests who are quartered below in the main cabin.

"Hold this for me," says Becky as she hands me the wine from my coat she's wearing and takes a seat on the berth.

She fishes around in her purse, comes up with a Swiss Army knife, and puts its corkscrew to work. After the cork pops out, she takes a long slug from the bottle and passes it to me.

"What are we going to do?" she sighs.

"What do you mean?"

"I must be insane."

"Why?"

Becky reaches over, grabs the bottle from between my knees, and takes another long drink.

"What am I doing sitting here in *When & If*, drinking with you? I should be home being a mother. Or at least off trying to find my jacket. Going to the police or something. I like that jacket. It gives me a big hug. And I don't even know if I like you. You don't give me a big hug."

She takes another slug of wine.

"In fact, did I ever tell you that I think you give about the worst hugs that are humanly possible? Hugging you is like hugging a statue. It was like that thirty years ago. And it's the same today. You know that?"

Gee, this is turning out to be such a swell date. We have moved from one romantic setting to another, and in each one things between Becky and me have decayed from bad to worse. I am so glad that I've come home to bury Tina—just about get accused of murdering her by my old buddies and take a knee between the legs about a hundred times from my boyhood flame.

I reach for the bottle, but Becky tosses it up to her mouth for another swallow.

"Maybe we should go home," I suggest. "This isn't really doing either of us a lot of good."

Becky gives a little laugh.

"Not a chance, Bagman. I'm just starting to have fun. Maybe if I drink enough of this wine, I can feel safe with you for once. That's what booze has always done for you, am I right? It makes you feel safe? Safe in the midst of chaos?"

"It has that effect," I murmur. "Or at least it used to."

"It has that effect." She mimics me with a stern face.

"Aw lighten up, Billy. Stop acting like you're above all this. Cut the crap."

"What?"

She takes another drink.

"Drop the mask. Maybe you really don't care about me. Maybe you just asked me to dinner tonight out of some vague sense of nostalgia or guilt that you're feeling. I don't know. And I'm not sure I even want to know. You've worn me out with worry. But stop pretending that you don't know anything about who killed Tina. Stop putting up the walls. Hell, maybe you killed her? Are you going to kill me? You can tell me. Because you know what? I don't care anymore."

I want to just get up and leave her to stew in the Merlot and her bizarre speculations. But something keeps me glued to that berth in the *When & If.* Out in the harbor the big white ferry *Islander* has thrown its engines into reverse and is braking for its landing at the Steamship Authority terminal. I wait until I see it safely into its landing and the static clears in my head. Then I speak.

"Look. Can you cut me a little slack?"

"Why?"

"Because I'm going to tell you what you asked for back in the Dog."

"What?"

"I remember something, okay?"

ψ ψ ψ ψ ψ

For me, Monday nights during this summer of 1964 reek of semen, beer, and blood. During the summer, Monday is the most important night of the week for teenagers on the Upper Cape. It's the night the Falmouth Drive-In lets a carload of people watch the movies for just one dollar. Buck Night. Family movie-goers stay at home and let the parking lot of the drive-in overflow with crowds of teenagers arriving in anything that will roll.

The James Bond film *Dr. No* is playing tonight.

"Come with us," Becky invites, when I pay my daily social call to her front porch. "Arlene's going to take daddy's car. Laurie and Caroline are coming, too. We've got room for you if you can stand being with a bunch of girls. It's going to be a bitchin' cool movie!"

I look at Becky and think about what she has just said, 'Bitchin' cool?'

A month or so ago, Becky left our neighborhood for a long visit with cousins in Los Angeles. It was her first big trip away from Woods Hole, and the day she left for the airport with her hair in Heidi braids, I thought, 'There goes my little sister in her blue Sunday-go-to-meetin' dress.'

Becky returned a few days ago speaking this new language. She has a golden tan like girls never get during the foggy summers we have on Cape Cod. In the funny clothes she wears—Mickey Mouse t-shirts, short-shorts, and flip-flops—she looks like she has added four inches to her legs above the knees. And her t-shirts bulge with breasts. Now when I look at her, daisies come to mind. Grown-up—almost over night. Never kissed. No boyfriend.

Sure, I can go to a bitchin' cool movie with Becky and pack into her dad's big, black Olds with a bunch of girls; I'll plan on it and meet up with them at Becky's a little after seven.

But something comes up to screw the program royal, as it always does.

Zal shows up at my side door right after my parents have finished dinner and gone down to the docks to go over Skipper Wade's books and pay off the crew after their last trip. Zal has beer on his breath, and he says I owe him money.

"What are you talking about?"

"The three bucks you lost to me last Friday. Pay up!"

Zal is right. He creamed me in a half dozen games of eight ball. I haven't paid him because I have this dream that one of these days I will win it all back. Besides, I want to save all the money I can to buy a German Shepherd puppy. My parents have always said "No dog, we don't have enough room." But I hope that if I show them I have saved $100 for a puppy, they might give in.

"I want a rematch," I challenge as Zal pushes his way into my bedroom and begins fingering the foot-tall model of the Planter's Mister Peanut where I stash the money I earn delivering the morning paper. "Hands off!"

I grab Mister Peanut.

"Now or never, earlobes," chuckles Zal as he flicks his fingers to the roots of my ears and gives a tug. "Now or never. The Gorgeous One needs a little extra cashola, now, for some more brewski and the drive-in. Gonna suck on some suds and watch Double-O Seven play hide the salami with Ursula Andress tonight. What a babe, huh?"

"Yeah," I agree thinking of Becky, hugging Mister Peanut against my chest, and deciding not to let Zal in on my plans for the night.

Then I add, "I'll whip you later; I'd hate to see you so broke you have to spend Buck Night at home watching Dick van Dyke on TV with your little sisters."

"Right, Bagman. Come on, bet me. Now or never, money bags!" With those words Zal feigns for my groin with his open hands, and as I bend to protect my jewels, he grabs Mister Peanut from me and hits the door running. I can already see we are headed for trouble.

By the time I catch up with Zal, we have traveled the four blocks around Eel Pond to Bo's Place, a pool hall near Neptune's Bar and the ferry landing. A pre-drive-in crowd of teens mills between jalopies and the attractions inside.

Walking in the door, I see Curly Sullivan holding Mister Peanut. At sixteen, Curly already has a clammer's body. His hands are the size of meat hooks. These make an odd combination with his small head and freckled cheeks—the genetic inheritance of parents who came to Woods Hole straight from Western Ireland. His razor-cut hair falls across his forehead like John F. Kennedy's.

"Zal says you're playin' some eight ball," laughs Curly. "And this is the prize. I'll keep it REAL safe." His breath smells like liquor.

'Jesus christ,' I mutter to myself. 'Why are things like this always happening to me?' I glance at the Coca Cola clock behind the soda counter. It is already twenty after six. How the hell am I going to make it back to Becky's by seven? I have to get this over.

"Rack 'em up," I grunt at Zal.

So we begin. In the first game, I win the break and sink two striped balls, but then Zal runs the table. The second game is more even, but it drags on as both Zal and I keep missing shots. The beer he drank somewhere before raiding my house seems to have slowed him down, and I keep watching the clock instead of focusing on the game. By seven o'clock half the balls are still left on the table. If I am going to get back to Becky's in time for my ride, I need to leave now. Just put down my cue stick and walk. But that leaves Curly and Zal with Mister Peanut. There is $64 in that plastic model. I can't take a chance on losing it. Just screw it! One more game. Maybe Becky will wait.

By the middle of the game, Zal has begun making rude remarks about my mother's sex life, a sure sign that I am getting to him.

"The Bagman's puttin' the ole' buddyfuck to you, Zal," observes Curly.

"Maybe the Gorgeous One needs to take a little powder." The observation comes from a bantam body that strides up to the side of the pool table and slaps down two quarters on the rail. "Next game."

Zal, Curly, and I look at the speaker, a guy in his mid-twenties. Dressed in neat tennis sneakers, tight blue jeans, and a Hawaiian-print shirt, Freddy Farnham looks like one of the guys in The Beach Boys. He has fine features, dark hair, and the dewy eyes some teenage girls can't resist.

"What a waste of a cute man," Tina judged once after she heard the rumor that Freddy prefers boys—a judgment confirmed by a social life that generally places Freddy at Bo's Place or cruising in his white Chevy Impala convertible with a clutch of high school footballers and basketball guys. Rumor has it that he gives blow jobs on demand, too. Yeah, he is queer, but almost everybody tolerates him because he has some hot wheels, buys us brewskis, and you can boss him around like a whipped dog.

"Who's asking you?" spits Zal. "Maybe we don't want you to have the next game." He speaks as if Freddy is some dorky classmate, not the guy who taught us biology last year.

"Don't be an ass. You need my help. You and me against Curly and Bagger. Deal?"

Zal looks at Curly and me.

"What's in it for us?" asks Curly with a smirk. I can't tell whether this remark carries some kind of homo undertone or whether Curly's question rings with genuine skepticism born of the knowledge that Freddy Farnham is possibly the best eight ball shooter in town.

"If my team loses, I'll buy the beer," shrugs Freddy.

"You drive to Buck-Night no matter what," bargains Zal as thoughts of Ursula Andress must be crossing his mind.

"Natch," smiles Freddy, grabbing a ball rack and beginning to trash the current game on the table. "Best out of three?"

I think about Becky in a Mickey Mouse t-shirt.

"I gotta go."

I lunge for Mister Peanut.

"Not so fast, Bagman. We be partners now."

Curly passes Mr. Peanut to Zal like a football.

Damn. These guys are pissing me off. Arlene and Becky are going to leave for the drive-in without me. But there is still hope. Freddy said he'd drive us all to Buck Night. I just have to nab a ride with Freddy the Fairy and catch up with Becky at the drive-in … if I can find her sister's car.

Maybe my luck with the ladies sucks, but I am on a roll with the pool cue. In our first game, Curly and I bounce back to win after Zal has nearly run the table. In the second, we have them all the way, and that is all she wrote.

"Party time," coos Curly.

At last Zal hands me Mr. Peanut after removing the money he claims I owe him.

"Rock 'n' roll, Bagman." Zal gives me a hard jab to the right shoulder.

Right. Maybe within the hour I can find Becky. A little beer might loosen me up. We have some time; it isn't dark yet.

'This is a mistake,' I think as I watch Freddy march out of the packy near the ferry landing with a big square case of quarts. 'Something's wrong here.'

"Silver Top?" complains Curly after the Chevy convertible begins wheeling out of town on the back road that runs north through the hills along Buzzards Bay. "Jesus christ, the man buys Silver Top. Women shit. My old lady drinks this stuff. What is he thinking? At least he could have bought some Narry."

I open the cardboard box and pass a 32-ounce bottle to each of the guys in the front seat.

"Ah, yes, I know this," goofs Zal with a phony Australian accent. From his seat at shotgun, he holds a quart of Silver Top high above the right side of the car and stares at it against the light of the setting sun. "Back in Sidney we used to drink the stuff day and night. Kept the man-eating sharks away. Pregnant porpoise piss, mate."

"What the fuck are you talkin' about?" blurts Curly, sitting on the bench seat between Freddy and Zal looking like a kid who has just been given a dead chick on Easter.

"Hey, you don't have to drink it if you don't think it's manly enough for a stud like Big Curly Sullivan."

Something about Freddy's tone of voice reminds me of biology class; and now it really hits me that Freddy is an adult. Twenty-three (or maybe twenty-four) years old. My old teacher, Mr. Farnham, the guy who made me dissect frogs. It seems strange being with him like this. I know other kids who have hung around with Freddy for a while, and being with Freddy Farnham like this doesn't seem to bother Zal or Curly; but—I don't know—I just feel weird. I shouldn't be here; I should be with Becky.

"Another," burps Curly as he throws his empty quart of Silver Top into the bushes along the road. Zal sticks an empty hand in my direction, too. These guys amaze me. I have barely taken three sips out of my beer. But maybe that is because I am having a hard time juggling it and Mister Peanut as the car lurches over the bumpy road.

The Chevy turns down a dirt road that comes to a dead end at the foot of three small mountains of sand. They rise in peaks in front of us and slide thirty feet down to Buzzards Bay. A defunct dredging operation for a manmade harbor. These are the gravel piles. Another place where kids come to park and party and drink, like the Knob and the golf course.

"My home away from home," announces Zal.

"So I've heard," says Freddy. "You're a popular guy."

Freddy delivers this remark without any hint of sarcasm or teasing, and he seems to have an accurate bead on Zal's social life so far this summer. Recently, I have seen a lot less of him since Zal established himself as a guy who can buy beer in the local packies. He has become surrounded by older kids who have cars and want to come drinking at the gravel piles, but need someone to buy.

"Yeah, my real name's Tony Curtis and I've been diddling Marilyn Monroe here every Friday night," boasts Zal.

Freddy seems to have had enough of Zal's ridicule and shoots back.

"God, you're beautiful, Zal—really beautiful … like a frigging sick squid. I bet none of you studs have the balls to go skinny dipping, huh?"

Freddy makes his eyebrows jump like Groucho Marx and begins peeling out of his shirt.

"Yeah … well … if I go, it's because it feels good. Because

I want to. Know what I mean?" boasts Curly. "Nobody makes me do anything I don't feel like. Fuck this dare shit."

"We don't have to prove anything to you, Freddy," says Zal. "Bagger and I already had skinny dipping in mind, didn't we, Bags."

Damn. Not me. Skinny dipping with Freddy the Fairy? I just want to be at the drive-in tracking down Becky. Get me the hell out of here.

Zal hands me his quart of beer to hold while he climbs out of the car, pulls the football t-shirt over his head, and drops his black Bermuda shorts over his ankles. He's not wearing underwear.

"Jesus christ, it's an ape man," marvels Freddy who must not have expected to see how much thick, black hair covers Zal's body.

Almost instantly, Curly drops his pants and follows Zal in a race over one of the sand piles and down the slope into Buzzards Bay.

"After you, Bagman," gestures Freddy toward the bay. He peels out of his clothes, sidles up beside me as I lean against the fender of the Impala, and pinches my butt cheek in his fingers.

"Jesus, what the hell?! I'm outta here." But the next thing I know I'm naked and making for the water like a man in a race against death. For maybe a minute I swim underwater toward the dark center of the bay to smooth away the shakiness that has suddenly overtaken my arms and legs when Freddy grabbed me.

I have barely surfaced when I hear a car radio begin blasting out Dion Warwick's voice singing "Walk on By."

"Shit," says Freddy. "Stay the hell away from that car, Reggie!"

"We ain't hurtin' nothin'. We just came to join the party; that's all!"

The speaker is Reggie Jones … yet another veteran of Freddy Farnham's biology class. He has three other black guys with him, including his main man Joey Hardison and two older guys wearing basketball jerseys from Barnstable High. One of the guys has helped himself to an unopened quart of our beer and is passing it around.

"We just thought we'd sit up here, have a quiet little drink, and watch all the Tina Toys play drop the soap with the blowboy." Freddy Farnham failed Reggie in bio, and Reggie has not forgotten.

"Let's kick some ass," growls Zal. He reaches down to the bay bottom and picks up two rocks.

"Wait," says Freddy.

"Booolshit," mutters Curly who picks up a half-dozen rocks in his claws. Then he charges out of the water firing rocks at the black guys who have just sat down on the lip of a gravel pile.

"Motherfuck ..." calls one of the guys as a rock hits home.

Zal gives a war cry as he runs at Curly's side and lets go with his rocks. Freddy and I follow behind as if some general has given us an order.

A sandstorm comes rolling down into our faces as the guys up top try to kick the mountain down on us. By the time I stagger up through the dust, Curly and Zal stand waving their fists at a gold Plymouth Valiant starting to churn up the dirt road.

"You better run, you chickenshits," bellows Zal.

"I'm gonna waste you, Reggie," adds Curly.

Two of the black guys shoot us moons through the back window.

"Sayonora, you corn-hole astronauts," calls Reggie as the Valiant disappears around a turn.

Corn-hole astronauts? What?

We all look at each other—naked and caked with mud and dust. All four of us sit down on the lip of a gravel pile.

"You're a fucking mess, Bagman," says Zal. "You gotta clean yourself up."

I feel the dirt between my toes and fingers. And I taste its grit in my mouth and smell it clotting like salt in my nostrils. As I get up and sprint down the gravel pile into the water, I have to wonder what the hell else can possibly go wrong on such a warm summer night.

Kids and cars pack the drive-in at sundown. Curly commandeered the driver's seat to Freddy's car, and as the last streaks of the evening's red and violet fade into the starlit Cape Cod night, Curly guides the Impala through the lanes between the rows of cars already poised to watch the film … or party.

The roar and crackle of souped-up jalopies mixes with the bass beat from radios and the mutter of movie voices seeping from tin speakers. A gang of girls wave to us and sing "The Duke of Earl" in a parked yellow Tempest convertible as we move through the ranks at a walker's pace. The peanut-popcorn-Pepsi-gasoline scent hangs in the air, and on the giant screen the previews roll.

I search for Becky in her dad's black Olds, but I haven't a clue to her whereabouts. Curly swerves into an open parking space two rows behind the building that houses the projection booth and snack bar. I have only witnessed Buck Night twice before, but I know this is where you park if you are only faintly interested in watching the movie. Kids come back here—out of the glare of the projector's beam—to drink and make out. You park another five or six rows back near the fence when people have sex or a rumble in mind.

"Chug-a-lug, Bagman," orders Zal. "Let's cruise this joint!"

"Indubitably," burps Curly. This might be the only big word he knows, and he learned it watching Bugs Bunny or Mr. Magoo. "Let's see if Reggie Jones dares to show his black ass."

I open my throat and let the last six or eight ounces of Silver Top bubble into my stomach and launch an immense belch.

"Lovely, manners," says Freddy with a little smirk on his face. "Are you drunk?"

"No way," I spit, springing out of the back seat and onto the trunk of the car—ready for anything.

"Then why the fuck are you still holding onto that goddamn doll?" asks Freddy.

Funny how I haven't noticed Mister Peanut clutched in my right hand.

"Get rid of that fuckin' thing before someone sees you with it, asshole," advises Zal.

"Time to ditch the fag," whispers Curly. Then louder, "See you later, Freddy. We gotta cruise some chicks. I guess you wouldn't understand."

"Dipshit ape." Freddy waves us away.

I stash Mister Peanut on the floor by the back seat.

The three of us beat it down to the front row of the parking lot then begin working our way through the throng of cars—walking up and down each row to see who has made the scene, where the action is. Curly and Zal are pumping kids for information about the location of Reggie and his friends.

Rounding a beat-up panel truck, I come face to face with a couple of linemen on the Clippers. Danny Sider and Chicky Boyle are wandering around giggling and searching for more beer. Chicky slaps Curly a high five, snickers, and stumbles off into the dark after Danny who claims he has to meet a babydoll for a blowjob.

"Beautiful people," laughs Curly.

"Douche bags," says Zal.

I can't say anything. A thick, coppery fluid has started to rise in my throat.

Next, Curly and Zal sneak up on the back of Rollo's Dodge and pile into the back seat. It is sort of a surprise invasion that catches Rollo with his tongue on Tina de Oliveira's right breast. Rollo points a pistol at us and tells us to "get fucking lost." What a guy. "Heeeeeeeyyyyyy, it's a pussy wagon," coos Zal. "The Bagger's nubile neighbors."

"Cunts," grunts Curly happily. "Oh, excuse me," Curly corrects himself. "I mean vaginas, birth canals, Dago echo chambers, Portagee dispose-alls."

By this time Curly has wandered right up to the passengers' side windows and is bending over looking in at Becky, her sister, and the two other girls from my block. They heard every word of Curly's monologue.

"Buzz OFF, pinhead," shouts Becky's sister Arlene.

"Oh they get cute when they're mad!"

"Who invited you, Curly?" asks Caroline, the other girl in the front seat. She is pretty, but she has a body that looks like she can bench press three hundred pounds.

"Not you, Amazon! I just came for a look at what you got here in the back seat." Curly gives a Howdy Doody smile at Becky. "The Bagman says little Becky-girl's about to bust out of her jeans!"

Becky flashes me a hurt look asking, 'How could you?'

I want to die or at least change my name. I have to explain.

My head pokes in the open window just inches from Becky and her cousin Laurie.

"Becky, he's full of shit. I never …"

"You're drunk," she says evenly. "Please just go off somewhere and …"

"Shitty shock absorbers. You got shock absorbers like Jello, Arlene," Zal says standing on the Oldsmobile's front bumper, rocking the car with his weight.

"What the hell have you been doing in this baby?" Zal cackles. He keeps rocking the car in ever-greater gyrations. You can hear the frame beat against the axles as the Oldsmobile bobs and bucks.

"I'm getting the police!" says Caroline springing out of the car.

Curly grabs her by the shoulders. Face to face they look

virtually the same size.

"I'm outta here." I feel drunk and stupid. As I stumble away into the dark, I look back. Curly and Caroline are trading slaps across the face. The guy hit girls. Shit. Zal has mounted the Oldsmobile's hood. He rises and falls, King Kong on a trampoline.

A police whistle screeches. Three cops appear out of nowhere and nail me with a spotlight. I take off. The ground rolls under my feet like the deck of the *Ellen B* running before a smoky sou'wester. Man, I have to sit down somewhere, even if it is in freaking Freddy's car.

A long, muted cry tumbling from my lips wakes me. Hands like big white spiders have been crawling all over me.

"Shssssssh." Freddy puts his left hand to my lips. "You were dreaming. It's okay. Everything's okay. Calm down."

I look around. I am still at the drive-in. On the screen James Bond sits at a dinner table with a Chinese-looking man who has black mechanical claws for hands. In the car, Freddy's right hand lies pressed between my legs.

"What the hell?"

He pulls his hand away and stares at it as if it is a piece of trash he has just found littering his car.

"I couldn't help myself. I didn't think you would mind."

"Why? Jesus christ. Why?" I back against the passenger door of the Impala.

"I thought you'd like it."

"You don't understand," I shriek. "You fucking faggot." Suddenly, I pounce onto the driver's side of the car. I hold Freddy by the lapels of his Hawaiian shirt. My knees press against his ribs. His head cocks back against the sideview mirror, and in the flickering light from the screen his face looks ten years old and blue.

"You don't have any idea," I scream again.

"Yes I do," he says in a small voice ... and then I think he begins to cry.

But I don't stop to be sure. I don't care. I run.

It seems like hours later when I finally find my way to Becky's car.

"What do you want?" Arlene challenges.

Bending down, I look inside the car for Becky.

"Becky ... please." I can barely get the words out. I'm breathing hard from my run.

"You okay?" her voice sounds from the darkness.

"I don't know. Can we talk?"

"Well, about what?" asks Becky. "I don't want to be a jerk, but I don't like you very much the way you are tonight."

"Ditch that drunken creep," Caroline shakes a fist at me. "I hope your friends are in jail!"

"Come-on, let's walk." Becky climbs out of the car, takes my hand, and leads me toward a fence that separates the far side of the drive-in from a meadow.

"What's wrong? Are you in trouble?"

I don't know where to begin. I just want to be with her.

"I've lost Mister Peanut," I say.

"What?"

I lost this Mister Peanut thing. It's like a model."

"Look at me. You're babbling. What's going on?" Becky stops walking and steps in front of me. She holds both my hands and looks deep into my eyes.

"Kiss her," calls a girl's voice.

"You're blocking the view!" someone bellows and honks their horn.

Becky drops one of my hands and starts leading me toward the fence again. She doesn't say anything until we sit down in some long grass and put our backs against the whitewashed fence boards.

"Now, what are you talking about?"

"A lot of things," I say. "Everything has gone wrong tonight … and now I have lost all of my money. It is in the Mister Peanut model, which I left in Freddy Farnham's car."

"You're money for the puppy?" Becky asks. We have talked a lot over the years about my getting a dog. When we were seven or eight a bunch of the kids in the neighborhood behind Eel Pond had scripted our own version of Lassie, only with a German shepherd. Becky liked to pretend she was the dog. We called her Duchess.

"Why can't you go back and get the money?"

I don't know what to say.

"Did Farnham do something to you?"

"Maybe it's not all his fault," I mumble. "I don't want to make any more trouble for him. I just can't …"

"Come on, I'm with you. He won't try anything."

She put her arm through mine and for a couple seconds laid her head on my shoulder.

"What are we going to do about you?" she sighs.

I wouldn't have moved if a car leaving the drive-in had not turned in our direction and pinned us in its headlights. A ground fog has developed, and in the lights from the car the drive-in looks to be floating in a cloud.

We reach the heart of the car lot, and a crowd of guys who have collected in the dark behind the snack bar start running past us.

Guys carrying bats and tire irons, and I can hear the clink of chains.

"What's going on?" I call.

"Rumble," shouts a voice that sounds like Chicky Boyle's.

"Sullivan and Zalarelli dropped a couple of niggers from Barnstable. Now there's a whole gang after them!"

"Stay out of it." Becky tugs on my arm.

On the screen Bond is creating havoc in some kind of missile silo. Warning horns trumpet.

In the car lot a siren whines. Two police cruisers shoot past. The flashing gumball machines on their roofs make the fog pulsate red. For a second, I stop walking and watch the progress of the police cars toward the back of the lot.

Becky tugs at me again.

"I don't like this. I want to find your Mister Peanut … or go back to my car. Now!"

"This way." We begin moving again in the direction of Freddy Farnham's car, but my mind is on Curly and Zal. By now they won't be anywhere near that crowd or those cops; they'll be hiding.

The headlights and red pursuit lights of the police turn back in our direction. Clusters of boys come running out of the dark in twos and threes. Around the drive-in car doors are slamming, engines racing, and cars are peeling toward the exit without their lights on. Reggie's gold Valiant almost runs down Becky and me before we can step out of the way. Three more cars speed by. Then a police car. On the screen a series of explosions spews smoke and fire and seems on the verge of vaporizing Jamaica. From the highway comes the roar of engines winding into high gear.

"This is sick," says Becky.

I have to agree.

"Let's forget it."

"What about the money?"

I shrug. I have had enough for one night. I don't want to face Farnham, and I also have a suspicion that Curly, Zal, or both of them might be hiding in Farnham's car. The last thing I want is to get Becky tangled up in the rumble.

A row of flood lights flash on at the top of the movie screen, and a Hammond organ begins blaring stupid music over the P.A. system.

"Don't quit. Come-on. The movie's over. It'll be easier now." Becky flashes me the cheery mask she uses with people at church.

So we head to the spot where I left Freddy Farnham's car. Down front in the parking lot quite a few cars are leaving— mostly younger kids with curfews. Others move to the dark rows behind the snack bar and wait for the lights to go down and the second feature to begin.

The ground fog buries us to our waists and makes me feel disoriented ... especially when I come to the place I thought Curly had parked Freddy's Impala. And it's not there.

"It's over. He left." I say staring at the vacant parking space.

"Maybe you're mistaken, or maybe he moved during all the commotion. Think about the puppy; think about all the money you saved. You've got to look."

I want to turn back. If I stand by the drive-in exit while cars are leaving, I can probably hitch a ride home. But Becky takes up my hand again and that is reason enough to keep going.

As we work our way toward the back of the lot veering back and forth among the cars up to their windshields in fog, neither of us talk. Becky holds my hand and leads me with the firmness of someone trying to distract herself from a nightmare. The second feature starts rolling, but I barely notice. Every step I take with Becky holding my hand drives me closer toward the decision that I should kiss her.

"Look, there it is!" Becky drops my hand and points.

In the corner of the last row of the lot, I can just make out the white Impala parked off by itself. The convertible top is up now. I wonder why Farnham has moved back here.

"Christ. What am I going to say?" I ask myself as much as Becky.

"Tell him the truth. How hard is that? You forgot some- thing, and you want it back. He's not going to try anything with me here."

"Okay."

I take her hand and walk quickly. At maybe twenty-yards

from the Impala, I can see two silhouettes in the front seat. We step closer, and the silhouette behind the steering wheel disappears from view. A shadowy figure of a boy in a slicker grips the dashboard and moans.

Becky squeezes my hand and stops.

"Ummmmmm," says the boy again. "Do me."

"Oh, my god," whispers Becky as a picture of what is taking place on the front seat of the Impala begins to form in her mind. Her voice trembles, and her nails dig into my hand.

"This is sick. It's too sick. I'm sorry." Suddenly, Becky begins running away.

When I catch up with her, she has stopped with her hand over her mouth as if she is about to vomit. She sobs.

"Why are you mixed up with such pitiful people?" Her hands push against my chest and she gives me a look that says, 'If you touch me, I'll scream.'

I think I hear a branch break. I smell smoke and a crush of images begins tumbling through my mind—marsh boots, the wail of a boat horn in the Sound.

Then I start shouting.

"Motherfucking sonuvabithin' faggot …"

As I swear, I cast about me and begin ripping the drive-in speakers from their stands, snapping them off their chords and throwing them in the general direction of Farnham's car.

When I stop, Becky has vanished.

13

Becky nuzzles up against my chest as we lounge against a pile of pillows on the schooner. To tell the truth, I don't know how much of the story she has heard because she is asleep when I finish. Her breath echoes like a slow, soft purr in the boat cabin. As I sit there listening and feeling her warm body heaving against my chest, an after shock from my memory of that night in the drive-in hits me.

ψ ψ ψ ψ ψ

She's gone. I wander up and down the rows of the drive-in for a while. Sometime after midnight I find Rollo and Tina in the Dodge and bum a ride home. They heard a rumor that the police are holding Zal.

More news comes my way the next afternoon while I'm cutting my parents lawn as payback for having stayed out later than my eleven o'clock curfew.

Danny Sider catches me as he passes my yard. He has a split lip and a bruised eye.

"We kicked ass in the rumble, me and Chicky and Curly," Danny brags. He goes on to tell me the rest.

The police had taken Zal into custody for fighting. His father had to pick him up at the station, and Zal has a hearing before a Falmouth magistrate this afternoon. The other news is that Freddy Farnham is in the hospital with a concussion and a broken jaw. Someone at the drive-in found him beaten up and unconscious in his car around one o'clock last night. He has slashes carved all over his back. Danny says a lot of kids saw me with Freddy. They figure that Freddy tried to get into my pants, and I jacked him up and carved on his back with the sharp end of a beer opener.

"What a fucking crock of shit!" I scream at Danny.

"Be cool," he says raising his hands in defense and back-pedaling up the street. "That faggot got what he's been asking for, for a long time. You're a hero."

Ψ Ψ Ψ Ψ Ψ

I don't think I'd tell Becky this part. In fact, now that I think about it, the whole story seems pretty random, unrelated to Tina's murder—or just about anything else—and pathetically juvenile. I hope that she fell asleep before I got to the part about the shadows in Freddy Farnham's car. Who needs to dredge up that stuff? Well, the good news is that Becky has stopped accusing me of things, like Tina's murder, and has crashed in my arms. I want to believe that after all of these years she finally has found a way to feel safe with me, but I know that her crashing here has more to do with the wine than with me or us.

I don't wake Becky until well past midnight. She is still in a daze when I lead her back to the wharf in front of the Black Dog and help her into her boat. Immediately she curls up on the floor in front of the windscreen and pulls Skipper Wade's yellow slicker over her like a blanket. For a second I think about having another look for her coat, but the Dog is closed and dark. It has been years since I have actually run a speedboat. But I guess you don't forget these things if you've grown up on the water. In no time I have the engine running, the lines cast off, and the boat roaring north approaching the winking red light of a buoy and the lighthouse at West Chop. The moon is not up. A thin layer of fog puts a murky veil over the water.

I guess I must have been in a bit of a daze from the wine, too, or maybe it is just shell shock from all that has happened in the last twenty-four hours, but I barely see the other boat until it's swerving across our bow doing about thirty knots and throwing up a wake that rolls the Mako sharply to the left.

"Jesus christ!" I shout automatically.

"What? What's going on?" calls Becky over the whine of our engine. She scrambles off the floor and pulls herself onto the bench seat beside me behind the windscreen and rubs her eyes with her fingertips.

"Shit!"

I pull back the throttle a bit to avoid hitting the dark boat in front of us as it veers back across our bow from left to right. When it just crosses our bow, it makes a sharp S-turn back in front of us, throwing a shower of water from its wake in our faces.

"What have you done, now?" Becky growls as if I have touched off someone's road rage on a highway with a dumb move of my own. "Just stop."

She stands, grabs the throttle out of my hand, and pulls the power completely off. The Mako bucks forward with rapid deceleration and the boat in front roars ahead.

"It came out of nowhere." I try to explain as Becky nudges me to her left with her hip, grabbing the wheel and starting to turn us back toward the safety of the inner harbor.

"Yeah right."

"I swear."

"How come lightning always strikes when you're around?"

"I don't know, but we're sitting ducks right now, and here it comes again."

The boat that cut us off has circled back on our left and

is bearing down on us from less than fifty yards like one of those blacked-out stealth fighters you see in pictures. More of a shadow than a boat. No running lights.

Becky gooses the throttle, feigns a left, then abruptly cranks the Mako in a sharp turn to the right to dodge what is now clearly an attack. She is only about two seconds into this steep accelerating turn when the other boat hits us. It is a glancing blow with the attacker's starboard bow against our port quarter, but the hit comes so hard that it throws both of us on the floor and shatters the night with the crunch of rupturing fiberglass.

As I stagger to my feet, I get my first close look at the other boat. It looks dark green or black. A sleek, open boat about twenty-five-feet long with a center consul, T-top, and a pair of big silver Yamahas hanging on the back. It could be somebody's plaything, but I get the feeling this is a workboat. You can smell the stench of fish or shellfish hanging in the air with the exhaust fumes. It wallows just forty feet off to port. The driver wears sunglasses and a dark wool watch cap pulled down over his ears and forehead. At this distance I can't tell how big he is. And I don't spend a lot of time staring. He has a double-barrel shotgun pointed at us. Becky's field coat is over his shoulders like a cape.

"My coat," shouts Becky. "You thief!"

"Duck!" I say pushing Becky back to the floor.

The shotgun blast blows the plastic windscreen on the Mako into a hundred knifes that come raining down on our heads.

Still on the floor, I reach up and brush a couple of shotgun pellets out of my hair as I hear the gunner powering up his engines and start toward us.

"He's got another shot left," I say thinking aloud.

"Screw him!" says Becky.

With those words she reaches up from the floor, spins

the wheel of the Mako in the direction of the on-coming boat, and rams the throttle forward. The second shotgun blast hits at just about the same moment that the two boats slam together with a bang that leaves me waiting for an explosion.

But when it doesn't come, I pop up and see that the driver of the other boat has been knocked down.

"Go!" I shout to Becky as she stands up to take the wheel of the Mako. "Go, go, go!"

Five seconds later we are screaming west and hugging the coast of the Vineyard with West Chop Lighthouse behind us. The other guy is more than one hundred yards astern , but gaining on us. I grab the mike for the VHF radio to call the Coast Guard, but the mike and radio have been peppered to death by the shotgun blasts.

Becky has the Mako running wide open and ripping along in the shadow of the bluffs and beaches on the west side of the island. The boat shakes as it skips over a light chop. Thank god the wind and seas have settled down because even in these calm conditions, the Mako is coming apart like a paper airplane held too close to a fan. Pieces of fiberglass from the blasted consul and windscreen are scattering everywhere. Worse, there is a split in the bow— almost right along the centerline—that seems to rip farther into the hull as we flow down the Sound. It is just a matter of time before the boat begins shipping enough water through the crack to sink us … or one side of the boat just peels away in the wind.

"Where are we going?" I ask.

"I don't know. Maybe Manemsha. Isn't there a Coast Guard Station there?"

"I think they closed it."

"Then we have to go back to Woods Hole."

"We can't make it." I say. The maniac behind us is already close to within seventy-five yards and if we veer north for the Coast Guard Station at Woods Hole's Little Harbor, our course change will shorten the distance between us and the other boat.

"How high was the tide?" asks Becky.

"What?"

"The tide back in Vineyard Haven. How high when we left?"

I have to think. When I had led Becky off the *When & If* we had to step down to the dock. But we had stepped down to the boat when we had boarded it about three hours earlier.

"At least half and rising."

"Good. Maybe I can lose him."

"How?"

"Lackeys Bay."

With those words, Becky swings the Mako to the northwest and aims us straight across Vineyard Sound toward Naushon Island.

"Are you crazy?"

I know Lackeys Bay. Well, at least I used to known it. As a kid we used to clam, oyster, fish, and generally fart around in what was actually just a large, rock-strewn, shallow cove near the northeast end of Naushon. It was a great place for small, slow boats like our canoes, fishing skiffs, and Beetle Cats. But the water is littered with boulders dropped by a receding glacier in the last Ice Age. It is a place just about guaranteed to rip the bottom out of a boat that can't see the rocks lurking just below the surface. A rising tide can add a foot or two of depth to the water in the bay and might give you a slightly better chance to clear some of the rocks. Not all.

But we are doomed out here on the Sound. And Becky knows that Lackeys has something that just might serve as an escape hatch. If you make it through the boulder field in the middle of the bay, you find two tidal creeks that run north around a small island into the deep water of the yacht anchorage at Hadley Harbor. From Hadley you are less than a half mile from Woods Hole, the Coast Guard, and safety. More rocks and low bridges booby trap the two creeks. But if we can avoid the rocks, we can slide the Mako under the bridges now that our windscreen has been blown away. The madman behind us has little chance. His windscreen is at least seven feet off his deck, and the T-top's canvas roof stretches on a frame of steel tubes above that. The bridges will snag his rig for certain.

"You know Lackeys?" I ask.

"Brandon and I fish for schoolies here every spring and fall. I've never been in there at dark, but, yeah, I remember the rocks. Anyway, if we pile up on a ledge we can get out and run ashore on Naushon, right? There's no running if he catches us out here."

She has a point. And if we don't do something clever in the next five minutes, we will tear this Mako to pieces or be in shotgun range … or both.

"I'll drive. You navigate," I say.

Just before I take the wheel I give one last glance astern. The black boat is only fifty yards behind. A pointed silhouette looms smack in the middle of the silver-green V of our wake.

"God, I wish we had some moonlight," says Becky as we close with the shadowy forest on the coast of Naushon. But there is no chance. The stars are bright, but not bright enough to penetrate the surface of the water or light up a snag.

"What about a searchlight?"

"Shoot, I forgot."

Becky begins digging through the locker under the driver's seat while I stand at the wheel. The force of the wind stings my eyes.

"Got it."

She is plugging it into an outlet on the side of the steering consul when I hear a faint pop and feel something sting my neck and back.

"Christ, oh christ!"

Becky is holding her left ear. I can see a dark web of blood lacing her hand and face.

"Freaking shotgun."

"I'm shot!"

I pull her hand away from her face. There is a steel pellet stuck in the cup of her ear just beneath the skin.

"You were!" I say, flicking the pellet out with the nail of my index finger.

"Damn! That stings!"

"Save it for a souvenir," I say dropping the steel shot in her hand.

"Adventures with the Bagman." She laughs faintly, mostly out of fear.

So do I. What else am I going to do? I start to turn to look over my shoulder, but stop myself. He is within shooting ranging. Steer the boat, man! And pray that the guys who laid up the fiberglass hull of this Mako weren't having a bad day.

Seconds later we are in Lackeys Bay, and I am asking Becky which way now. The east or west creek?

"East," she says over the whine of the engine and the rattling of ripping fiberglass.

Becky snaps on the searchlight. For a second it is so bright that all I can see are spots in front of my eyes. But then the spots resolve themselves into boulders dead ahead.

I swerve right and wait for the sickening crunch of a rock strike as Becky shouts directions.

"Left. More. Right. Right. Go right. Straight. Stay straight. It's deep here. Straight for the bridge. Don't even think about slowing down!"

The Mako chatters forward at thirty knots. Up ahead at just twenty-five yards, I see a low bridge spanning a creek maybe fifteen-feet wide that cuts between the knolls of two islands. In the searchlight beam the scene looks like a set in a black and white movie. We are going to thread this needle if we can avoid just two more rocks I see ahead in the search-light beam.

"Heads up," shouts Becky.

She means for me to duck. Still, I can't help it. I have to look back one last time. But when I turn, all I can see is black. It is like that dark workboat, its driver, and his shotgun have been just another of my nightmares.

"What the fuck was that all about?" I spit after our Mako limps into the still waters of Hadley Harbor where a handful of sailboats swing to anchors and moorings.

"Do you always need to swear?"

"Sorry. It's the adrenaline."

"Somebody tried to kill us."

"That pretty much sums things up."

"He destroyed my boat."

"I don't think it was a random act."

"Why?"

"He stole your coat."

"Oh, jesus."

"Exactly."

"This has something to do with Tina."

"What's the connection?"

Becky takes over steering and guides the Mako out of Hadley Harbor toward the nearby lights of the ferry terminal, the Oceanographic docks, and Eel Pond.

"You don't want to know what I'm thinking," she says over the mutter of the engine.

"Why?"

"You. I'm thinking you're the connection."

"Please! I really have had enough of everybody pointing fingers at me as if I killed …"

Becky cuts me off with the slash of her hand through the dark.

"What the hell's wrong with you, Billy? Save your poor-me story for Curly Sullivan. Jesus christ. Someone just destroyed my boat and tried to kill us. Don't tell me you're not involved! Don't tell me you never hooked up with her during all these years you've *both* been in New York. Don't even try. I know your obsession with her didn't end in high school. Just call the police!"

14

I emerge from the Canal Street subway stop. The street is still wet from an earlier shower, awash in blurs of yellow and red lights from the cars and shops. But the sky has cleared. A steel pan band is playing "No Woman No Cry" for spare change, and you can smell the wet earth of the park at Washington Square, lilacs, and new leaves.

I'm late coming home from work as usual, and I know Sukey is stewing in our apartment, dreaming up wise cracks about her amazing, invisible husband. The best I can do to improve the situation is to bring flowers. So I stop at a vendor's display, sniffing a bunch of daffodils. Then I hear a strange yet familiar voice at my back.

"Roses always work ... Bagger."

Tina. Or Noelle. Neptune's daughter. I recognize her the moment I turn to meet the voice. She has on a gabardine trench coat over jeans. Her hair is tucked up under a green berét, and she's wearing catty sunglasses that take me right back to the Shade Queen in ninth grade.

"Holy shit!"

She cocks her head, pulls off her glasses, gives me that golden smile that always made me feel about ten feet tall.

"Is that how you greet an old friend?"

She throws her arms around me, kisses me on both cheeks, and draws me into a hug. After long seconds she steps back to look at me.

"You age well, cutie."

"I'm speechless. Damn!"

"After all these years, huh?"

"I never expected ..."

She smiles again.

"Why? We both live in the Village. Didn't you think it was inevitable? Sometime?"

My heart feels ready to explode.

"I ... I ... give me some words."

"You're supposed to tell me I look fabulous."

I gulp for air. She still looks more like Cher than Cher. "Christ, better than that."

"Now you're talking. Good boy."

Suddenly I seem to find myself and give her a wise-ass grin.

"Hey. What do I call you?"

She makes a little fist, pops out her eyes at me in mock anger, jabs me in the ribs, and shrugs. "The Shade Queen, Tina the Tease. You remember don't you?"

"Come on, Tina."

"There you go, Bags. See. I've found you. Right here on Canal Street."

Her eyes wander over my face. She puts her hands on my cheeks and moves them slowly over my nose and lips, pressing the skin back at the corners of my jaw, conjuring the boy she remembers to rise again. Then she picks up a long stem red rose from the vendor's bucket and hands it to me.

"I owe you one."

Something seems to crack open in the back of my head. Suddenly I need to make a confession.

"I still have the picture you sent me after you took off," I shrug. "Dumb, huh? Still holding on to the past."

Her black eyes search mine.

"Oh, Bags. Can we talk?"

I picture Sukey working up a steam at home, think I should call her, finger the phone in my jacket pocket, can't think of a lie, and let it drop.

"Where do you want to go?"

"Walk with me."

People on the street are starting to look at her as if they suspect a celebrity in their presence. She puts her shades back on, pulls up the collar of her coat, and takes my hand.

"Come on. I know a place. We'll get some wine."

I feel something chilling and hollow in my guts. It is the feeling that I used to get before football games or a boxing match.

The bottle of Moët we have been sharing is almost empty. The grass under my butt no longer feels wet. We have been sitting here leaning against a tree in the churchyard garden of Saint Luke's-in-the-Fields for quite some time.

We are side-by-side, her head is on my shoulder. In the last hour she has unfolded thirty years of tortured history, taking her from hippie chick to rock celebrity spouse. She has talked about what a failure of a mother she is. How her own mother drank herself to death in Vegas fifteen years ago. How Neptune is still running his bar at the age of seventy-one, except when she takes him to St. Barts for a month every winter. How he still refuses to think of her as anything but his little mermaid. How Butch is a cheating prick.

I give her my own twisted tale of the sports writing I love and the marriage I've all but abandoned. Like me, she has almost never gone back to Woods Hole.

"I get all sick inside when I think about going back," I say. "I just can't make myself."

"I know. But just once I'd like to go back there and show them that Neptune's Daughter is somebody."

"Forget about Woods Hole."

"I can't. I've tried, believe me. But I fucking can't. It always comes back to me. All of you wild-ass, fishy boys. Especially you."

"I'm not worth the trouble." I mean it, and I am beginning to feel uneasy with this conversation.

"Talk to me. We used to talk a lot back in those days. Strange. And you used to watch me some nights. Watch me go with other guys. Like at the fish pier when you used to sit in the dark up there in the wheel house of Skipper Wade's boat. I made it easy for you. Just like I made it easy for you to find me tonight. I always liked to feel you watching. Why did you watch me?"

I'm not going to answer that. Something seethes inside me. So she set me up back then to be the freaking audience for her sick deeds. And she set me up tonight. This was no chance meeting, no act of fate. Tina stalked me. Planned that I would bump into her, and has dragged me to this churchyard out of some twisted need to revisit a hundred acts of teenage sex, violence, and betrayal with one of the only people who has shared the nightmare. What in god's name am I doing here with this woman … while my own marriage is sliding down the tubes?

I stand up, pulling her to her feet. The church walls are pressing in around us.

"Look. It's late. I gotta go."

"Fuck you!" A wild huskiness has come into her voice.

She spins away, putting her back to me. She stares into the yellowish green glow of the city sky over the peaks of the church roof. Her chest heaves as if it is trying to cough up a ball of feathers and scales and bones.

"Just fuck you."

I hear something snap.

Then I am on her, pressing her against the hard stone wall of the church. Covering her mouth with mine.

Her tongue jams into my throat, hot and spiced with wine. Our hips feel welded together with lightning.

"Fucking jesus!" She bites at my neck. Rams a hand down the back of my pants.

I picture a lion dragging a wildebeest to the ground, ripping open a loin and feasting even as the prey's front legs still stretch to run. I seize a handful of her blouse where it buttons below the neckline.

Her fingers drive into my rectum. I tear the blouse right down the front. The bra shreds like it is nothing at all. Tina's breasts still taste like sugar and sea salt.

Her fingers claw inside me, pulling me against her as she shimmies out of her jeans.

I release my belt, feel a freight train shaking in my thighs. Don't know where I am.

"Do me!"

Somewhere a siren howls. Something deep inside me staggers.

"I can't do this." The words burst from my throat with a sob.

Tina pushes me back, slamming my heart with a sharp jab from the heel of her hand. A storm of tears breaks over her face. Then both her fists beat my chest.

I just stand there and let her flail. Like this is some kind of holy obligation I have been ducking for decades.

Suddenly she stops, stands up straight. Her hands tug up her jeans and button the trench coat. She pulls on her berét and sunglasses.

"I'm better than you," she spits and walks off into the bright lights. "I'm better than all of you."

"You always were," I call after her.

Then I add softly, "That's the problem."

I have no idea what I mean.

15

Shaky. I am still feeling downright shaky from last night's attack when it comes time to bury Tina. I don't know why Becky and I didn't go the police last night. Maybe it would have made it all too real. Meanwhile, the town smolders with curiosity about the spectacle of a celebrity death in our midst. The word "zoo" pretty much describes the scene as Woods Hole gathers to bury Neptune's daughter at one in the afternoon.

Just getting to the church is an ordeal. TV trucks and cop cars have the whole street blocked. Reporters with microphones, palm tops, and cell phones fill the sidewalks. My parents and I have to park in one of the ferry parking lots and hike up the bike path and through the cemetery to get to the church.

There must be two thousand people outside watching while the TV crews and flocks of photographers shoot close-ups as the limos roll up to disgorge a who's-who in the rock n' roll hall of fame. The air vibrates with a harsh buzz. For some reason the spectacle makes me so tense I just put my head down, take my mother's hand, and push through the crowd toward the door. Meanwhile, I hear people screeching and sighing as the royalty of rock arrive to pay their last respects. It's like a freaking red carpet. Of course, the one-and-only Butch Werlin doesn't make it. They still have him under suicide watch back in New York.

The only limo I watch empty itself is the one that mystifies almost all of the gawkers.

An enormous old man in a black suit, slouching on a cane as he emerges from the car. A thick tousle of gray hair and a huge mustache blurs his face. I am marveling at his impossible mustache when I see twin fourteen-year-old girls moving to either side of him to help him walk. Tina's daughters. They look nothing like their sexy mother did at that age; these girls have "French nannies" and "Swiss boarding school" written all over their bobbed black hair and charcoal suits. They look scared to death. Poor kids.

"Whose that?" asks someone.

"Burt Lancaster?"

"I thought he was dead?"

"He looks like it."

"That's Neptune," I grumble.

"Who?"

"Her father, fool. Have a little respect!" I say.

My mother squeezes my hand and pushes me into the church.

It seems like half of Woods Hole has already crushed into the sanctuary at Blessed Sacrament when we finally walk. Except for the faces of superstars wearing their mourning masks, the faces in the pews are the same faces I remember from my childhood—the ruddy faces of men who have known decades working the decks of fish boats; the furrowed, squint-eyed brows of captains; booze-wrecked cheeks of deckhands; and pale, tragic mouths of the women who have made a life of waiting for such men. Women in these fishing towns—whether Portuguese, Irish, Italian, or black—always seem to end up looking like Madonnas drawn by a sad Spanish painter.

Most of the women sit wrapped in their overcoats. The men among them look uneasy in their cheap, dark suits. At the organ, May Bell Knight plays Bach's, "Jesus, Joy of Man's Desiring." Two altar boys move around the nave lighting candles and filling the air with the smell that my mother always called "frank incense." Mounted on trestles before the altar lies Tina's coffin. Chrome and open. My final good-bye is coming.

Ψ Ψ Ψ Ψ Ψ

The telephone rings. It's Tina.

"Can you get a boat, Bagger. I really need to see you tonight."

A boat? We have the *Ellen B*, but I don't think a sixty-five-foot fish boat is what she has in mind. There is Rollo's bass boat, but he is always checking on it, and I can't risk him catching me borrowing it … or seeing me with Tina. Then there are the Beetle Cats bobbing on their moorings off the yacht club, waiting for the Sea Scouts to show up the next morning for sailing school.

"How about we go for a sail?"

"You're the captain."

"I'll meet you at the end of the fish pier about nine."

"What's this about?"

She heaves a deep sigh.

"Just come, Bags. Okay? Just be there for me."

It's a fine mid-summer night with the moon waxing full when Tina slips off the pier into my stolen Beetle Cat. The wind comes at about ten knots out of the south, ruffling her long black hair. She looks different. No make-up, no skin-tight dress, or red pumps. Just dark blue shorts and a high school sweatshirt.

"Where are we going?"

"Out of here. Take me far away. Just sail … until there is nothing left of this place."

I hear a hitch in her voice. She is on the verge of tears. And suddenly she throws herself on me as I sit in the bottom of the little sailboat. She wraps her arms around my neck, squeezing me and crying. The boat rocks and drifts out into the moon-drenched harbor.

Eventually, she settles back into the cove of my arm. I trim the sheet and we scoot through Woods Hole Passage, past Devil's Foot and into Buzzards Bay. I steer west along the wooded shores of Naushon Island that glow light blue in the moonshine. She nuzzles my old cotton sweater, and I think maybe we can just sail on like this forever. I'm not going to say anything to break the spell.

"My mother left this morning. Just flat out fucking packed up her bag, took the car, and left. Gone!"

"What?"

She starts to cry again. Buckets of tears.

God, what can I say? Here is something I can't even imagine, not even in the drama that is Tina's life.

"She's such a slut. She's been cheating on him for years. My fucking mother's a dirty joke in half the bars on the Cape. Jesus christ. Sneaking off while dad works fifteen hours a day. Fuck her. Just fuck her!"

Woods Hole is a small town; I've heard the rumors— "like mother like daughter"—and always tried to put them out of my mind. Fucking around I can understand. But this? Walking out on your daughter? I feel the need to say something. I want to comfort her, but I don't know how.

"I'm sure she loves you."

"Bullshit!"

She backs away from me toward the bow of the boat and points her finger at me like a knife. Her face twists into vicious shapes and her chin quivers.

"Yeah, she loves me, Bags. You know what she said before she walked out the door? She said, 'You and your old man will be better off without me, honey. I'm poison to myself and everyone else. Live your own life. Forget about me.' You call that love? Just fuck you, Bagger. And fuck her. The bitch didn't even give me a hug. She just turned around and walked down the steps with her bag!"

I picture the scene in my mind. Tina's copper-haired mother half-toasted, juiced up on some kind of hooch or maybe reds, stumbling down the stairs from the apartment over the bar. Suitcase clattering. Tina in her nightshirt at the top of the steps, only half-awake, bleary-eyed, mouth open in a silent plea, arms reaching out after the ghost. Neptune downstairs in the bar, his gray handlebar mustache drooping just like his eyes, shuttling around empty kegs, pretending his life isn't coming apart and his wife isn't leaving their baby. Jesus christ!

"Hold me. Just hold me."

I let the sheet and the tiller go. Then I wrap her in my arms again, and smell the faint scent of Jade. But mostly I smell baby powder and fear. The boat drifts up on a beach of a small island in the Weepeckets.

We kiss. I feel her tongue begging for something in my mouth. Her hands slide under my sweater, down the plain of my belly, and into my jeans.

"Make love to me." Her voice sounds sure and steady.

So I do. In the bottom of the sailboat. After all of those years, all the failures, and all of the other lovers.

We couple like young animals who only know what God and their instincts tell them. Love without the help of Jewish wine or Crisco or sappy music. While the stars swirl around the moon.

The next day I place a rose outside her door. And Tina has left town forever. Without so much as a good-bye, a phone call, or a note. When I find out, I don't know whether to cheer for her escape or scream for my own emptiness.

ψ ψ ψ ψ ψ

I find myself in a line of mourners shuffling toward the coffin.

It must be thirty years since I have been to a fish town funeral, and I have forgotten how you can smell the fear of death oozing into the room. The only antidote is a bizarre ritual of physical leave-taking in which the survivors file forward before the service begins to look the corpse in the face. Far ahead of me I see Curly, Rollo, and Reggie with their wives, who look like the mothers of girls I knew in school. Becky already sits in her family's pew with her parents, who haven't changed in thirty years. She looks stunning in a midnight-blue satin dress—but still frozen in shock from last night. I hope I can catch her eye. Now that I have slept on the madness of our attack, I need to talk to her about what happened at the Black Dog, on the *When & If*, and—especially—later on our way home in the boat. We have to talk. Things are getting way out of hand, and Becky and I definitely need to visit Curly's police boys. But now Becky weaves her fingers together in prayer, fixing her eyes on the crucifix on the wall behind the altar and never looks my way.

I come to Tina's coffin before I have a chance to think about what I might see or do, and I almost choke—out of surprise—when I actually see the body. I swear the figure in the casket has been made up in the image of Disney's *Sleeping Beauty*. In death she is still stunning. Tina lies amid champagne-colored quilts in a white bridal dress of silk brocade with an empire neck that highlights her fine features. She holds a bouquet of forget-me-nots in her hands, and her lips glisten a subtle pink like a child's. Her hair falls black and long over her chest just the way I remember it did on that Valentine's Day long ago when she modeled a burgundy sweater for me in a dark living room. From ten feet away the effect is magical … and it still is. I can't hate her anymore … or love her either. But I wish she would open her eyes, flash me that magical smile one last time, and make me feel whole for a moment.

In line in front of me, my mother bends over Tina, and

murmurs, "Lord Jesus, be with us in this the hour of our need."
Then my mother kisses Tina's forehead and makes room for
me to make my peace with a woman I have been trying to
bury for thirty years. It takes my breath away. I don't know
what to say. And I notice that a witchy-looking woman behind me in line is watching me with blatant fascination. So
I bend over in a rush and stare into Tina's face. For a second,
time seems to stop and the details of that face strike me. On
close inspection, the long, thick eyelashes show their coats of
mascara. The wrinkles beneath the make-up on the forehead
break the illusion of Sleeping Beauty and give Tina a look
that I can only describe as the face of a person who has died
confused. It is a weird look—part child, part adult. Even with
her eyes closed, she still offers up a hint of that golden smile,
and I want to feel it just a little longer …

"Come-on!" whispers the witch behind me in a long, gray
leather duster and goofy-looking stirrup slacks.

I pretend I don't hear her and ponder for a second or two
more, searching for something to say to this goddess who has
left a lot of boys in Woods Hole with broken hearts. But in
the end nothing comes to mind, and I stand there like a man
who has come to keep a promise that he can't remember. So
I kiss the wrinkles on Tina's forehead, and for an instant she
lives again. I see her in her rabbit coat standing alongside the
railroad tracks between the beach and Oyster Pond, flashing
a leg at the engineer on one of the last freight trains ever to
leave Woods Hole and shouting "Take me with you!" I can
smell Jade and hear her husky voice saying "Play it as it lays,
Bagger."

Then she is gone, and I wonder how I have tied myself to
the mystery of her murder. I feel like crying, and I don't know
why. It is the strangest feeling because crying is something
I haven't done in years. Just then Zal appears from out of
nowhere, looking like the Pope, rubbing a hand across my
shoulders, and saying "Ride this out, Bagger."

The rest of the funeral service passes by me in a blur. All I notice is the wail of Neptune's raspy old voice, like a ferryboat horn, when the sexton closes the coffin. He wraps his grand-daughters in his arms and seems to grit his teeth so hard that the flesh on his cheeks shakes. Once this old whaler looked like a titan to me—dark, thick, mustached, and barrel-chested like the actor Anthony Quinn. Now, he looks withered with age and grief, a hobbled skeleton of a giant, a Cape Cod Portagee grandfather in a black suit.

His eyes stare vacantly straight ahead as if he is seeing something far away or long ago, and I wonder where a father's mind might take him at a time like this. Only the handlebar mustache still seems larger than life. It makes his face look like it has a pair of gray wings that might lift it off his neck at any moment. I get down on my knees in the pew and pray for Neptune, his granddaughters … and us all. What have we lost? Who have we killed?

I walk to the cemetery with Reggie and his wife, but when we get to the hillside graveyard, I feel this overwhelming urge to be alone. So I let the crowd get between me and my old friend and then I kind of drift off to the edge of the flock. I see the pallbearers—men who have been ushers in the church since we were kids—carry the coffin into the crowd surrounding the grave on the hillside, and then I kind of space out. I am thinking about how the weather feels like a snow is coming, then a woman's arm hooks through mine and tightens the pressure like a wrestler.

"I haven't been this scared in thirty years," says the woman's voice. "This isn't over. And you're right there in the middle of it all, aren't you, Billy? I know what you did to her. I saw you. Remember me?"

Frankly I don't. Well, not at first anyway. The woman locked onto my arm is the same witch in the leather duster and stirrup pants who was behind me in line when we paid our respects to Tina. She looks like a mummy or Vanessa Redgrave playing a Holocaust victim. Her short, mousy hair is brittle and pokes off her skull in irregular spikes. The flesh droops off her cheeks in gray, blotchy folds. Only after I look into this person's blurry blue eyes do I recognize her. Jesus. She is Sandy Dillard, Tina's cousin. And here we are back in the cemetery again.

16

It's Halloween night 1962. The film showing at the Elizabeth Cinema is *Blood of Dracula*, and I have permission to see the Halloween show, even though it is Thursday and we have school the next day. A gang of us is going. Couples. Tina and Zal have been going out together since early September so they are together. Smitty is with his forever-steady Lily. Rollo is with the loud-mouth of the tenth-grade class, Joyce. And I have a blind date with Tina's cousin, Sandy Dillard.

In the locker room after JV football practice today, the guys had been wired for the up-coming evening … particularly Zal.

"I'm gonna get me some ass tonight," he squealed in imitation of Reggie Jones. "Little baby-girl pppppppooooontang!"

"Yeeeaaaaaah," we all murmured. Zal spoke for us all. Horny as tom cats.

We pack into the back row of the theater under the balcony—boy-girl-boy-girl—the seats stink of stale popcorn, whiskey, and semen stains. The only parts of the movie I watch are a few Technicolor images of thunderstorms rolling through the Carpathian peaks, a rain-pelted castle, and a brace of black horses rushing a carriage through the mud on a twisting mountain road.

We all go to the movies to make out. This girl I barely know automatically turns face to face with me, and we begin painting each other's cheeks with saliva. The first kiss is a long, wet suffocating affair that makes me shiver as my tongue probes and Sandy refuses to open her mouth for deep kissing. She wiggles ambiguously as my fingers graze the lower curves of her bra.

Then suddenly the fingers of her left hand drive their nails into my right wrist. I can feel her nails drawing blood.

"What are you trying to do to me?" she gasps and shrugs forward to shake off my right hand and arm.

Sandy reaches around Zal's shoulder to her right and taps Tina on the head until the girl breaks her clutch with Zal.

"We have to go to the bathroom," Tina announces and the two girls vanish.

Zal raises his hands to the sky as if beseeching God for an answer.

"What the fuck did you do?" he challenges me.

I shrug. I have no clue. All I know is that I am getting a really strange feeling sitting there in the dark to the left of Joyce with her right knee pumping against my thigh as she stretches out across three seats and tries to suck dessert from Rollo's lips.

In the gloom to my right beyond Rollo, I can see Smitty's face pressing into the v-neck of Lily's bright green pullover. Her right hand rolls the waist line of his pants below his hips; his bum cheeks squirm to help her. Meanwhile, here Zal and I sit with our hands in our laps watching Dracula drain the blood from the neck of a maiden. Jesus christ.

It is pathetic, but I have almost found a way to take my mind off the girls' vanishing act. I begin to picture some kind of interplay between events on the screen and the scene unfolding between Joyce and Rollo. They have their hands in each other's pants, and I can see their torsos squirm as they stroke. On screen we have the chase scene. Dracula is hot with blood lust, stalking his male secretary through the maze of corridors in the vampire's castle. My attention divides as if watching a split-image ... wondering if Joyce and Rollo might bring each other down at the very moment Dracula gets his man. But before I can discover whether some bizarre harmony actually binds the real and imaginary, Zal interrupts.

"Fucking dikes!" he says in a voice that turns a dozen heads our way. His arm reaches across and massages my shoulder and the back of my neck for a couple of seconds.

"Shut up!" says a bunch of people.

I can't care less.

We are shuffling toward the exits when Tina and Sandy finally come out of the ladies room. They are giggling. They stink of cigarettes, fresh lipstick, chocolate, and apricot brandy. And they wiggle their butts like … like I don't know what. Like only fifteen-year-old girls can. We are all waiting under the theater marquis for someone's parents to give us a ride back to Woods Hole when Tina starts in with the needling.

"I bet you guys are too chicken," she challenges. "I bet you don't have the guts to walk home on the tracks and go into the cemetery at night. I bet you're afraid to piss on old Captain Ezra's grave." She speaks her words loudly—fired by the apricot brandy and whatever else she and Sandy have done in the ladies room.

"Joyce's mother's comin' for us," announces Lily.

"Yeah, some other time," shrugs Joyce.

"Well, I'd like to see it," continues Tina. "I bet these guys don't have the balls to go home through that cemetery. I bet they're too afraid of spooks and Captain Ezra."

For all of us, Captain Ezra Harding stands out as a symbol of untouchable power. We have heard stories about how he and his family had built a whaling empire in our town more than one hundred years ago. We have seen photographs of his fleet of whaling ships anchored in Great Harbor, and we can lead you to the ruins of his mansion on the knoll in the woods near the golf course. In Memorial Day parades, we marched as Sea Scouts and Girl Scouts to lay wreaths, stand at attention, and watch the Legionnaires fire their salutes at Captain Ezra's grave. To us children of fishermen, Captain Ezra Harding and his family, grown prosperous and respected on whaling, had everything we didn't. They are our aristocrats, not the wealthy folks who come down from Boston for their summers at Penzance Point, Quissett, Falmouth Heights, and the Vineyard. Even in death, Captain Ezra is the name that comes to our minds when we think of someone who has wealth and power beyond the scale of Blessed Sacrament Church or even Sam Cahoon, who's been running the fish wharf for decades.

"It's a done deal," drawls Zal. "We're going to the cemetery. We're not just going to piss on the Captain's gravestone … we're going to play Bizz Buzz on his bones!"

Zal reaches into the inside pocket of his windbreaker and produces an unopened pint of Seagram's Seven Crown whiskey.

"Fuckin' A," says Rollo. "Drinkin' games with the spooks."

"Give me some of that," urges Tina. She pulls the bottle away from Zal, twists off the cap, takes a long swallow, and passes it to Sandy.

"Jesus, put that away. There are people all around," cautions Smitty, reminding us that we are fewer than five steps beyond the lighted marquis of the theater.

"We're outta here!" Tina takes another long pull from the open whiskey bottle, hands it to me, and leads our troupe up the street. Lily and Joyce gasp with open mouths as we march into the dark. Four boys and two girls.

I take a sip from the bottle and swallow. I never have had whiskey before, and its sharp, steely taste makes me shudder. Tina laughs at my sour face.

We get to the cemetery fast … thanks to Rollo knocking over about a dozen garbage cans set out for trash pick-up as we walk between rows of cottages along Shore Street. With the cans clanging as they hit the pavement and beginning to roll into the street, we burst into a sprint. Lights flash on in some of the darkened houses.

"Sunamabitch!" curses a thick Italian accent.

"Trick or treat," shrieks Sandy.

We race a quarter of a mile down Surf Drive until we pick up the railroad tracks to Woods Hole. And we keep on running until we reach Blessed Sacrament's cemetery rising on a hillside south of the tracks. Out of breath, we tumble on the grass among the tombstones … laughing.

"Rollo, you're a madman," howls Zal.

"Un-fucking-real," gasps Smitty. "The Bagman took off like Johnny Unitas."

Suddenly, everybody seems to be staring at me as I lie on my back gasping for air.

"You're pretty quiet, Bags," Zal props his head on his elbow and gives me a hard look. His straight black hair falls over half his face. "That whiskey too much for you?"

"Our Mr. Bagger is a milk and cookies boy; these little baby dolls gonna drink him right under the table," explains Rollo.

"Fuck you," I shoot back and grab the whiskey from Zal.

"Eat me, Rollo!" Zal chimes in just to stir the shit.

"Wassh that," slurs Sandy.

"Yeah, watch the mouth!" says Tina. "Ladez presen."

"Oh, 'scuse me!" Zal's voice has raised an octave. The alcohol must be hitting him.

"Can't I show a little sympathy for my friend?" he adds.

"We don' haff ta hear that fish boat talk." Sandy sits up in the grass. Her torso totters, and she reaches out swiftly to the right with braced arms and catches herself from toppling over. She looks like she is preparing to do a push up.

It is the first time all night I have really taken a good look at Sandy. She is a wispy-looking kid—hardly sexy—small and thin with straight, shoulder-length brown hair that seems to have been blown into a tangle around her face by the wind.

Strands stick to the sweat on her pale cheeks and forehead in a way that makes me remember her as the girl who some-times plays left field in our after-school softball games. That oversized, navy pullover and red suede skirt can't disguise what looks like the hips of a ten-year-old boy. The only things that make her stand out are her blurry blue eyes.

I know almost nothing of her home life, but when we were in grade school, kids said Sandy's mother hung around with Tina's mom in the bars east of Mashpee. But I don't know that for sure. Sandy and I live in different quarters of town. I can't really call her a friend—just a kid from school, Tina's cousin, a blind date that hasn't worked out, a drunken girl.

She closes her eyes and mumbles, "I think I wanna go hum."

"Me, too," says Tina.

'Good idea,' I think. The tombstones are beginning to swim around me.

"Aw hey, baby, I was just foolin' around," Zal begins. He raises off his back and puts his arm around Tina's who's sit-ting there staring off into the dark with her legs crossed and her arms folded across her chest.

"Why don't you guys leave us alone for a while?" he asks.

"Go up to Captain Ezra's monument and start Bizz Buzz."

He hands the whiskey to Rollo.

"We'll be along when my baby feels better," Zal says to us. Then he puts both his arms around Tina from behind her and cuddles her back against his chest and begins whispering things we can't hear.

So we leave … Rollo, Smitty, Sandy, and I, staggering a bit and passing the whiskey bottle among us as we weave our way uphill through the cemetery toward where we think old Ezra's monument stands. But we can't find it—even after three or four criss-crossings of the high ground. So much for Bizz Buzz.

"I'm gettin' the creeps," mutters Smitty at one point. "I know where that grave is, but I can't find it. It's like the thing disappeared or something. Like I'm not in the right graveyard."

"Spooks," giggles Sandy.

"Man, they're puttin' one on us. Fuckin' Ezra and his buddies are jacking us around," says Rollo. "They ain't gonna let a bunch o' punks piss on 'em."

"I don't want to piss on anybody; I just want to know where the hell I am," I confess.

I feel lost and dizzy and lie down on the steps of a monument. Smitty drops down beside me.

"You shits!" grumbles Rollo. "You're too wasted to even play one round of Bizz Buzz … how are we ever goin' to find Zal and Tina?"

"They're probably playin' tonsil hockey and gettin' grass stains on their assholes," chuckles Smitty. "Whadda they care about us?"

"Yeah, well I'm not gonna si' here freezin' all night waitin' for 'um ta fin' us. I'm gonna fin' at girl and we're gonna go hum," mutters Sandy.

I watch her disappear into the shadows before I close my eyes and try to chase the whirly-twirly feeling out of my head.

"Stop hugging yourself and find me that whiskey bottle!" Zal is standing over me. He has a weird grin on his face.

On the step above me, Smitty sits up and rubs his face with both hands, then looks around.

"Am I in hell?" he asks.

"Right," chirps Zal finding the whiskey where Rollo left it on the doorsill of a mausoleum.

"And you're about to have a drink with a REAL man!" He takes a swig from the bottle and waves it at Smitty.

"You got … laid?" Smitty pushes the bottle away from his face. "Tina, haul your ashes, man?"

"Bullshit," I judge. "Coco the chimp wouldn't screw you."

In my experience, girls are saving themselves for marriage.

"Hey, if you don't believe me, Bags, you can either smell my dick or walk down into the children's corner of the cemetery and see if Rollo isn't gettin' his rocks off right now. She loves it. See for yourself. Maybe she'll even give you pencil-dicks a ride if you can get it up."

'Shit, she's only fifteen,' I think.

Zal drags Smitty and me to our feet and leads us with his arms around our shoulders two hundred yards or so into the lowest corner of the cemetery where the unmarked graves for dead infants lie among a few headstones for children who died in their first years. The place seems lifeless until we get close enough to hear Rollo's pocket radio issuing forth the soft voices of the Platters singing "Smoke Gets in Your Eyes." Near the source of the music, Rollo's bare buttocks hump away on top of Tina while his pants snarl around his sneakers.

She is naked except for her sweater rolled up to her arm-pits, and her knees cock up in the air, rocking or shivering with Rollo's thrusts. Her left arm clutches Rollo around the neck, and she makes deep panting noises—almost growls.

Rollo keeps saying he loves her, and it seems strange to me that kind of talk doesn't make Zal jealous or something. But he just stands there watching with an odd little grin on his face like he's just discovered a secret.

I have never actually seen sex before, and my first thought is 'Jesus, somebody ought to throw a blanket over these two.'

"Ah hell!" moans Smitty. He clearly isn't happy about the spectacle before his eyes.

"You're next," laughs Zal. "My baby wants to show the Smithman what fur!"

"Not me," Smitty shakes his head. "This is one bad fuckin' scene, Zal! I'm going home."

Just like that, Smitty disappears in the mist.

"What about Bagger?" Rollo grunts from the ground.

"He's a chickenshit. Bagger's just a little pud knocker." This last insult Zal says in falsetto, imitating Sandy.

I explode. "Fuck off. What do you know?"

"Hurry up, Rollo!" I urge.

But in my heart I am hoping Rollo and Tina will take all night ... or that she will tear herself free and run.

Suddenly Rollo sprawls onto his back in the grass—smiling, with both hands pressing against his groin.

"Go Bagman. Show us how." Zal gives me a push toward Tina's inert body.

I stumble and fall on my face.

"Be a man!" I hear Rollo call.

Then someone grabs my pants from behind and jerks them down around my knees. When I look up I see Tina's left foot directly in front of my nose. Her right leg splays off at an angle with the knee raised like the woman we saw giving birth in a health class film. A slick of sweat, semen, cut grass, and brittle oak leaves cover her from her knees to her breasts. They seem flat and childlike with the nipples rising and falling on her heaving chest.

Then she moans, and I look up at her head as it lies on her shoulder. Her eyelids are half closed ... but those brown eyes watch me.

For seconds neither of us moves. We just look at each other. The words from "Angel Baby" pour from Rollo's radio.

Slowly Tina stretches her left arm down to me, takes my hand, and pulls me up beside her.

"Just don't hurt me," she says and wraps me in a bear hug. Her voice sounds low and dead like the women trapped in Dracula's castle.

Then we kiss, and even though I am drunk it is a kiss I will always remember. It is a kiss that engages our thrusting tongues for just a split-second ... then quickly backs off to lips against lips and cheeks and eyes ... then the hollow places at the bases of necks.

"Just pretend," I say so only Tina can hear me.

She puts her hands behind my head and presses my face into the tangle of hair around her neck. Slowly her thighs begin to roll as her legs grasp my hips and bring me into their rhythm. My penis—barely aroused—pushes against the dry ground. I hold my eyes shut tight.

"Fuck her silly, you bald-assed pansy," somebody calls.

"Make him moan," a voice laughs.

Tina's breath comes wet and hot.

I open my eyes. And as I look off among the dark tomb-stones of little kids to my left, I think I see Sandy Dillard propped against a small white monument, blinking herself awake. For a second, her blurry blue eyes seem to lock on me, until I bury my face in the tangle of dark hair at Tina's neck and we reel against each other.

Then I think I hear a branch snap and a fish boat or ferry bleating in the Sound.

"Leave me alone," I shout. "Leave me the fuck alone!"

I swing my arms in a frenzy. My hands seize on flesh and bone … and hang on. I taste tears.

A scream fills my ears, and my eyes shoot open.

"Don't hurt me. Please don't hurt me. Please," sobs Tina.

She looks up at me wide-eyed. My hands hold her wrists pinned against the ground above her head.

"Oh shit," I stutter and let go of her hands. "I didn't mean …"

"What's wrong with you? Are you crazy?!" Tina spits and squirms away from me onto her belly.

"I'm sorry," I say and reach out to touch her cheek.

"We better clear outta here," warns Rollo. "Shit, it's after eleven. I'm gonna be fish meal. Come on!"

I look around for Sandy, but she is nowhere in sight.

Rollo takes a long look at the night's aftermath—an empty bottle of whiskey, a naked girl pulling into the fetal position against a broken headstone, and a white mask settling over

Zal's face. Then I see Rollo snatch his radio and something else off the ground before dashing toward the streetlights.

"Christ, now what?" mutters Zal. Then he looks at me sitting on the grass with my head in my hands.

"Pull up your pants for god's sake, Bagger. We got a problem!"

Zal walks over to Tina who lies on her side, pulled up in a ball inside her sweater. He shakes her shoulders gently and calls her name, but she doesn't move.

"She's passed out. We got to get her dressed and home. If the cops catch us. Jesus."

For the next five or ten minutes Zal and I scurry around on our hands and knees looking for Tina's clothes and gear. Eventually, we find her skirt, garter belt, stockings, shoes, jacket, and bag … we can't find her panties.

"How the hell do we ever dress her with no undies," grumbles Zal as if he feels we have reached a dead end. "Where in god's name do you think …"

Then it hits me. "Rollo must have taken them. I saw him grab something when he was leaving."

"Jesus christ, that sick fuckin' thief took a souvenir. What next?"

"Put on her other things," I urge. "We don't have all night."

Somehow, working together, we manage to get Tina into her garter belt and skirt. Her body feels like a sack of sugar, and there is no way we are going to get her stockings on her. So we stuff them in her jacket pockets, pull her arms into her jacket, and try to stand her up. Hopeless.

"Man, she's gonna sleep all night if we don't think of something to wake her up," whines Zal. "We need some cold water or something."

"Right. And the cemetery has spigots scattered around for grounds care. We can put her head under one," I say.

After searching for a few minutes I locate one that works. Zal and I carry Tina slinging between our shoulders, and—

thank god—the cold water splashing on her cheeks revives her well enough to get her up and moving in slow steps. She walks between us. The three of us hold each other like chorus girls. Nobody speaks.

As we approach Neptune's and her apartment, the church clock strikes midnight.

"Are we in trouble?" I ask seriously.

"Nothin' ta worryabout," mumbles Tina seeing that the lights are out in her apartment, but the side-stoop light still burns. "Mom's out partying somewheres. Dad's still workin' inna bar."

"I can take her from here," whispers Zal and he nods his head for me to get lost.

Tina drops her hand from my waist.

"Get some help," she murmurs. Her hand raises and points at my chest. "Get some help, Bagger."

Then she throws her arms around Zal. I hear sobbing as I walk away. When I look back, I see Tina and Zal's silhouettes against the yellow glow of the stoop light. Zal has his shirttail in his hand wiping away the tears on Tina's face.

Skipper Wade meets me as I try to tip toe in the back door of our house. He slams me against the wall in the kitchen, growls that it is an hour past my curfew, and grounds me indefinitely. The next day I hear the kids in social studies teasing Tina—calling her the Shade Queen—for wearing plastic, heart-shaped sunglasses to class. After school Sandy Dillard calls to me.

"I saw what you did last night in the cemetery," she growls. "You better keep your mouth shut up about it … or you'll regret this the rest of your life."

17

Zal finishes reading the 23 Psalm, and the undertaker's men lower Tina's coffin into the grave. Sandy Dillard lets go of my arm and looks me hard in the eyes.

"You remember, don't you? I can see it in your eyes. You know who killed ..."

"I feel sick," I mumble and start jogging up the hill. I can't stay a second longer. Behind a monument I bend over and wretch like a drunk who has been empty for days. When I pull myself together, Sandy Dillard and everyone else has vanished.

Ψ Ψ Ψ Ψ Ψ

It's been almost twelve months since the gang bang, and I am beginning to wonder if I am ever going to escape from my private little hell. I feel the urge to spill my guts to Zal and Becky—to try to explain about all the crazy stuff with smoke, boat horns, knives, and marsh boots swirling through my head. But I hardly see either of them ..., which is probably a good thing because how do you tell your friends that some kind of alien force is taking over your brain.

Besides, my class schedule keeps me away from Zal and Becky at school, and our chances of getting together after school have shrunken to almost nothing. At football the coaches shunt me off to practice with the jayvees while Zal plays with the varsity. And since we have different practice schedules and work-out on different fields, Zal and I rarely even get the chance to snap towels at each other in the locker room. On the weekends I try to get together with him, but every time I call his little sisters tell me he is out with a mystery friend from "down the Cape." They say this friend has a maroon Corvette that he lets Zal drive. According to his sisters' accounts, Zal has "such a hard-on over that car that he can't even remember he has sisters … let alone old friends."

So much for brotherhood.

Sometimes I feel like sliding by Becky's house on my way home from practice, but her boyfriend Terry's car always seems to be parked out front. So Becky and I don't really say much to each other except for when she calls me about church stuff. She wants me to go to Blessed Sacrament with her to make plans for a young people's Halloween party, but I find excuses to be unavailable. Church is really not a place I want to be these days, and I guess I want to punish her. But even without my daily doses of Becky and Zal, I don't feel lonely. I have boxing with Daryl and the other Golden Glove guys.

Walking out the door after dinner for a sparring session with Daryl and Mugs, I hear two masked persons come charging up the sidewalk at me.

"Get him," shouts the figure wearing what looks like a black choir robe from church and a plastic Dracula mask.

The voice sounds familiar, and I am on the verge of identifying it when the other spook lets go with a banshee shriek that catches me so off-guard that I freeze. In an instant, the shrieking spook in a choir robe and a rubber hag's mask snatches my gym bag from my hand and flings it to Dracula. In one fluid motion he catches the bag and sends it sailing onto the roof of my house.

"Gotcha, Bagger!" laughs the vampire pointing his index fingers at me as if they are pistols.

Something cold clicks around my right wrist.

"Weeeee …" howls the hag. She jerks my right hand high overhead—and as the sleeve of the robe falls away—I see that a set of tin handcuffs binds me to an arm I have dreamed about half my life.

With her free hand, Becky pulls off her hag's face and combs the worst of the snarls out of her hair.

"You're coming with us," says Zal dropping the Dracula mask.

"Gonna have to put off beating on somebody for another day." Becky smiles her Shirley Temple smile. Her eyes dance, and she seems so pleased with herself.

"Don't even think of causing any problems or I'll scratch your cheeks off," she adds, waving long fingernails coated with a bloody paste next to my face.

"It's the witching hour, Bagman, and you're going to the spook show with us." Zal slips a choir robe over my head and snaps a hard-plastic Frankenstein mask against my face.

Immediately, I pull it off.

"I've got other plans," I snap, but secretly I am a bit curious about what Becky and Zal have cooked up. These two have been more or less at war for years.

"Face it, you've been kidnapped," chuckles Becky. "You can't escape. Give in, will ya? We're going to raise some hell!"

Zal pulls a three-pound bag of popping corn kernels out from under his black robe. He plops the bag in my hand cuffed to Becky's.

"Don't spill it," he says. "It's open!"

Zal produces another set of handcuffs and clips himself to my free arm. Almost as soon as he has locked onto me, Becky grabs a handful of corn and flings it against the storm door of my house. It sounds like the glass is shattering.

Becky screams and takes off running with Zal and me in tow.

The houses on Millfield Street have tiny front lawns

so—as we gallop up the middle of the street—Zal and Becky have no difficulty hitting every house they wish. That is about every second dwelling on both sides of the street. While they raise hell, all I can do is keep pace and listen to the rain of corn on windows, porches, and metal awnings. When I look back over my shoulder, I see lights coming on over porches and people running out into the street.

Zal and Becky don't stop throwing corn or running until we tumble behind the screen of shrubs surrounding the statue of the Virgin Mary in front of Blessed Sacrament Church.

"I'm sweating like a …" I begin.

"Shsssh, the cops are coming," Becky pinches my wrist.

"They must have gotten a dozen calls," laughs Zal.

"More," I gasp. "You just trashed four blocks of the town."

"You love it, Bagger. You love being B-A-D." Zal grabs for the chest of my black robe and tries to give my left nipple a titty twist. I bat his arm away.

"Boys!" grumbles Becky.

"Someday you're going to pay, Zal." I am serious.

"Like how; you want a shot at boxing the crap out of me?" He has slipped into his sarcastic voice.

"Yeah, dickhead. Box me."

"Come off it," growls Becky. "Bullet Bob's got his cruiser stopped right out front. Shut up!"

"Anytime, loverboy," Zal hisses.

Becky rolls her eyes at me.

A searchlight beam swings into our bushes. I feel Becky's fingers lace into mine. Zal's palm cups over my knuckles. The light shoots right through the arbor and almost blinds us. We make like mud turtles. I hold my breath. The light swings away and probes bushes farther along the foundation of the church. Becky heaves a great sigh. I gasp for air. The light swings back. The pulse of the blood pumping through my friends' hands ripple through my fingers, and the throbbing runs right up my arms into my ears. When I look at Becky, she has her eyes squeezed tight. Zal is gritting his teeth so hard his jaw muscles bulge like cords.

Suddenly, the light goes out, and I hear the cruiser click into gear and start to roll away. A sound like some lovesick hippo fills the air.

Becky jumps to her knees. "Was that a belch?"

"Sorry," cackles Zal. "Cops give me indigestion."

"I must be crazy. What am I doing here with you two?"

"Going to a dance party," says Zal. "It was your idea, remember? Show the Bagger a good time. Cheer him up … is what you said."

So that's it. Here is the reason behind this improbable alliance between Zal and Becky. This is a "Give the Bagger a Helping Hand" night.

We all stand up.

"Look, guys, thanks but I really don't need this," I say. "I'm not in the mood to go to a dance, okay?"

"See, I told you he would never …"

"Stop!" shouts Becky. Her lower lip bulges. She clinches her hands into two fists and hammers Zal and me simultaneously in the centers of our chests.

"Leave. Just get out of here. Go drink beer … or beat each other up. Just go. Please!"

Becky pulls a bobby pin from her pocket and uses it as a key to unlock our toy handcuffs. Zal and I just stand there like statues.

"Come on," I say at last, pulling my mask over my face and hooking my arms through my friends' elbows.

We walk around to the back of Blessed Sacrament where the church has built a new wing for its primary school. A crowd in Halloween costumes presses through the double doors. Inside the large recreation room is bathed in smoky, red spotlights. Tons of kids in masks and costumes are slopping and twisting to music. Judging by people's height, a third of the high school must have turned out for this event …, which is no surprise in a town where most of us are Catholic and the church has been sponsoring these seasonal dances for as long as anyone can remember. I figure that I know most of these kids, but except for two dark-skinned mummies who I guess to be Reggie Jones and Hucklebabe—I can't begin to guess the people behind the masks.

Among the crowd I see Bambi, Captain Hook, the Wicked Witch of the West, Snow White, six nurses, four hobos, three astronauts, five Cleopatras, several GI's in head bandages, and a cardboard shell fashioned to look like a rocket … a dick … or is it Mr. Peanut?

The touch of Becky's hand in mine breaks my fascination. Leslie Gore's "It's My Party" pours from the speakers, and Becky wants Zal and me to slop with her—two-on-one. She gives us each a hand and leads us into the crowd of dancers. The easy sway of her hips sets the rhythm, and Becky telegraphs every change in our routine with crisp tugs on our hands. Zal and I follow along just as we did in those conga lines back in grade school. We cross over, switch sides, and sometimes Becky twirls as she slides between Zal and me. Our choir robes swish against each other. No one misses a step. By the middle of the song Becky begins to sing along; then she catches Zal's and my eyes and gives her head one of those 'I-must-be-crazy' shakes. I can tell that behind her hag's mask she is smiling. I think all three of us are.

I can dance like this all night. But then the officers of the Catholic Youth Organization stop the music after a few songs to arrange a line dance. Everybody is six or seven years too old for such a party game; but since the CYO officers are also the high school's head cheerleader, the president of the senior class, and our quarterback, the crowd goes along with this nonsense. The faint smell of beer on people's breath offers another clue to the gang's willingness.

As the DJ spins a fifties standby called "The Midnight Stroll," the boys form a line on one side of the room and the girls on the other. The couple that pairs up at the head of the line has to dance a stroll down the "aisle" between the two lines. When the dancers get halfway down the aisle, they have to unmask and finish their stroll. In the meantime, the boys and girls in the line clap and sing along to the music while they shuffle slowly to the head of the lines to couple up.

The way the CYO leaders set things up, Zal and I end up near the head of the boys line, and when I count down the girls line to see who I might get as a partner, my arithmetic settles on one of two possibilities—either a rather plump female wearing a black body stocking and a cat mask or a slim, curvy girl in a sequin tutu and a plastic Tinkerbelle mask. Becky is way down the line somewhere. I won't be seeing her for a while.

As it turns out, Zal gets the cat. For a second, I watch as they start their stroll in hopes of learning the identity of the black cat, but I never get a chance to watch when she un-masks because Tinkerbelle and I have already started our own stroll. The first thing I notice as we start down the aisle is how rough Tinkerbelle's hands are as we hold on to each other. Then when the music calls us to take several steps together like a couple in a waltz, I see her eyes behind the cutouts in the mask. They look enormous, dark brown and—like the hand—familiar.

We have just finished our waltz steps when we reach the halfway point and I pull off my mask. When Tinkerbelle sees my face, both her hands fly to her mask for a second. Then she spins her back toward me and dashes for a door leading from the rec room into the main part of the church. Suddenly, there I stand without a partner. Unmasked. A thousand eyes watching me. I can't finish the stroll alone. Sweat pours from my scalp.

There is nothing for me to do except make a quick bow, give a so-long wave to the crowd, and beat it for the exit Tinkerbelle has taken. It isn't that I want to follow her as much as that I just want to escape all of those masked eyes staring at me … and find a place where I can sit down by myself in the dark and try to figure out what is going on.

The sound of music fades to soft bubbling as I make my way through the darkened corridor that opens into the sanctuary. I haven't been here since Zal, Becky, and I came for Midnight Mass on Christmas Eve. Both Zal and I had been drinking beer before, and one of the ushers asked us to leave because Zal developed a case of the hiccups. That was fine with me. Coming had been Becky's idea. I didn't need this place, still don't. Lately, I have been coming to the conclusion that forces other than Jesus Christ are ruling the world. Forget Confession. I am glad the Catholic Church gives my parents so much peace, but for me it has become simply a collection of pretty amazing stories.

But I like this sanctuary … especially when it is dark and nobody is here. The oak benches have a smoothness that invites me to lounge back and kick my feet up. The lights from the street lamps plays in the stained glass and make clusters of purple, red, and gold flecks high up on the ceiling. I always think of this sanctuary smelling like perfume, shaving cream, and the stale B.O. of old fishermen's suits. But tonight I smell the incense left by the censer during the evening Mass, the scent of the lilies, and just a hint of red wine.

Breaking the stillness I hear someone sniff as if holding back a sob. The noise comes from somewhere in the gloom near the altar.

"Tinkerbelle?" I call.

No answer. Then a sniff.

"Tinkerbelle is that you?"

"What do you think?"

I get up and move toward the sound.

"Are you, okay?"

No answer. I keep walking down the center aisle until I see the shadow of a girl's head leaning back against one of the pews.

"Are you okay?" I ask again.

She says my name. I know that voice.

"Yes?"

"Leave me the fuck alone!!!"

The shadow rises out of the pew, tries to run, and crashes into me. My hands catch her upper arms, and she grasps my elbows to keep us both from losing our balance. The pale face with those enormous brown eyes gazes at me as if I am some kind of monster.

"Christ!"

Tinkerbelle is Tina.

"You want to try FUCKING me, is that it?" she screams. "Or do you just want to FAKE IT one more time?"

She shakes free of my grip and drives the knuckles of both her hands up under my testicles. The pain shoots right out of my ears. I drop flat on the floor.

I don't know how long I have been lying here, but I remember coming to and passing out two or three times before I feel a hand lifting up the back of my head.

18

After we buried Tina, I didn't go looking for Becky. I didn't go looking for Curly Sullivan to unburden my tale of ambush by boat on Vineyard Sound. I just sit around my parents' living room, picturing Tina's murder. *Something slashes over her back like a cold whip or a lightning strike. An arm tightens around her waist. Trying to ride her.*

Maybe Sandy Dillard and the others are right; I know something about who killed Tina. But what? I remember Becky's words about finding the place where someone licks their wounds. Where is that? What happened there? The only antidote to these questions is to take myself out for a long jog. Maybe something will come to me.

When I start out the door in my black tights, red running shell, and gloves, I have no clear direction in mind, but ten minutes into the exercise, I realize that I am running over the course of my old paper route—exactly—in reverse. At one point I pass Rollo's house and see his mother with her head wrapped in a babushka raking leaves. She had been a pretty woman back in the sixties, and even now, more than thirty years later, she still is. As I pass her, our eyes meet and her jaw drops with recognition.

"Hi, Helen," I wave and continue down the road as if our meeting is still an everyday part of our lives.

"Still running," she muses after me as I put distance between us. "When are you going to …"

"Takin' care of business!" I call over my shoulder, but the

voice isn't mine. The words have escaped my mouth with such speed and force that I do not even consider them before speaking.

'Where the hell did that come from?' I ask myself ... and then I trip over a frost heave in the pavement and tumble "ass over tea kettle" as Skipper Wade says.

'He's back again,' I think as I roll onto my feet. 'The freaking Bagger's back.'

The air moves in and out of my lungs with effort, and my legs begin to feel as heavy as iron. I pass Zal's old home. His father had sold it a few years ago, but nothing seems to have changed.

At the end of my paper route, I begin to veer toward home around the west side of Eel Pond, but the Bagger's voice sounds like a siren in my head and screams, "Not yet you Tina Toy; we're not done!"

I turn back away from Eel Pond and the heart of the village, and head toward the ferry landing and the railroad tracks. But where the tracks had been, there is now a paved bike trail that leads past Little Harbor, Blessed Sacrament cemetery, Oyster Pond, and Surf Drive Beach to Falmouth. The clouds in the sky gather in a gray overcast. Dust devils stir the leaves as I detour off the bike path and into the graveyard where a backhoe is mounding fresh dirt over Tina's grave. The monuments in the cemetery look like images in an old black-and-white photo. I keep jogging through the potter's field where the children and paupers lie, where Tina had given Bagger the first of those kisses he still can't forget—where he had been a party to Tina's change into the Shade Queen.

"Christ, I'm sorry," I say as I pass among the line of tiny gravestones and rotting wooden crosses.

I half expect some ghost to whisper forgiveness ... but I hear nothing. The only sound is the moan of a boat horn way out on Vineyard Sound. The air feels heavy and wet with an early-season snow coming.

By the time I circle back onto the rail trail, fat flakes have begun to fall in veils. With the snow in the air, the woods along the trail begin to shimmer as if composed of millions of steel filings stirred by a magnet. I run on toward Falmouth, and as I run—I don't know why—I begin to sing half-aloud "Stay" by Maurice Williams. I can't put any images to the song, but I sense that the song is coming to me from those days when the Bagger had turned madman for a while. Singing feels good, and so I listen to the Bagger's voice and vaguely keep note of the moan of the boat that seems to be searching for Great Harbor in the mounting storm.

By the time I reach the point where the bike path crosses the old railroad bridge at Nobska Road and follow the railway bed as it stretches toward the beach, the wind has whipped the snow into a blizzard. I hear the groan of the boat horn out in the Sound, and for some reason I imagine a steam engine and its freight train at my back. It is close enough to sound like a distant—but constant—chuffing and clanking of chains.

I keep singing …

"Oh, won't you stay …"

"Just a little bit longer …"

Something other than my muscles seem to drive my legs as I jog east on the bike path between the snowy woods. Ahead I can hear the waves crashing on the beach where the tracks break out of the thick trees. The train puffs at my back.

'I dare you to stay right here running in the middle of the tracks,' I hear the Bagger say. 'If that train catches up with you, well, what the hell. You deserve it. There is no such thing as coincidence.'

I'm game.

"Never back down" was my motto in high school. But I like the way the poet Tennyson had put it in his poem "Ulysses," … "To strive, to seek, to find, and not to yield." This is the quote I keep folded in my wallet.

As I reach the end of the woods, I begin to sprint. Out in

front of me—maybe 300 yards—through the blizzard I see the silhouettes of the cattails at Oyster Pond on the left and the beginning of the beach to my right. On a knoll that juts out from the wooded slope above the pond, I can just make out a huge rock and a small clearing behind it.

For a few seconds I think I have beaten the imaginary train. Then, at my back the snort of the locomotive's steam exhaust begins echoing between the hills. At any second the train will burst through a curtain of swirling snow. The engineer might catch a glimpse of a shadow like a boy's, running in the middle of the tracks. Then he will reach for his cord to blow a warning. But before the whistle sounds, the train will overrun the shadow and tear on north at thirty miles an hour … leaving the trainman to wonder whether he had seen anything at all. I'm not going to make it. The Bagger isn't going to win this dare. I am dead meat.

My legs slow to a jog … then a trot. I wait. In a second or two the wave of hot air that always builds up about ten yards in front of a speeding train will strike me.

I stretch my neck and sing loudly …

"Just take a little chance …"

"And leave it all behind, yeah …"

The hot air hits me at the exact moment the locomotive's whistle shatters my song. The last thing I see is the image of Tina. She sits up ahead on the left—high atop the boulder on the knoll overlooking Oyster Pond. She is fourteen years old, dressed in blue jeans and a high school sweatshirt. Long, black hair hangs over her shoulders. Her arms stretch toward me.

"JUMP!" she shrieks.

I smell smoke. The air leaves my lungs, legs ripping at their roots … howling … leaping …

I lie among the poison ivy and blackberry stalks at the edge of the bike trail for a long time. My chest burns as I gulp for air. The flakes begin to cover my tights and running shell like flour.

I am still alive. I have beaten the train.

When I finally catch my breath I stand up, dust myself off, walk the last fifty yards up the footpath that breaks from the bike trail, and mount the knoll on the western edge of Oyster Pond. The boulder looks smaller—more like a tree stump—than the pulpit it had seemed just a few minutes ago. Tina is gone. Snow coats everything—the rock, the trees overhead, the thickets of prickers, the withering leaves of poison ivy, and the cattails down in the marsh. Even the water of Oyster Pond glows white like a long lost skating pond.

For a couple of minutes I sit down where I had imagined seeing Tina. The only sign of life is the sound of some distant gulls squawking as they patrol the surfline of the beach looking for fish. This is a place my grandfather called "the Jungle," and the boulder is "Hobo Rock." God, how many times have I visited this place in my dreams?

The Jungle never used to bring images of death or killing to my mind. I had first seen it when I was about seven or eight. That must have been 1955. My grandfather Happy, who had spent the better part of his life dory fishing on Georges Banks, introduced me to the Jungle one June day when my parents were working. That afternoon, he said he felt like having an adventure. He drove me in his old, gray Pontiac down to the freight depot near the ferry landing.

"Billy, we hike east from here, and you're going to see a puffer-belly," he promoted.

"Puffer-bellies" were what my grandfather called steam locomotives—the little, smoking water guzzlers that the dying Cape Cod railroad still used even after the wealthier lines had shifted over to diesel-powered trains.

"Puffer-bellies are grand machines like the coasting and fishing schooners," Happy said. "Old-time America." He wanted me to see them before they were all gone so I could understand a bit about what built this country.

According to my grandfather, the place to watch for the

puffer-bellies was the Jungle. He said a "jungle" was what hobos called a camp. Once we had one right here by Oyster Pond because it had been a good place for hobos, out-of-work sailors, and unemployed fishermen to wait for the freights and in the meantime cast lines off the beach for stripers and blues.

"This was just about the end of the line, and as close as a lot of 'bos would ever get to the Big Rock Candy Mountain, as near as a seaman might fetch Fiddler's Green," he remarked during our first visit. "Why if you wanted, you could hop a freight or a work boat anywhere in the east and end up here in the Jungle for the summer where the living was easy."

He also said that during the Depression, thirty or forty men might be camping in the Jungle for part or all of the summer— "boat fellas and rail fellas, men out of work, lookin' or just wanderin'."

Sometimes back during those dark days, long before my time, he would go down to the Jungle—even though he had his own little fishing schooner and a family—and bring along trash fish, like hake and monkfish, vegetables from the garden, and tobacco. Mail Pouch and Redman's. Then he'd hang around a bit just to hear the stories of the hobos and the seamen. They were real travelers, had seen it all.

But when he showed me the Jungle, not many traveling men were coming through. Still, every once in a while, you would see a fellow riding in a boxcar, or you might catch a glimpse of a campfire in the Jungle. But mostly, it was a perfect spot to camp, really. And Happy showed me why.

The Jungle sits on a knoll fifteen feet above the tracks and Oyster Pond—out of the way of a storm tide or a derailment. It has a floor of tall, soft grass for lounging around and a surrounding forest of oaks and maples for windbreaks and firewood. The Jungle has a spring with sweet water and Hobo Rock gives a bit of shelter under its crags and offers a great perch on top.

When I was young, from Hobo Rock I could watch the ferries streaming back and forth to the Vineyard, or see day draggers like Skipper Wade coming in from working the shoals. Back in the day, from this spot a hobo could pick out the best car to ride on a freight outbound from the ferry landing with a load emptied or some refer cars with fresh fish. Or he could keep watch for the "bull." The detective who worked for the railroad had to come along to break heads with his Billy club because the railroad didn't fancy freeloading hobos on its property. Best of all, Hobo Rock was a place to sit and tell your story. And to just think.

"Yeah boy, it's a grand place," said Happy, looking wise and confident like President Eisenhower. "Like a pulpit."

He'd seen an old seaman sit up there and tell tales to twenty fellas down below, with a fire going. He heard a story about back before the First World War when men fished the offshore banks aboard the sleek fishing schooners like the "Gertie," the *Gertrude L. Thebaud.* No power on many boats back then. No trucks. The local boys still fished and lobstered from catboats in those days. Set tub trawl out in the rifts in the bottom of the Sound. Big fat schooners built down east in Maine and the railroads were all you had to move goods up and down the coast. Lot of local coastermen were legends— toughs and ladies' men with names like Captain Zeb Tilton and his mate Charlie Sayle on the *Alice Wentworth*. Men who could love a lady or head off into a gale just for entertainment. Free and easy. "What a life," said Happy.

Later when I was thirteen, and my grandfather no longer came to the Jungle to do his dreaming about riding the rails or racing home from Georges under a full press of sail, I found myself drawn back there. I walked the rusty rails to the Jungle on bright afternoons when the shadow from the Quissett Hills began to fall across Oyster Pond, the tracks, and the beach.

Somehow watching a pair of ferries coming from different directions to pass and meet out in the Sound brought a kind of stillness to my mind that I've heard people talk about when they describe why they sit somewhere by themselves and stare out at the sea for hours. The flash of bluefish running the bait, the swoop of gulls, and the scent of the sea breeze can transport you. That's the truth.

On those days, I remembered my time with Happy ... pouring cocoa made with Pet Milk from his thermos into a dented tin cap, and tasting our sandwiches of peanut butter, orange marmalade, and mayonnaise on wheat. I saw the pictures my grandfather had painted with his stories about the Jungle, old-time passenger trains like the "Flying Dude," and days when Vineyard Sound seemed like a field of working sail.

In my mind, I joined the *Alice Wentworth* running toward Edgartown with her tanbark sails set wing and wing, Captain Zeb Tilton at the helm. Her green hull surfed down the three-foot seas, leaving a trail of diamonds in the quarter wake. As the cabin boy, I heated the cocoa on a fat coal stove we had back aft in the doghouse ...

I felt at total peace with my visits to the Jungle, my memories of Happy.

But now, even with the snow quieting the earth, a noise starts to grow in my head. It's the hurricaine I want to forget.

19

A branch snaps in the woods.

"So what the fuck you doin' all by yourself in the Jungle, Bagman?"

The rough voice calls me back from a sail on the Alice Wentworth. Two boys in their teens appear from the path that runs down through the woods to the Jungle. One looks like some kind of big ape; the other is as short and slight as a girl. The two of them stand there smoking in their marsh boots, dark pants, white t-shirts, and hand-me-down slickers. Oaks cast shadows on their faces. When they step into a pool of sunlight, I see that the intruders are two classmates of mine, Danny Sider and Chicky Boyle.

I hear a click and see a switchblade open in Chicky's hand.

"How's it hangin', Bagger?"

I feel dazed. I still have one foot aboard the Alice Wentworth.

Chicky smirks and fingers the blade of his knife with his thumb. Then he speaks.

"Didn't anyone ever tell you a lot of really nasty shit happens here? Like this is the place where the bums get drunk and buggar each other?"

I shrug. How am I suppose to answer this guy? I can't say I was dreaming about schooners and steam trains and my grandfather.

"Maybe the Bagman likes nasty shit," observes Danny.

"We've got some nasty shit right here, Bagman. Why don't you come on down here off that rock and help us with it. Just hooked it out of some drunk's car up on Luscombe Avenue a couple minutes ago."

Danny pulls out a bottle of Thunderbird wine from inside his jacket.

"Yeah, come on down from there and have some nasty shit with us, Bags," coaxes Chicky. He swaggers across the grass carpet of the Jungle and approaches Hobo Rock. "You ain't afraid, are ya? You don't think we'd do anything to hurt ya? You're my man, Bagger. Come on down and be cool. You ain't too good for us are ya?"

Chicky has his fingers hooked in his belt loops. The switchblade flashes above his waist. He is a big kid—almost full-grown compared to me. The story is that Chicky flunked some grade a while ago in elementary school, and last year he failed eighth grade ... so even though he is sixteen years old he is in my class. He has a tall, raw-boned and big-shouldered body that makes him a thug at football, but he has bad eyes. They are so bad that he has to wear thick glasses that the kids call Coke bottles behind his back. The glasses, combined with his pasty white skin, zits, dirty brown hair, and a broken front tooth, give his face a clownish look when he smiles as he's doing right now.

This year he has been in math and English with me, and he hasn't really been knocking the tops off the tests ... even though it is his second time around. Girls call him the "Four-eyed Flunky." His response to such comments is to tell them to go fuck their mamas ... which seems a bit strange to me but always makes him burst into this weird hee-hah laugh.

But until two weeks ago, when he slashed Big-Chandra Page after she pulled her knife on Chicky at school, most kids considered Chicky harmless. I really haven't made up my mind about that. I guess that the best tack to take with this guy is to be friendly. So sometimes I let Chicky copy my math homework, and once I helped him write an English composition. But I don't really want to drink Thunderbird with him in the Jungle, and that switchblade looks like bad news.

If I jump off Hobo Rock—right then—I can make an easy getaway down the tracks. In my sneakers I can out-run Chicky who's loaded down in all that gear. But what will I gain by running away? Would it allow Chicky and Danny to feel like they can bully me at will from here on out? That's how things seem to work; you have to face up to people and events or you are dead. Besides, Danny and I were friends for a while last fall and winter; maybe I am over-reacting to Chicky and the knife. Maybe it won't hurt to just fake a couple swigs of Thunderbird and hit the trail with a little dignity.

Six months ago Danny and I had both ended up playing guard on the CYO basketball team. We always walked home from practice together, and Danny kept me laughing with a rude wit that he turned on himself.

"I don't know why I play this game," he complained after one of his scoreless performances on the court. "I'm so short, Mickey Mouse couldn't fuck my ear."

Another time Danny told me that he affected girls "like a fart in an elevator."

He made me laugh, but Danny's constant smoking kind of turned me off. Then one night on the way home from the gym, he showed me a can of gasoline he had swiped from somebody and stashed in the bushes. He said he was going to torch the garage of a girl who had dumped him that day at school; how would I like to come along and watch the show? Nope. After that night I found reasons to keep my distance.

"You gonna make a fuckin' statue of yourself up there on that rock, Bagman, or are you gonna come on down and share in the low life?" asks Danny as he flops onto the grass and starts to fiddle with a transistor radio. He clicks his fingers and begins to sing along in a monotone to "Kansas City."

Danny takes a slug of the wine and shouts, "What's the word?"

"Thunderbird!" choruses Chicky.

"What's the price?" Danny points at me.

"Fifty twice." I know the ad slogan ... and I guess I just better slide down onto the grass and play along for a few minutes. Really, it will be better than taking off like some chickenshit.

Almost immediately after he starts drinking, Chicky begins rambling on about Tina. What a fox, man. Prime, grade-A Portagee tenderloin. Lips like bar cherries. Titties like smooth, warm bags of semen. And those black and red panties she was flashing in math class gave some great beaver shots that could give you a hard on for a week. She has a sweet little pussy. A bitch whore's wet pussy that loves a cock like Herman. Doesn't the Bagman like to play hide the linguiça with her?

Chicky lies back on one elbow. His other arm stretches to his groin where—with knife in hand—he begins massaging a bulge at his crotch. The way he keeps right on talking and laughing it seems to me that Chicky isn't even conscious that he is masturbating. Now, with the mention of a cock like Herman, Chicky slides open his fly and produces an erection the size of a cucumber ... beginning to weep semen. This is really sick and messed up, and I gather myself to go.

"Herman's a lonely little meat loaf," muses Chicky as he stares at his cock, stroking it with the right hand that still holds the open switchblade and talking to it like a pet.

"See, Herman needs some lovin'; he's missing Tina, the hot, wet cunt of a lovin' baby girl faggot whore," adds Chicky as he breaks into a fit of hoarse laughter. Has Tina messed with Chicky? Is she crazy?

I start to rise, but I have barely gotten my tail off the ground when Chicky collars me with one hand and holds the switchblade to my cheek. His face is inches away from mine; he grins wildly and rubs a bit of semen from his knife hand along the edge of my mouth.

"Jack me off, asshole, or I'll cut your face so bad no bitch—not even your mother—will look at you!" His breath smells like smoke.

"What the hell?"

"Do it, motherfuck!" Chicky pins me down on my back. "And do it nice and slow like you love Herman, like our little dolly girl Tina love's Herman."

I try to scream, but my throat feels clogged with fish bones.

"Just do it, Bagger," slurs Danny who is already feeling the wine. "Don't get yourself hurt, man. Just do it. It's no big deal."

"Right, Bagger. Just do this little thing for poor lonely Herman. Just do it right and nobody gets hurt. Nobody's gonna know about this except Herman and me and Danny. And Danny's not gonna say shit. Ain't that right?"

"Fuckin' A. Just do it, Bagger," Danny's voice seems distant like he's been through all this before.

"Don't keep Herman waiting; sometimes that makes him crazy. Then you never know what …"

What choice do I have? I put my hand around his prick. After a while I feel Chicky slip away from me and onto his back.

"Don't move. Just lie there," he groans. "Hold the knife, Danny."

Chicky passes the switchblade to Danny who hitches up behind my head to keep the knife pricking under my chin. Smoke from his cigarette drifts into my face.

"That's better." Chicky presses the side of his body against mine. "Herman loves this shit."

I turn my head in the opposite direction and try to will my soul away from this time and this place. I see one of the boxy white Steamship Authority ferries coming out of Vineyard Haven across the Sound. Three fat robins pluck for worms in the dirt on the other side of the Jungle, and a pair of great blue herons wades for minnows in the pond. Gulls screech and wheel over a school of bait fish. They muffle the sound of Chicky singing along with the radio, "Come on, baby, let's do the twist; come on, baby, it goes like …"

Hours seem to pass and still Herman stays erect.

I picture a steam train approaching from the north, accelerating and puffing as it runs down the slight grade from West Falmouth to Woods Hole and the ferry landing. I imagine each grade crossing meet and pass with every hoot of the whistle. I want to be on that train.

"Roll on your belly!" Chicky pinches my left earlobe and begins to twist.

"No way!" I shout. "You said you'd let me go!"

"Herman changed his mind. Roll over. Now! Cut him if he doesn't move NOW, Danny. Herman's on fire!"

I hear the train approaching. The engineer is pulling on the whistle cord to signal for Depot Avenue. Danny presses the knife under my chin and turns the edge against my throat. I roll on my belly. God help me.

"Pull his pants down. Herman wants to see his hot little hiney."

Danny throws a choke hold around my neck, and I feel the knife slit the back of my belt in half. Someone rips my pants down around my ankles. My knees knock against each other.

"Come on, man. You don't really want to do this," I plead. My fingers tear at each other against my belly. I keep my eyes closed tight.

"It's Herman, man. He loves you. He doesn't take no for an answer!"

I hear Danny chuckle and feel him hand the knife over to Chicky and slide away. The train's whistle sounds closer— Locust Street crossing now.

I feel Chicky put his cold arm around my bare waist and pull himself close.

"Herman wants it," he whispers in my right ear. And he

knows you want it too. You DO want it, don't you? You love it. You like Herman in your hand and you're gonna like him even better between your legs. He's hot for you, Bagman. You made him into a fuckin' hot rod. You only THINK you like girls, but Herman knows you want HIM. You want to be Herman's faggot whore, don't you? Don't you?"

Chicky begins to cackle to himself. I can feel his hands rubbing my back and my legs, I smell the smoke on his breath. His facial stubble grates against my shoulder. A leg slides over mine.

The train moans again. Just a half mile away. Chuffing, spewing steam from its pistons. I picture the engine swaying as it heads into the turn at the north end of Salt Pond.

Heavy panting. Sweat against my face and legs. God, fingers probing my rectum. Knife blade thrusting right up inside my nose.

"Come on, say it. You want to be Herman's faggot whore."

Something slashes over my back like a cold whip. Twice. An arm tightens around my waist. Chicky tries to ride me.

"You want to fuck? Say it. Fuck me!"

Ohhhhh, no. Please.

Air leaves my lungs. Legs ripping apart at their roots. Eyes opening. Knife flashing right alongside my nose. Train rumbling past. The cold whip slashing across my back again. Stretching for the train in my mind. Trying to ride out of …

"Oh, mama!" Howling, thrusting, lightning.

JUMP.

JUMPJUMPJUMPJUMPPPPPPPPPPPPPPPP PPPPPPPPP … … … … …

I roll to my left as if some kind of explosion has gone off inside me. My shoulder smashes into Chicky's rib cage as he tumbles under me. A loud grunt passes from his lips, and the knife flies free across the Jungle. As my momentum rocks me onto my feet, Chicky stumbles after me, grabbing for my waist.

"Faggot …" he bellows.

His fingernails claw into the flesh just below the lobes of

my hips ... but he loses his grip as I stumble away. A second later I'm running clutching my open pants to my waist. I ignore the searing pain.

"You're dead. I'm gonna kill you!" shouts Chicky over the clanking of the freight train in my mind.

Lurching up hill on the path that leads to Oyster Pond Road, I look back over my shoulder. Chicky Boyle stands there where the trail leads away from the Jungle. His pants are still bunched around his ankles, and Herman waves in the air like a headless snake. Both Chicky's arms stretch out to me with the middle fingers raised.

"Faggot whore," he crows again.

Through the trees I can see Danny Sider perched on Hobo Rock. He is all hunched up like a troll, doing the weirdest thing. He is crossing himself the way we do in church.

I run all the way to Becky's house. She is in the street practicing baton twirling with two younger girls from the neighborhood. I call them the Sugarplum Fairies because they are always prancing around to music like the creatures in The Nutcracker.

"What happened to you?" Becky stops twirling when she sees me.

"Just a fight," I tell her ... already half-believing my lie. I don't say with whom, and I love her for not asking.

She frowns.

"Am I bad?"

Becky motions for the two other fairies to get lost for a while. Then she puts her hands on her hips and steps back for a broader perspective. In her blue jeans, gray pull-over, and Heidi braids, Becky looks like she lives in that world we used to watch on Lassie.

"Not bad. Just a bit of a mess. Look here."

She leads me to the sideview mirror of her parents' Oldsmobile and cocks it toward my face.

I can hardly believe what I see. My nose and throat are

not cut. No bruises. No tear tracks. All I see is a bit of dirt on my left cheek and mussed hair. Besides that, my shirttail needs tucking in, I've lost both halves of my belt, and my sneakers are mud-flecked and loaded with soil. Now that it is over—and I am here—what happened in the Jungle doesn't look like any big deal. Really.

All I have to do is comb my hair with my fingers, tuck my shirttail in, and empty my shoes. Becky wets the cuff of her sweatshirt with her tongue and wipes the dirt off my cheek.

"Okay. You're fine. Your parents will never know."

"Sure?"

"Absolutely. Don't I always make you look good?"

Becky pinches my belly to make me laugh then skips aside.

"Go away, crazy boy … and come back after dinner. I want to talk."

"I'm okay?" I ask again.

"Yes. Don't be so paranoid. Your parents love you. They won't notice a thing."

She is right. When I drift home for dinner after watching the Sugarplum Fairies reconvene and resume their prancing and twirling to the tones of the car radio, my parents don't say a word.

That night I put some of my mother's burn ointment on the zigzags that the switchblade sliced across my back … and hope to god that Chicky Boyle and Danny Sider won't say anything. My life will be hell if it gets all over town that I have been the Four-eyed Flunky's whore. This is the kind of thing I know—even now—that I should tell somebody about, at least Becky and Zal. But I just can't. Shit. I just want to kill someone.

20

When I climb down from my perch on Hobo Rock and start a slow jog home along the snowy bike path to Woods Hole, the old urge to rip something to pieces is pulsing in my hands. I know what I have to do. But instead, I just want to go to bed when I get home.

My parents leave me alone and let me go off to my room. They don't see or act like they don't see how messed up I am when I walk in the door. I think a lot of fishermen's families are like ours. This world has more than enough death to go around, but in a fishing town sudden, violent death is as common as the changes in the weather. Fishing is still listed as the most dangerous job in America by those who keep track of such things. Friends and loved ones go out to sea; and too many don't come back. And even when fishermen come home, I think plenty of them bring the chaos they've seen at sea ashore to kill each other and themselves with cigarettes, booze, fights, and cars. It's the fishing families' way of coping with violent death to make a public show of leave-taking at a funeral. Then we kind of withdraw from each other to build walls against the fear and death in private so we will be ready for the next time.

I am still in bed the next morning when I finally do what I know I need to do. I call Zal. He answers his phone on the second ring. He says he's been expecting my call. He saw me with Sandy Dillard at the internent, and Becky called him to tell him about our rotten time at dinner on the Vineyard and the ambush that followed. Curly had told him he saw me throwing up in the cemetery.

"You want to go for a sail?" he asks.

"It's snowing."

"That was yesterday. Look outside."

I push back the thick gray curtains over my window. The sun is blazing on Eel Pond so brightly that the skiffs and sailboats are little more than silhouettes in the glare. Man, New England weather; who can fathom its changes?

"Come on, Bagman. The sea calls."

"I don't know." Sailboats were my life once, but now they seem like furniture from another man's youth.

There is a long pause, and I hear Zal sigh at the other end of the phone line.

"Look, I know some old ghosts have jumped you; I'm sorry. I figured coming back here wouldn't be easy for you. Still, I didn't quite picture how hard it might be. But we need you here. You're our best hope for getting this killer."

"I got raped," I blurt.

"I know."

"You know? How the fuck do you know?"

"When you're a priest you hear things, Bags. Understand?"

"What? Like confession?"

"Let's just say I know. I'm really, really sorry."

"He carved up my back. With Z's. Like Rollo's dog. Like Freddy Farnham. Like Tina."

"You'll like my boat. Let's take her down to the Elizabeth Islands. I need this too. Please?"

I hear a sadness in Zal's voice. Almost a desperation that I have never heard before. And it reminds me that he has goblins to shake off, too. Not just from our youth, but think of the secrets people must place in his custody in the confessional.

"Where's the boat?"

"Quissett."

The sight of Zal's boat is enough to convince me I've done the right thing by agreeing to a sail. What a little ship. Her name is *Amazing Grace*. And my god! She looks like a half-size sister of Zeb Tilton's *Alice Wentworth*. Wood. About forty-five-feet long. She has a green hull, white trim, flush deck with a dog house aft and tanbark sails. The steering station has a wheel box and a cast iron Edson steering wheel painted silver just like the original coasting schooners.

"Damn!"

"I built her."

"She's a Vineyard coaster."

"I found some plans. Several schooners. Mixed them together. Scaled them down. She took me ten years."

"I had no idea."

"She was my secret. My therapy. I put her together in a barn down in Mashpee."

"When …"

"Just launched her last spring. And the summer's swept by so fast I hardly had a chance to really sail her much. I think she ought to have one last sail before I strip her sails and put her away for the winter. Don't you?"

"I'm drooling. She's like something out of a dream."

"A time machine."

"Yeah. That."

By ten o'clock we have dropped the mooring, set sails, and are sliding west down Buzzards Bay between the north shore of Naushon Island and the islets of the Weepeckets. We wear thick sweaters and slickers, but the air temperature is already climbing toward seventy degrees and a classic Indian summer day. The wind comes clear and easy at about ten knots out of the east, and *Amazing Grace* slips along at five knots in nearly calm seas. She has her foresail set out to port and her mainsail to starboard … what the old schoonermen had called "sailing like an open Bible."

I steer and fall into the old rhythm of sailing from the days when my Sea Scouts pals and I had explored the eighteen-mile chain of the Elizabeth Islands in our Beetle Cats. The rush of *Amazing Grace's* bow wave sings a call-and-response chorus with the screech of the gulls and the creaking of the rigging. Scents of wild grapes carry off the land. Ashore off to port, the sassafras, maples, and high brush on the low hills of Naushon flash red and brown with a few swatches of yellow and orange. Buzzards Bay looks like a pale blue blanket spreading out ahead of us all the way to the islands of Cuttyhunk and Penikese to the west at the mouth of the bay.

This is the going to sea that I sometimes still dream of, my grandfather's schooner days. Not like all of those summers on the *Ellen B* with Skipper Wade, heading out to Lucas Shoal or the Middle Ground with the constant growl of her eight-cylinder Detroit and the heavy scent of fish, diesel, and armpits. That kind of going to sea in a rolling old Eastern-rig was work and—sometimes—danger. This sailing is something else all together.

We don't talk for a long time. Zal tinkers with the set of the sails and the tension of the lanyards and deadeyes in the standing rigging. Then he disappears below deck and starts rattling around in the galley. Five minutes later he climbs back on deck with two mugs steaming in his fists.

"What's that," I ask.

"Truth serum."

"Really."

"Green tea and Virgin Islands rum."

"Now we're talkin'."

"That's right," Zal smiles as he hands me a mug.

He raises his drink, and pauses with his mug raised high.

I can see him getting ready to propose yet another toast to Tina and then changes his mind.

A smile gathers at the corners of his mouth.

"Fair winds and silky seas."

"Fuckin' A."

Zal nods his head and we both stare out to sea.

"Goddamn. I guess I need to talk," I say after a long while. "About this rape stuff."

"You never told anybody? Not even Sukey?"

I shake my head no.

"Look, I'm not very good at this kind of thing, maybe we should ..."

"Just start. Just start with a picture you remember."

I take a long sip of the spiked tea. The sweetness of the rum rises in my sinuses.

"You know a place near Oyster Pond called Hobo Rock ..."

A half hour later I have finish my story about Chicky, Danny, a switchblade, Herman, and a fantasy freight train. We have peeled out of our slickers, and Zal has taken over the helm. *Amazing Grace* continues to the westward, steady as the earth, still sailing like an open Bible with Kettle Cove on Naushon just off to port. I remember times years ago when both confession at church and sailing had made me feel like I could fly. But not now. Now I feel as low and skanky as the ingots of lead ballast in the schooner's bilge.

"Why do I still feel like shit? I think I know who killed Tina. Isn't that what everybody wants from me?"

"I want you to come clean. I want you to get the monkey off your back, Bags."

"What do you mean?"

"I think there's more to tell."

"Yeah, right!"

"Well why do you think that you never told anybody about your rape?"

"I dunno. I felt ashamed. Isn't that the usual deal?"

"Not for everybody. But, it's different, for people who have other reasons to feel shame, isn't it?"

"Shame about what?"

"Maybe you can tell me."

I shake my head. This conversation is garbage. Worse than garbage. It stinks like a whole deck of dead porgies. I look at the granite boulders on the shore of Naushon and a point called the Rams Head. I wish I was one of those rocks.

"You want to know about Tina. Am I right? Everybody wants to know about Tina and me. Jesus, two nights ago Becky was all over me about Tina."

"So?"

"So, okay, Tina and I had a sort of secret thing for a while. In tenth and eleventh grade."

"Behind Rollo's back?"

"And Curly's, okay? But I wasn't banging her."

"Really?"

"Really."

Ψ Ψ Ψ Ψ Ψ

"Here, drink some of this," offers Tina.

I can't focus my eyes. The pain in my testicles feels like some kind of detonation deep in my body that spews cold steam from my eyes and ears. But I feel a paper cup pressing against my lips, and I taste pineapple juice.

"Where the hell …"

"You're in church."

Somewhere off in the distance I hear Maurice Williams singing and I think of Becky, the CYO Halloween party, and "The Midnight Stroll." But the rough skin of the fingers behind my neck tells me this is not Becky.

"Tina?"

"I'm sorry. I just wanted to hurt you."

Now, I remember what happened. She'd fork-lifted my balls to the moon with her fists so hard I'd tasted blood. I must have passed out.

"Forget it," I cough. "I deserved it."

"Yes and no."

"I'm an asshole."

"No, you're just a guy. Just another fish town boy … but I always thought you were different. I don't know why."

I feel the air rush out of my lungs like a moan.

For a long time Tina falls silent and still. After a while she reaches out and takes my left hand in one of hers. Eventually, her long arms wrap around my shoulders and rock me. She sings quietly along with the music drifting in from the dance. The song is "It's All right" by Curtis Mayfield and the Impressions.

We stay like that for a long time on the floor of the sanctuary. I rub my hands along her calves softly, and I feel her lips on the side of my head. I turn, and for a second we kiss. It is just like the beginning of that kiss—lips against lips, lips against eyes, lips against necks—that we shared a year ago in the cemetery, the same kiss we shared on St. Valentine's Day. A kiss that tries to whisper some kind of understanding … before I break it off.

"Somebody messed with you," says Tina. "I picked you at that New Year's Eve dance in ninth grade because you're just like me. I wanted you to fuck me that Valentine's Day because … because we're the same."

I hear a branch snap, and I smell smoke.

"It's none of your goddamn business," I blurt. "I could have died!"

"You don't have to say anything, okay? Just listen. Listen to me, Bagger."

Ψ Ψ Ψ Ψ Ψ

"So we began meeting. Almost every Thursday night that winter, through the spring of tenth grade, and right on through eleventh grade—in the sanctuary of your church, Father."

"And?"

"The church was always unlocked. We used to curl up on the floor in the nave behind the statue of Saint Peter."

"You made out in the chapel?"

"Fuck you, man. I knew I shouldn't have gotten into this."

"I'm sorry, Bags."

"You ought to be. It's not like you're some innocent bystander!"

I shoot Zal a burning look and then turn away to stare off to port at terns working a school of bait in Robinsons Hole, the channel between Naushon and Pasque Island.

"What are you talking about?"

"Have you forgotten the cemetery, the freaking gang bang?"

My friend the priest's olive skin turns as pale and gray as the terns screeching off to leeward.

"You think I don't feel responsible here, Bags? You think a day goes by without me praying for forgiveness? I know what I did to Tina. I know I started something that turned her sick inside, caused her to wear those ridiculous sunglasses for almost a year, drove her out of town, and all the rest. It was like I had killed her. You think that I need you to remind me when I've got God? Every day I hated me, and I hated Tina. I wished we were dead. Now one of us is … and *still* none of this is over."

For some reason I have never thought of all our high school madness from Zal's point of view before. And now here it is. Maybe even the reason Mr. High School Bad Ass had turned into a man of the cloth. He is on a mission for redemption. He'd joined the priesthood to save himself. My god, what we won't do to get right with our souls. But for once I seem to know something Father Zal doesn't.

"You didn't start anything."

"What do you mean?"

"Tina told me things."

Zal gives me a squinting look. He doesn't understand.

"Those nights in the church, when we held each other."

"Yeah?"

"She forgave us for the gang bang. But I don't think she forgave herself."

"It works that way with victims. The guilt just eats you up."

"I don't think you understand. Tina was already damaged goods when she pulled our train in the cemetery. She knew what she was doing."

Zal's jaw muscles flex.

"You think that excuses us?"

"No. And neither did she, but listen, will you?"

ψ ψ ψ ψ ψ

"Look," she says. "I know what he did to you. I couldn't talk about it back in ninth grade when I was with you. But now. We have cut through some shit. You and me."

My butt shifts on the hard floor of the sanctuary. A jolt runs through my brain like a hot spike. Suddenly Tina's breath smells of Thunderbird wine and stale cigarettes. I try to push her away. But she presses her head to my chest and hugs me like a straight jacket.

"I don't know what you mean."

"Come on, Bags, do you think you're the only one he messes with?"

"You're way off base."

I want to go. I try to stand. I have to run.

"Listen, goddamn you! Chicky told me everything. He bragged about it. He got me too, Bags. See? Before he ever got to you. And after. I was coming home from school, and he asked me if I wanted to see a dead shark. He took me out to an empty houseboat at Devil's Foot. He put a knife to my throat. And he … he raped me. He fucked me until I hoped he would kill me and it would be all over. And then he fucked me the way he fucked you. Herman fucked me. He just fucked and fucked and fucked and ..."

She is shivering. Tina's body feels like a block of ice in my arms.

"I was only twelve. I didn't even have my period yet, and he fucked me, Bagger. He made me bleed ribbons of pink blood down my legs to my ankles. My shoes. My goddamn white tennis shoes. He wrecked my fucking shoes. They were sticky with blood. Later he made me suck him. It was the fall, and he made me suck him off after school in that old houseboat. He told me if I didn't do it he'd kill me. I'd wake up on fire some night with the whole bar burning down around me. Kill my parents. He made me do it in Neptune's car when he was working in the bar. Sometimes he brought beer bottles and other things to put inside me. Then he started bringing a gun. He fucked me in the ass with a goddamn gun in my mouth. It went on for months, until he said I bored and disgusted him. Then he told me no other boy would ever want me. He told me I'd always be his whore. His bitch whore. Well I showed him didn't I? And now he wants me back. Well screw him. I don't care how he threatens me anymore. He's going to have to wait in line. Boys love me, Bagger. Lots of boys."

"They love you. We all love you," I say. And it is the truth. If Tina set out to prove to Chicky Boyle and the world that she can make the entire male population of Woods Hole and Falmouth under age twenty-five fall for her, she is doing one hell of a job.

"I feel disgusting. I'm such a slut. But you know what? I'm totally my own girl now. I choose who and when. Do you know what it's like to have that kind of power?"

I shake my head. I have no clue. As far as I can tell life is a constant struggle for purchase. Chicky Boyle hasn't made that any easier for me.

"When you're bad, nothing can hurt you." Her voice sounds a thousand years old.

ψ ψ ψ ψ ψ

"Sometimes I still think she was right." I tell Zal.

"She's dead," he says. "Bad didn't save her from a stake through the chest, did it?"

"I didn't save her either," I say. Jesus, the words just jump out of my mouth before I can even think about them.

A gust of wind catches *Amazing Grace,* and the schooner heels over hard to starboard.

"What are you talking about? It wasn't your job to save her."

All of a sudden I am crying.

"She came to me, man! She told me her worst secrets. We were the same. Chicky's whores. And I did nothing. For more than a year. We met in the church and just freaking *talked* about Chicky. It was weird. We told each other every sick detail about what he did to us. And we wondered for hours about why. Why he did it. Why we let him. Who had done what to him? And who else he was fucking over. It was as if we were members of his fan club in some sick way. And we talked about all of the crazy things we had done—couldn't stop doing—since Chicky had gotten us. And after all of this, she still fucked him sometimes, you know. Can you believe it? Out at the houseboats. He beat her! That bastard! I should have jacked him up so bad he couldn't even remember who Herman was. I should have driven a marlinspike through him, or gone to the fucking police. But I did nothing. Nothing season after season. And then she left town. Split. Not even a good-bye."

"You listened. You never walked away from her. You were her friend. That's more than I did."

"You didn't know."

"I didn't want to. And I didn't want to know about you and Chicky. So who's the real coward here?"

"Jesus, but this is a happy sail."

Zal is staring astern at Robinsons Hole. There is a boat ripping toward us out of the channel between the islands, screaming toward us at about thirty knots. Water flies back from its bows like silver wings. The hull looks dark green or black. An open boat about twenty-five-feet long with a center consul, T-top, and a pair of big silver outboards hanging on the back.

"That's the guy from the other night!"

"No doubt," mumbles Zal.

"Call the Coast Guard."

"And what do I say? We *think* this guy is *about* to harass us? Besides whatever happens, it will be all over in the next ten minutes. The Coasties' helicopter can't even get here that fast from their base at Otis."

Right.

"You don't have a gun aboard, do you?"

Zal gives me a look like I am crazy, then disappears below. When he comes up, he is carrying an old metal ammo box with a 12-gauge flare pistol and a handful of flare cartridges.

"Christ, I feel like I'm in some Hollywood thriller," I laugh. My god, how many movies have I seen where the desperate yacht crew resorts to a flare gun for defense against raiders?

"Got a better idea, Bagman?"

"Maybe," I say. "Look at that."

Ahead a wall of fog has begun boiling over the tops of the Elizabeth Islands. Already the fog is pouring through Quicks Hole Passage from Vineyard Sound into Buzzards Bay ... less than a half mile ahead. Immediately, Zal sees the strategy. If we can beat this bastard to the fog, there is a chance we can lose him in it. And maybe escape. We have radar; the other guy doesn't.

Zal passes me the flare gun, re-trims the sails, and takes the wheel. Then we wait to see what the speedboat is going to do next. I am picturing how we must look like a ship sailing into the fog in a Winslow Homer painting titled something like "Dirty Weather" when the first round comes aboard. The raider's shot hits *Amazing Grace* with a slap, splintering the port cabin side and taking out a window. He is using his shotgun again, this time firing what seems like deer slugs not pellets.

"Shit!" I yell as I duck a second after the fact and pluck slivers of pine and glass out of my sweater. I feel pissed. Pissed at Tina for dying so easily. Pissed at myself for coming back to Woods Hole. Pissed at Zal for coaxing me out on the sail. Pissed that I have put myself in a position to let Chicky Boyle fuck with me again.

"It's fucking Chicky, isn't it?" I shout at Zal. "You know all about this don't you? Every dirty little detail from Tina's murder right on down to this current horse shit. Mother fucker!"

"Shut up and shoot, Bagman."

In all my years growing up with a fisherman and messing around in boats, I've fired off no more than three or four flares, and those were from the deck of the *Ellen B* after watching the Fourth of July fireworks of Falmouth Heights. I have absolutely no memory of a flare's range or speed or sink rate. So I just guess about how much to lead my target and fire.

The flare falls twenty yards short of the raider, and even though sunglasses and a dark wool watch cap hide most of his face, I can see him laughing as he takes aim with the shot gun braced on his boat's consul.

With the fog, the wind has come around southeast at about fifteen knots and our little schooner is already plunging into the fog bank when a second slug takes out the compass with a shower of glass. The air around us now shimmers with mist, and visibility has dropped to less than one hundred yards.

"Get on it, Bags!"

I fire back. The flare goes off with a pop and arches like a red meteor across the water.

The driver swerves left, almost disappearing in the thickening fog, and the flare falls harmlessly into the empty bay.

"He's reloading!" Zal's voice has a shrill edge.

'Aim and fire, asshole,' I think as I begin jamming another flare into the pistol. 'This fucker's going to have us at point-blank range in seconds.'

"Duck," shouts Zal.

Before I can even look up, he grabs me by the sweater and pulls me down on the schooner's cockpit sole. We hit with a bang as a slug buzzes overhead and buries itself into the round clock-like face of the depth sounder with a fizz and flash of sparks.

I don't even stop to think. I just pop up and take aim. The speedboat is only thirty yards behind us now, and this time I point the pistol at the masked face and squeeze the trigger. Fuck you, Chicky. Just fuck you!

The flare goes off with a hiss, and in the thickening fog it lights up the space between our two boats like a deep red sunburst. I see spots in front of my eyes. My head fills with the scent of gun powder and the tang of burning magnesium.

"Die, you prick!"

When my vision clears, there is nothing behind us, beside us, or in front of us but fog.

Zal gives me a hand-held bearing compass to replace the shattered compass in the binnacle.

"Steer two zero zero," he whispers and dives below deck to look at his radar screen. The only way this bastard can find us is by guessing at our course and listening for us. Since we have no engine running for him to home in on, we might give him the slip if the fog holds, we steer an unlikely course, and keep quiet. A few seconds later, Zal returns and points off to port at about our ten o'clock position. I turn my head in that direction and hear the low whine of outboards, speeding up and slowing down. The sorry prick is already in front of us.

"Right to two three zero," whispers Zal. "He thinks we're headed into Quicks Hole Passage, and he's going to wait for us there. We'll stay out here in the Bay."

The whine of the outboard's engines vanishes.

"He's more than a quarter mile at our seven o'clock sitting right by the buoy in Quicks. He thinks that with this wind we'll have to tack through the passage, and one of our tacks is bound to take us right up to that buoy … where he'll be waiting. Smart guy."

"But we're not going to play."

"That's right. We're going home. Ready about."

The fog and breeze holds. Two hours later, radar brings us safely back to Quissett Harbor.

"What do you want to do now?" Zal asks.

"Tell people; fucking put Chicky away!"

"It may not be that easy."

"I've already waited way too long."

'Like thirty years,' I think.

21

Zal, Curly, Rollo, Reggie, Becky, and I sit together in Fish Monger's Café at the entrance to the Eel Pond Channel. It has been dark outside for over an hour. Becky tells her story of the assault on her Mako two nights ago. Zal describes the afternoon's attack on *Amazing Grace*. And over the scent of hazelnut and scones, I unfold the story of my rape by Chicky Boyle in the Jungle back in 1962.

As I finish telling them, I feel out of breath. Steam and smoke and blood catch in my throat. My friends stare silently at the empty coffee mugs. Becky covers my hand with hers.

"That's all I know. Chicky Boyle raped me, and he raped Tina. He was on Nomans the night of the gunfight. He followed us there. To scare us off Tina. To prove he still had power over her, over all or us. I'd bank on that. He carved up the dog's back just like he carved up mine. I saw my cuts in the mirror. The more I think about it, the more I think that he could have been the one who slashed Freddy Farnham—the guy I saw with Freddy in the Impala had a jacket like Chicky's. I think I saw him stalking Tina way back on Valentine's Day in ninth grade. And I don't think he ever really stopped. He's the one who beat her up during the spring of tenth grade. She told me. He always wanted to control her. Then one day he got up the courage, went down to New York, found her, and killed her. And I'll bet you that he's the guy in the black watch cap with the shotgun."

"I don't think so," Curly mutters.

"Why? Why the hell not?"

"Chicky Boyle's buried not more than a hundred yards from Tina. He's right next to Smitty in the veterans' section of the cemetery. They got it in Nam—1968," says Reggie.

"On the same night," adds Rollo. "A bunch of those guys enlisted in the Marines together. They went on the buddy system so they were all in the same unit, the same squad. One night they got jumped in their sleep up in the Northern Highlands. The VC dusted them."

"How do you know?" asks Zal. He has a funny, overly-earnest look on his face that makes me think he knows more than he is letting on or that he thinks Rollo is lying.

"Danny Sider told me when he got back, man. Danny was there, too. The three of them were out on fucking patrol. Somehow when the VC attacked, they failed to finish Danny off. The other guys got staked to the ground right through their chests. Danny just got all cut up."

Rollo pauses, and the skin on his cheeks goes gray. His eyes dart around to each of us as if he is trying to see if we buy his story.

"Honest to christ! He told me. It was like right after Danny got back. Right after we buried Smitty and Chicky. We were drinking down at Blackbeard's, and Danny fucking lets loose with this story."

"So you say."

I don't know why I am challenging Rollo, but he just sort of pisses me off. Hell, he has pissed me off for more than thirty years. The smug bastard always seems to have the right answer. Inside information. Stories that always seem to protect Rollo or make him look like the victim or the hero. Well, screw him. If Chicky didn't kill Tina, maybe Rollo did. He'd wanted her, or wanted her dead, for years. In fact, hadn't he once said he wished we were all dead? The sick bastard had never gotten over Tina, that was as obvious as the veins in his waxy nose. Maybe the stake and the slashed back were just his cover, a convenient copycat thing. Hell, maybe the guy in the dark speedboat with the shotgun was Rollo!

"This is no shit. Danny pulled off the shirt and showed me the scars. Zigzags all over his chest."

"Cut the crap, Rollo. Why don't you ask him where he was the night Tina died, Curly? Maybe he took a little excursion to New York with a marlinspike."

"Fuck you, Bagger. Everybody here knows I was in Blackbeard's. What's you're fucking alibi, man? Tell me that! You were in New York, you ..."

"Hey, you two!" Becky glares from me to Rollo and back again. "Grow up!"

"Yeah, stow it, gentlemen!" Reggie throws a red cardboard file folder on the table, labeled "Werlin/ de Oliveira Murder."

"Curly checked you out. You're both clean." He clears his throat. Then he adds softly, "So is Father Zal."

Zal has been staring somberly at the table as if he is locked in some private struggle to hold a few of his own demons at bay. But now he raises his eyes and twists his head around to give Curly a raw look of disbelief.

Curly shrugs his shoulders and sucks on the inside of his right cheek.

"Sorry, Father. Reggie told me to check out everybody who'd ever been hurt or wanted to hurt Tina. Do I need to say more?"

The word "gang bang" hangs over us like the pregnant elephant in the room that nobody wants to talk about.

Zal begins to unconsciously massage his left cheek with his hand. Rollo fumbles with a pack of butts. I look at Becky's face, hoping for a little warmth or wisdom from those green eyes. But she is staring out the window at the Eel Pond drawbridge as it tilts open above the canal for a small fishing boat to pass. You can hear the machinery clink.

"What about Reggie?" I say. "Tina told me she did you, man. She said you showed her how to ride the Snake in the back seat of your Valiant in Sippiwissett woods? She said it was just your little secret."

Reggie curls up his lip at me and drums his fingers on the table.

At last Curly speaks.

"I had some state dicks check him out on the sly, guys. We had to cover all the bases. The mayor is clean. He was home with the wife and kiddies the night Tina died."

"Asshole." Reggie is pissed.

Curly shifts his mammoth body in the chair.

"Why are all you looking at me? You think the big, dumb Mick cop killed her? You think I went to New York and put Tina on a spit because she shit all over my head in eleventh grade? That fucking cunt! I wouldn't waste the wood. I was up in West Falmouth screwing Sandy Dillard the night Tina died. Go ahead and ask her. So fuck off. And that just about covers it for suspects, doesn't it?"

"Well … it looks like you missed at least two, Curly," Zal says.

Curly shifts in his chair again. Then Reggie speaks up. "Look, man, Chicky wasn't even on our radar screen; hell, he's been dead for more than thirty years." The mayor's voice has an edge like 'don't mess white boy.'

"Two?" asks Curly.

Becky turns her eyes back to the table as she gathers each of us into her gaze.

"I didn't imagine that someone stole my coat and tried to kill me the other night."

Curly makes a soft whistling sound.

"Somebody still knows something he's not telling us or we're missing something here."

This is crazy. What in god's name are we doing tearing up each other like a bunch of angry teenagers. Can I just get up and walk away from this whole nightmare? Is it all just as simple as walking out a door and never looking back?

I stand up to go, but Zal grabs my wrist.

"Show us your scars."

I give him a fuck-off look. I've bared enough of myself for one day.

"Bags, just this one last thing, okay?"

So I peel out of my shirt. People at the other tables stare.

"What's to see; they're—Z's! Just like Tina and Wanger and Freddy Farnham."

"Sit down," says Reggie. "You're making a spectacle of us."

"I don't see anything," says Rollo. "Maybe you just made this stuff up, Bagman."

"In your dreams!"

"Enough!" Becky is up to her ears with us.

"Are we talking about all these little lines like lightning bolts?" asks Curly. He presses his fat mitt against my back.

"Yeah, I guess I see what your saying, Bags. A bunch of Z's."

"Look closer," says Zal. "What do you see? Connect the dots."

I feel like a road map.

Becky traces the faint threads of scar tissue on my back with her finger. "Those aren't Z's; they're S's." She pauses and puts her hands in front of her face as if she is praying.

Finally, she stares into my eyes and speaks.

"You had your eyes closed when Chicky raped you, didn't you Billy? It could have been someone else who sliced you. And he put his initial on your back. It could have been Danny Sider."

"It wasn't his mother." I don't mean to be sarcastic; these kinds of things just seem to come out of my mouth sometimes.

I see Becky exchange looks with Zal and frown for an instant.

"Let's go find that fucker." Reggie pounds the table. "The man's got a lot of explaining to do!"

"Are you okay?" asks Becky squeezing my hand. Before I can answer she leans over and gives me a hug. I smell grass and cherry pie.

"Just totally swell," I say.

22

For years Danny Sider has been living as a caretaker on Pasque Island at Robinsons Hole. He keeps some chickens and goats—maybe a pig—and gardens some. And he takes in a little bit of cash from his Army disability check. Does some clamming in the bays and holes of the Elizabeth Islands. The guy keeps to himself. When he comes into town—even in the summer—he wears gloves, an overcoat, sunglasses, and always has some kind of hat pulled down over his ears and forehead. His cheeks look like someone has scrubbed them with a wire brush. People only see him when he shows up to buy a jug of wine at the packy or make Saturday night confession at Blessed Sacrament. As the story goes, Danny had gotten a bad case of Agent Orange trying to work his way back to the base camp through the jungle after his buddies died in Nam.

"They say his body's all messed up," says Curly. "Let's just go see for ourselves."

The six of us push the beer cans, McDonald wrappers, and fishing tackle off the seats of Rollo's old McKenzie bass boat. I can't believe it is still afloat. The thing has to be fifty years old. But the boat screams when Rollo opens the throttle as soon as we get out of Eel Pond.

Darkness settles over Vineyard Sound. We race south along the coast of Naushon Island towards Robinsons Hole, the gut that divides Naushon from Pasque. The wind comes stiff and cold out of the north, but the tide must be on the ebb because we have smooth water.

As we pick up the buoyed channel into Robinsons, no lights shine from the farmhouse on Pasque. A few goats skitter into the brush when we land the bass boat at the small stone wharf. Tied at the head of the wharf sits a black, center consul boat. It has a pair of clam rakes aboard, a T-top with a black hole the size of a baseball through it, and a starboard gunwale shredded to pieces in two places, midships and near the bow. No question, it is the boat that attacked Becky and me on our way back from the Vineyard, the boat that stocked Zal and me aboard *Amazing Grace*.

There are footprints on the muddy trail, leading away from the wharf and up a steep hill on a path through the scrub brush. Curly leads us along the tracks to a low concrete building all but buried in the hillside a hundred feet above the Sound. From as close as twenty yards it just looks like a part of the hill, overgrown with poison ivy turned yellow and brown with the onset of winter. I think I smell coal smoke.

The tracks lead under a pair of heavy metal doors into what must have been a coast-watcher's bunker or a gun emplacement built to stop German U-boats from coming up the Sound in World War II. In all the years we poked around these private wilderness islands, none of us had ever guessed there was a bunker hidden up on the crest of Pasque. We knew about the ones on Naushon that overlooked Buzzards Bay, but not this one. Amazing.

Curly gives a hard tug on the doors, but they seem to be barred from the inside. The six of us head off around the bunker, and on the backside of the hill covering it we find stairs leading down below ground level to an open doorway. Hulks of rusted machinery and small metal hopper cars fill Curly's flashlight beam as it searches the interior. The hopper cars sit on narrow railway tracks that lead off into a dark tunnel. The large room looks like it had once been a machine shop for this abandoned fortress. When Reggie throws a rock across the room into the dark, a chicken flushes and flies into the flashlight's beam in a flapping blur of white feathers. We all jump. Becky grabs my arm with both of hers.

"Follow me," urges Curly as he leads us through a maze of machines to a door at the far end of the shop. A dusty, orange sign hangs next to the pealing green door, "Safety First."

The door yields to Curly's touch, and the next thing I know the six of us are standing in Danny's den. A large pot-belly coal stove hisses in the near corner of the room giving the place a hot sulfur smell. Rollo opens the stove's large front hatch, and the light of the fire bathes the room in flickering shades of orange and wavering shadows. We spread out and walk around the room, stepping softly. Nobody speaks.

Except for a galvanized washtub filled with a few pots and dirty dishes, a book case jammed with foods like pasta and rice, and an old table decorated with a kerosene lamp, the only other objects of note in this room are steamer trunks. There must be more than a dozen with their lids open and contents strewn all around the room as if Danny has been rummaging for something. The place looks like a theatrical prop shop. Women's clothing of every shape and description lay everywhere. House dresses to evening gowns, bikinis to grandma's girdles, skirts, tights, furs. And Becky's burgundy field coat.

"The guy seems to have a thing for women," says Rollo.

"Looks like he's been raiding the Goodwill drop boxes for years," adds Curly.

"Quite a lingerie collection." Reggie picks up a flame red bra and wiggles his fingers through the peek-a-boo nipple holes.

"He's really sick," whispers Becky.

Zal raises his eyebrows and nods.

"Well you got to love his heroes." After everything that has happened to me in the last twenty-four hours I have begun to feel overrun with a sense of irony.

"What?" asks Zal.

I point to the movie posters Danny has used to decorate

his walls. James Dean, the Terminator, and Robert DeNiro in *The Deer Hunter*.

"Wild things," says Becky. "A bunch of wild animals!"

I turn to Zal, "That's what this is all about; isn't it, Father Zalarelli? Don't be so fucking coy. You knew about all of this, didn't you? Danny told you about all this stuff in confession, but you didn't stop it. You just let this sick shit breed until …"

"Jesus christ, Bagger, I know you've had a hard time, but would you leave him alone! He's a priest for god's sake. Isn't anything sacred?" asks Curly.

"Shut up you chumps and come look at this," calls Reggie.

"I want to take my coat and go home," says Becky. "This whole thing is a nightmare."

She is right. I know it. I want to say I am sorry to her and to Zal, but the words won't come out. I feel like I have a cobra rising in my throat as I watch Becky start for the door.

"He's sorry," says Zal grabbing her hand. "Forgive him. You know what he's been through; you know what he's gone through to get us this close to the killer?"

Becky looks at me. Tears well in her eyes. She stretches out her free hand to me, and I take it. Together Becky, Zal, and I follow the other men into a back room of this apartment in the bunker.

Against the right-hand wall stands an unmade bed piled with ragged quilts. When Curly swings his flashlight's beam across to the left side of the room, we see a workbench that Danny seems to have converted into a kind of make-up table. Wig stands with blonde, black, and red women's wigs sit at the far end of the long table. At the middle of the table are more wig stands covered with what looks like Hollywood-quality rubber masks of women's faces. One has the smooth, blank features of a white teenager. Another is the face of an adult black lady. A third is an old Asian woman whose cheeks have begun to settle into jowls. At the near end of the table sits a small collection of chemical bottles and make-up tubes surrounding a latex impression that Danny seems to be using for a mold to make a new mask.

"Shit, it's Tina." Rollo is peering into the impression.

Curly brings his flashlight directly on the mold. There is no doubt in my mind. This is the face of the woman I kissed good-by yesterday ... turned inside out like a dish. Reggie holds up the mold. You can look right into the eyes. They are opaque and open. This is not the look of the face in the coffin. It is the look I remember seeing on her face on those nights so long ago in the cemetery and when the Crisco can slipped out of my hand. On the nights when I had screamed. It was the face of fear, a person looking eye-to-eye with death.

"What's all that?" asks Becky pointing through the gloom to decorations on the wall at the back of the room.

Curly shines the light on the wall as we follow him for a closer look. One side of the wall—at least six feet wide—has newspaper clippings of Tina/Noelle pasted side-by-side all the way from the floor to the ceiling. There are old high school yearbook pictures, portraits, and casuals of Tina dancing across a studio in a dark leotard. There are some snapshots of Tina posing on the merry-go-round at the elementary school. She has on the rabbit coat I remember. In one photo she stands on the playground between Danny and Chicky. She has her arms around both boys' waists, and the photographer catches her just at the moment when she is stretching to give Chicky a kiss on the cheek. In another snapshot the camera has snapped her in a hug with Danny; she is taller. That has to be back in the—jesus—seventh grade when Tina was twelve. Back when Chicky had taken her out to the houseboat to see the dead shark.

Next to these memories are scores of newspaper and magazine photos of Tina after she became Noelle and started her glamorous life with Butch Werlin. One relatively recent photo from *Rolling Stone* shows Noelle sunning herself topless in a beach chair on the deck of her home on Fire Island. Across the photo someone has scrawled with a red marker "BITCH FAGGOT WHORE."

Separate from the Tina collection by a couple of feet stands a gathering of small portraits tacked to the wall in neat rows. They are the kind of pictures we got every year in school and gave away by the dozen to friends. Danny's collection includes every guy in town who had ever gone out with Tina. Me, Zal, Smitty, Rollo, Curly, and even Reggie. Smitty's picture has an S carved across his face. There is also a carved up picture of Freddy Farnham and an 8 x 10 Marine Corps photo of Chicky Boyle in his dress blues … with an S carved across it. In the lower, right-hand corner of the photograph Chicky had scrawled, "To Danny Bitch—Semper Fi!"

"See the pictures. The creep wants to do us all. Everybody who ever got between him and Tina," groans Curly.

"It's more than that," sighs Becky. "Look at all of this stuff. Something terrible happened to Danny. Something really sick."

"There's your murder weapon." Curly points at a canvas ditty bag like fishermen use to keep their tools for mending nets and splicing line. The old bag is filled with ash marlinspikes, like the ones that killed Tina and Rollo's dog.

"I want this bastard out of circulation now." Reggie kicks the floor.

I think I understand everything.

"He wanted to ruin everything in Tina's …"

"Jesus, the bastard keeps souvenirs!" Rollo stands frozen, pointing to the floor inside a metal closet he has just opened. Curly's flashlight swings to the spot and illuminates the mummified carcass of a black lab. It has leathery lightning bolts carved on its back and a spike through the chest. After more than thirty years we've found Wanger.

ψ ψ ψ ψ ψ

The whine of an outboard engine screeches through my dreams. It comes out of the purple night like an animal on the hunt. When I open my eyes, I see Zal, Rollo, and Smitty curled up in their sleeping bags around the fire like dead men, despite the sound of the outboard. The boat swerves into the lagoon, and in the glow of the campfire I can see the pale faces of Chicky Boyle at the wheel and Danny Sider standing in the stern with a rifle in his hands. The boat's silver wake breaks on the beach as it pulls away to the east. Wanger starts chasing the wake down the beach and barking fiercely. I stumble to my feet to follow. Something is wrong. We have company. I don't know why it doesn't cross my mind to wake the others.

I try to run, but the best my body can manage is a broad-gaited stagger. My arms flail at the air as if trying to grab handholds to pull me down the beach after the outboard and Wanger. Several times I stumble, hit the sand with a shoulder, and roll back onto my feet again. At some point I look up and see Rollo's bass boat ahead of me and realize that I am running the wrong direction. I have lost the outboard, Chicky, Danny, and Rollo's dog. This is bad shit. I know I have to wake the others. I have to. But first I think I better get to Rollo's boat and grab Rollo's hunting knife. Forget a gun, Chicky and Danny used a knife on me. Tonight it is my turn to make the bastards know what it feels like to have a blade at your throat. The Bagman will have his day.

But I don't. It takes me forever, rooting around in the dark cuddy of the boat for the hunting knife, and by the time I put my hands on it, I feel too dizzy to move another step. I just think I'll lie down on one of the berths and close my eyes for a second to clear my head.

The next thing I know, Smitty is shaking me awake. Shooting has started. And I can't remember why I am holding a knife.

23

The six of us are still standing in Danny's bedroom when Curly hisses. "Shut up, I see a flashlight beam; he's coming!"

Curly snaps off his light, but Danny must have seen it because I catch a glimpse of his silhouette pause at the entrance to his den and stare hard in our direction before turning back toward the little railway tunnel that leads off the machine shop. Reggie starts to run, and the rest of us take off after him. Rollo sees another flashlight in the corner and grabs it before we head down into the tunnel.

I think how strange it is that the tracks leading down into this long-abandoned bunker have a polished sheen to them like tracks that trains run over regularly. But any ideas I have of finding a nice clean, industrial place vanishes when Rollo flashes his light around at the rotting concrete walls. Huge brown and yellow spiders perch in the corners of thousands of funnel webs. We stop running, but charge ahead imitating Curly's long strides. Five minutes into the tunnel, the spider webs disappear and the walls bloom with mushrooms and sheets of orange nitre that drip off the rocks like thick pudding. Every once in a while we pause, turn off the flashlights, and listen. We can hear the clatter of Danny's shoes. His headlamp shines with a faint white glow.

"I smell shit," says Rollo sniffing the air.

"Right!"

"I do too," says Becky, "It's coming from up ahead."

As we continue along the tracks the smell gets stronger

until we reach a spot where the ceiling of the shaft has long ago caved in and left a mound of rock and broken concrete slabs piled five feet deep across the tracks. Smack up against this debris sits one of the metal hopper cars covered with a patina of straw and dirt, stinking of manure. Fertilizer.

"Smells like our boy has been doing a bit of gardening," judges Reggie. "Let's go see."

Reggie grabs Curly's flashlight and begins scrambling over the cave-in. As we follow, Rollo shines his light nervously overhead. The ceiling yawns away into darkness. A faint shower of water sprays out of the blackness and splatters on my face. For thirty yards or so we creep along over the mounds of rubble with our heads ducked down. Then, as suddenly as the cave-in begins, it ends and the tracks reappear. Now, a stream or rusty water a foot wide rushes along the right side of the tracks. Curly grabs back his flashlight and begins leading the way again. We march forward. From where I walk at the very back of the group, our shadows move like dancers on the walls.

Curly stops.

"Shit. The goddamn tunnel splits!"

Ahead we see a railway switch and the tracks break off in two directions.

Rollo shuts off his light.

"Listen."

Curly douses his light too. The darkness shimmers with a greenish light that isn't exactly light, more like a haze.

"I hear splashing."

"Which way, Father?" asks Curly.

"I'd follow the stream."

Off we go, following the water down the shaft to the right. We haven't gone more than a hundred yards farther when we come to a point where a pool of water begins covering the floor of the tunnel and the tracks.

"This sucks," grumbles Rollo.

"Don't chicken out on us now," Curly wades into the water.

"If it gets over my knees, I'm out of here," whines Rollo.

"Be cool!"

Eventually, the water does reach our knees, but it is surprisingly warm and all six of us slog on until the tunnel seems to rise a little and the tracks climb out of the water. Ahead the walls of the narrow shaft veer away from the tracks in opposite directions and we find ourselves in an immense gallery. Thick pillars of concrete support the ceiling at twenty-foot intervals as far as the flashlights can illuminate.

"It's a fucking maze."

"Jesus christ, would you shut up Rollo," fires back Curly. "Haven't you ever been in a powder magazine. This is where the army guys stored the shells for their guns. It's the end of the line. He's in here. We'll find—"

A burst of automatic rifle fire cuts Curly off. Concrete dust flies. We fall to the floor and scramble behind one of the pillars. Bullets ricochet around the gallery. Small pieces of concrete ceiling fall in soft clunks and hiss.

"He's got an M-16," says Curly in a calm, lowered voice. "We got to split up and try to flank him. Rollo, give your light to Zal and come with Reggie and me. Becky, Bagger, Zal, you get down behind this pillar. Flash the light, get his attention, draw his fire so we can find him."

"Take your best shot, asshole," screams Zal as he flashes the light to our right while Curly, Reggie, and Rollo scuttle off in the dark to our left. I can't believe how his voice has changed. The priest has vanished. This is the voice of the cowboy I knew back in high school, and it has real venom in it.

"Run for your lives you fucking Tina Toy faggot whores," shouts Danny. I know that voice. It is the voice in the dark from Nomans, from more than three decades ago. No question about it.

A burst of gunfire rings out. Zal clicks off the light. Rounds hit the ground from an angle at our left. Becky screams. Concrete dust stings my nose and throat.

"Come on," whispers Zal. "We have to move. He grabs Becky's hand and begins crawling through the dirt toward the right.

I follow. More shots—five or six in a second—hit the floor behind me. I scramble ahead and into the dark. Zal's hand grabs me around the wrist and pulls me behind a three-foot high mound of debris left from a cave-in. We lie with our heads close enough to feel each other's breath. Our bodies splay out like spokes on a wheel.

"Piss poor," shouts Zal. This time he keeps the light off.

Another burst tears through the air, and I can hear the rounds plow into the mound of debris in front of us. Dirt and small rocks fall from the ceiling on our bodies. I can feel Becky shivering beside me. When I try to wrap my arm around her, I feel Zal's already there.

"Come and get us you pussy-whipped peckerhead," I shout. I can feel Zal's free arm tense around me as I scream.

"You're gonna die," shouts Danny as he flashes a light in our direction for a second then rips off another burst of gunfire. This time it hits the ceiling overhead. Concrete and dirt splatter over my back and legs like a wet sand bag.

Becky coughs, "What do we do now?"

"Hope those other guys can flank him ... and pray," says Zal.

I try to make a joke. "If I have to die, what would be better than to go down with a priest's arm around me? You're not gay are you, Zal?" I tease.

"That's nobody's business!" His voice has a huskiness that cuts me like a knife.

"That's the whole point isn't it?" I ask as if my friend has just delivered me an insight.

"The whole point about what?" asks Becky.

I open my mouth, I can't say what I mean, what I know.

But it has something to do with the adrenaline, confusion, and bitterness that has surrounded our lives for almost as long as we have known each other."

"Come on, Billy. About what?"

I still can't find the words, but a picture of a carnival thrill ride called the Tilt-A-Whirl pops into my head. It is a kind of high-speed merry-go-round that tilts on end and spins you until the world turns into a blur, the snake rises in your throat and your crotch aches.

"Love," I choke ... and suddenly I feel tears welling in my eyes.

Danny's M-16 splatters into the ceiling again, and the chunks of concrete and dirt begin to bury us.

"Merciful Father," begins Zal.

I stretch my arms over my friends' heads like shields and hold on tight.

The next thing I hear is Curly's service magnum discharge in three ear-ringing booms.

"Ah, bitch motherfucker!"

Danny's squeal echoes off the walls.

Lights flash on, and for a half a minute I am more or less blind. Then shapes and colors begin to emerge before my eyes just as I hear the rattle of the M-16. Zal grabs my wrist again. A second later he is on his feet running with Becky and me in hand. Behind us the ceiling collapses in a cloud of dust. Ahead stands a hopper car mounded over with manure. Beyond that the gallery seems filled with a garden of plants growing almost to the ceiling. We duck for cover behind the manure hopper but no more shots sound.

"Give it up, Danny. It's over, buddy," calls Rollo who has gotten brave.

"Up yours, fucker!"

I see Curly, Reggie, and Rollo scuttling toward us from the left. Curly is pointing at dark, sticky splotches on the floor that lead into the underground garden of tall green plants.

Danny's blood. Lots of it. Reggie picks up a chunk of shattered concrete and lobs it off into the garden to startle Danny and draw fire. Nothing happens, and the three men fan out and start into the plants. Looking closer, I can see that the plants grow from individual pots. The leaves are full and shiny with five distinct fronds. Marijuana. Danny has a pot farm down here. Jesus.

Suddenly, a long burst of gunfire erupts from the other side of the jungle, and shredded plant leaves fill the air. Then Curly's pistol booms again.

When the leaves settle I hear Curly's voice.

"Zal, you better come fast."

We all fall in behind him as he follows the bloody trail through the jungle of pot.

Then we break out of the little forest, and I see the strangest thing. There, splayed across several bales of marijuana, lies the woman we buried only yesterday. Noelle Werlin, Tina de Oliveira. Neptune's daughter is doing her best to look like the Great American Bitch Goddess with the same surprised look I remember from Valentine's Day 1963. Her black mane of hair swirls around her head and strands streak across her long eyelashes and crimson lips. She looks like a streetwalker in a form-fitting, red sequin tunic and gold lame tights that run down her legs into a pair of fashion jogging shoes. In one hand she holds an M-16; a miner's lamp dangles from the strap in her other hand. As she breathes, blood blooms on her lips and sputters from several wounds in her breast.

"Last rites," begs Tina.

But the voice has none of the husky spirit of the girl's voice that had spilled its secrets to the Bagman in a dark church. The voice is Danny's.

Zal stoops to his knees and makes the sign of the cross on the forehead of the man hidden behind the mask of Tina.

"Confession," coughs the voice that still seems a distortion, some weird new permutation of Tina de Oliveira.

Zal nods and bends his ear so close that the blood from those pretty lips smears his cheeks. Everyone hears the words through the sobs.

"Chicky fucked me like a dog; he fucked me twice a week just like I fucked Freddy Farnham ... and called me his bitch faggot whore. He fucked me like he fucked her. He called me Tina .... We loved her."

That is all. Those dark eyes—Tina's, Danny's—close and die.

"Amen," whispers Zal.

"Amen," mutters the rest of us automatically.

24

As soon as the five of us come out of the bunker after the shooting, Curly radios the police and Coast Guard. The next thing I know an armada of police launches, cabin cruisers, and Coast Guard assault boats crowd at the little wharf on Robinsons Hole. A bunch of detectives descend on us, and before I can even wave "so long" to Zal or Becky, they split us up and shuttle us off into separate boats to take our statements.

The heat inside the police cabin cruiser is pretty welcoming. Snow has started coming down again, and I feel like I have been shivering for years. After my statement, for some stupid reason I keep trying to watch for when they bring the body out, but the night is too dark. One of those morbid things people do, I guess. Like I need to see that dead goddess one more time, just to prove all of this stuff really happened. Just like I had wanted to see Wanger's body on Nomans so many years ago.

The detective, a skinny little guy named Hannah who took my statement, didn't want a whole lot from me—just the basics about how I know everybody, why I had come here, and what happened in the bunker. He wanted to know who shot first, and how "the victim" died. He said he hoped I could back up Curly's story. The public was pretty sensitive to insinuations of excessive use of force. Hannah didn't want to see his boss saddled with a bad rap. Anyway, I told the detective the short version of what happened and let him give me a ride home to Eel Pond in a Boston Whaler.

What a mess. Just like about a hundred other times in my life, my mother tried to prepare one of my favorite dinners, and I show up late. My folks usually eat dinner at six o'clock sharp, and it is at least nine o'clock when I walk in the door. Even before I see the scowl on Skipper Wade's face as he thumbs through the newspaper in the living room, I smell the acrid scent of peas going dry in a pot and codfish over-heating in the oven.

"You don't even want to know what happened," I sigh.

"You owe us the truth, mister," grumbles my father. Even at seventy-four years of age the old fisherman can muster an edge. And for a moment I feel as if I should salute when he drops the paper at the side of his chair and rises to attention like pictures I have seen of old sailing captains.

"Sit and eat, you two," calls my mother from the kitchen. "Deaths and funerals are hard things."

Seconds later she shuffles the cod, the peas, and the baked potatoes onto the table and sits down with my father and me. She is no longer the dark-haired beauty she had been when we were a family back in the sixties, but she still has the fresh cheeks and bright eyes of a woman who looks forward to every day.

Without a word, my father stretches out his hands to clasp my mother's and mine. Then he says grace. His voice resonates with the words "Heavenly Father, Bless this food ..."

My eyes give in to an old habit and close. For a second or two life seems just as it did when I was a kid ... before Valentine's Day at Tina's, that spring day in the Jungle, rabbit hunting, and all the rest. I don't think I pray. But before I open my eyes again, I find Zal and Becky's adult faces roaming through my head. I know that the three of us have been through hell ... and that—as my father said—I owed my parents the truth.

We pick at the dinner for a while. Then I tell them about the death I witnessed in the bunker and just about everything that led up to it. How all of this pretty much marked Danny Sider as Tina's killer even though nobody yet has actually placed him in New York the night that she died. I leave out the gory details, of course. My parents don't need absolute authenticity about my rape, that was for sure. Why should they suffer over things that happened so long ago, things that can't be changed? And I leave out my new suspicion about Zal's being gay and the emptiness I experience every time I have seen Becky since 1963 … because … I don't know.

"We tried to protect you from things like that." My mother is quietly crying.

"I'm sorry, buddy." My father is stunned beyond words.

"It's okay," I say. "I think the nightmare's over."

Then the phone rings. And it doesn't stop ringing until we unplug it an hour later. All my adult life I've worked in the media business, and I think I know what it means to be hungry for a story. But I'm telling you, some of these reporters aren't even people; they're sharks. Like the first woman who spoke to my mother on the phone. She said she was from some TV station or another. Then she told my mother that she had heard that her son—ME—was caught up in some kind of sex and drug cult assassination plot against celebrity women like Noelle Werlin and Madonna. What did my mother think about my impending indictment?

Tell me, where do these sharks come up with such garbage? Do they make it up to provoke some kind of quotable response from regular people like my mom … or do they just race off to scoop sensational interviews before they get their facts straight? I write sports for a decent paper, and I'll tell you I'd be fired if I carried on like these sharks. I mean at the Times you don't go into an interview—even when you smell a story—with nothing but some twisted rumor. You have to check things out. Like last week a source told me Bill Parcell was going to blow off the head coaching job with the Jets.

"He doesn't even care if he gets the Jets into the Super Bowl this year; Parcell is going to walk on his contract. Done deal," said my source. Juicy story. But I wasn't going to write it unless

I could confirm it. You think Parcell was going to help me with that … in the middle of the football season? Should I have called his mother and said that I heard her son is caught up in some kind of Mafia gambling vendetta that wants him out of New York or dead? No chance. You don't have to hurt old ladies to get a story.

After the TV satellite truck shows up outside on the street, we turn off all the lights and go down into the back room to watch home movies. My dad loves them. When I was a kid—from the time I was about six until I was out of high school—my dad shot reels of eight millimeter. About a year ago he got a cousin of mine to convert all the old film over to video. My mom says Skipper Wade watches them more than he watches *Jeopardy*.

That's what the Bagwells are doing tonight … no matter what the media says. I'm not destroying evidence of sex and drug cult assassinations or talking to my lawyer: I am watching old movies of fourth grade swimming parties at the Weepeckets on the Forth of July.

My dad has lots of shots of women like my mother and Becky's in bathing suits carrying casserole dishes, men like Zal's father playing horseshoes, and kids floating around Buzzards Bay in truck inner tubes that look like giant lifesavers. My friends and I are all there … but none of us are together. Zal shows up next to the charcoal grill with his belly hanging out and a hot dog in each hand; Becky waves to us in her Heidi braids from somebody's beached speedboat. I swing out over the water from a halyard on Skipper Wade's *Ellen B* like some kind of scrawny Tarzan who then loses his grip and belly flops into the water.

Even after my parents pack it in and go to bed, I keep watching the tapes reel on and on to a soundtrack of saxophone blues. After some footage comes on showing an eleventh grade football game against the Vineyard, I crack a beer, plug in the phone, and call Zal. I need to talk. He says he has to do an early morning Mass … but why don't I come by the rectory at about ten o'clock. We can go for a long jog. Then I ask him for a favor—Becky's number.

I wake to the smell of waffles, maple syrup, and linguiça; and I know that my mother has made her only child his special breakfast for a reason.

"You're going to need your strength today," she says. "A lot of people want to talk to you, and—well—you can't hide forever."

So for the next two hours I play defense, fielding calls that come in from places as different as *The Falmouth Enterprise*, *The Boston Globe*, *Good Morning America*, and *Geraldo*. I even get a call from the city editor back in New York at the Times. Everybody wants to know all the details of Danny's bunker and how Danny and I knew Noelle Werlin, that is, Tina. I get pretty good at saying, "Right now, this is private. No comment."

But as we talk, I do learn from the city editor in New York that some computer hackers in San Diego have broken into the Falmouth's Police computers and got Curly's narrative of the shoot-out as well as a memo naming me "the key witness," the guy who has seen Danny's twisted soul at work from beginning to end. The hackers also accessed Danny's Marine Corps records and are offering the whole package for $10,000 to the media. There have been plenty of buyers … so maybe I ought to lose myself in the Bahamas or some place far away for a few weeks unless I want to be pestered to death. Now I understand why the TV satellite trucks are parked up and down the street in front of my parents' house.

The city editor also tells me that there is a rumor floating around that someone named Charles Boyle has been a silent player in Noelle Werlin's murder. What do I know about that?

"He's been dead for more than thirty years," I say. "Check his Marine Corps records and notice how he died. You won't be disappointed."

Suddenly, I feel like throwing up and excuse myself from the call. I want to crawl under a rock somewhere and hide.

Even though it is a half hour before Zal told me to come for a jog, I just can't sit in this house and field another phone call. So I pull on an old pair of high school track sweats I find in a drawer in the attic and cover my head with an old blue, wool watch cap I used to wear on cold days when I went fishing with Skipper Wade. I think the high school stuff might disguise me as a local—maybe even a kid—at a distance. At least I will look less conspicuous than I might in my black tights and running shell. I slip out the back door and through the bushes into the neighbor's rear yard and follow the back streets to Blessed Sacrament without a soul seeing me. It was easy, really, with the help of my mother who stepped out the front door and began sweeping her porch to distract the media.

The weather is great. Yet another Indian summer day. The snow is melting, and you can see your reflection in the puddles it leaves on the pavement. It is not until I reach Blessed Sacrament and see the wet blades of grass in front of the church shining like a field of emeralds that I remember that I have forgotten to call Becky. Something sinks in my stomach.

Not a single media person hovers in view when a nun lets me into the rectory. Zal has just come in from Mass when I enter his quarters, and he is still wearing his robes and skull cap. Dressed like that, Zal looks strange.

As he leads me into his kitchen and pours us both glasses of orange juice, Zal cocks an eyebrow at me and warns, "Don't even say it, Bagman."

"What?"

"That I look like a woman, that cross-dressing is getting to be something of a fashion craze around Woods Hole. I know what kind of stuff goes through your fetid brain."

"Was I staring? I was just wondering where you got your halo."

"And I was just wondering why you're dressed like a case of arrested development. You look like a refugee from the sixties."

Then, as my friend ruffles past me on the way to his dressing room to change, he gives me three rapid-fire noogies to the left arm. Good old Zal.

When he reappears in a blue Gortex running suit, Zal is smiling, "I'm going to run you ragged this morning, Bagger."

And he does. From the moment Zal ushers me out the rectory door and leads me down to the bike path on the old railroad bed back toward the ferry landing and the village, I know that somehow this run is the last round of that boxing match we never finished. When I go out for my usual jogs, I'm no slouch with pace. Maybe I run six-and-a-half-minute miles or so, for a half-dozen miles. But Zal has us cranking out steady six-minute miles … and he isn't even breathing hard.

We wheel passed Neptune's Bar.

I can't do more than catch a glimpse of the windows to the upstairs living room where Tina had once danced for me in a burgundy, v-neck sweater. But for just an instant or two I smell the scent of Jade and hear "The Duke of Earl" playing on the phonograph before Zal reads my mind and coaches, "Let her go, Bags."

Suddenly, I feel mean; I can't help it. What the hell does Zal know? He doesn't have a media carnival playing in front of his house? Nobody has called him the "key witness."

"Maybe it's easier for you because you're GAY!" I growl. There it is, isn't it? I've spit out my suspicions.

"I knew this was coming," he sighs. Then he picks up the pace a notch as we pass the guard house on Bar Neck Road and start out toward Penzance Point where almost all of the summer mansions have been closed for the season.

"Go ahead Bagger … let … me have it!" Zal forces out between steps.

"You were … such … a macho … prick," I begin. It's hard to get the words out with my breathing.

Zal doesn't say anything. When we veer off the road and hit the stony beach on Buzzards Bay, I expect him to slow down a little, but he keeps on pounding along.

"Let it go," breathes Zal.

I don't know why, but I felt Chicky Boyle riding my back again, and I see Danny sitting on Hobo Rock.

"You're a fuck … ing Tina Toy …"

"Yeah?"

"That's what … you … called ME!"

"You think that … I've forgotten?"

His question leaves me with no response. I guess I just never thought that he would remember how he provoked me during that boxing match in eleventh grade.

We run on in silence to the north end of the beach and then take a trail up the hill into some woods and a neighborhood of homes where the scientists from WHOI and the MBL live. Maybe on a slower run I might have had some vision of Tina or Becky back in high school or heard a snatch of some song from those days. But now my heart is pounding so loud that I can barely picture the patch of earth where I am going to place my next step.

That's all I focus on, my heart pounding for the next mile as we head north out of town and up a steep hill. Meanwhile, the words "faggot whore" keep tumbling through my head.

Finally, we veer off onto the fairways of the Woods Hole Golf Club. Here, Zal makes a sharp right and we begin to scale a hill. As we chuff up the face of the hill, sweat fills my eyes, and everything begins to look brown and hazy. Out in front Zal seems to be running even faster, his legs driving like pistons, pulling away from me. We must have gone on like this for at least five minutes, veering over the fairways from hole to hole. It is too late in the season for any golfers to be out. Zal is just a distant shadow, and I want to quit. Then I hear those words "faggot whore" rattling through my brain again, and I know I have to catch him. I know I have to ask him something.

Near the crest of a hill, I catch up with Zal. Abruptly, he stops, and I know where we are. Back in the sixties we had made a career out of partying here with the rich girls who had come down to the Cape for the summer. Now a herd of more than a dozen deer are grazing on the same turf. As the deer perk up at the sound of our breathing and watch, Zal leads me to a knoll that makes for a vista on Vineyard Sound. Across the Sound you can see the black hull of the topsail passenger schooner *Shenandoah* out for a fall sail. Probably her last of the season.

Suddenly, I feel my legs quivering.

"Sit down?" says Zal more as an invitation than a question. He nods to the vista and takes a seat. I follow like a man on a string. My legs seem to be sinking in mud, and sunbursts keep blotting out patches of my vision.

"Go ahead and ask," he says, his breathing already slow and steady.

"Why?" I gasp for breath. I still feel my heart pounding at my temples so I tear off my watch cap and face south into the breeze. Vineyard Sound seems to disappear like a silver mirror in a golden haze.

"Why what?"

"Why … did you … call me a faggot whore. How … how could you when …"

breathing and words are still too difficult.

"Oh, come off it, Bags. You know the answer. I wore a mask just like you. Just like everybody. For protection. Do you think I could stand the thought of what I was? I hated it."

"So you took it … out on me?"

"Do you think I could have told you the truth?"

He has a point.

"But that night in the cemetery with Tina? How could … you have done that and … and been gay?"

"A sick act. As they say, denial is not just a river in Africa."

"And the time you made Becky look like a slut … at the movies just for my benefit. An act? Thanks, Father."

"Look, you have a right to be angry. But it's not like you didn't do crazy, wild things to me."

"I was hurting."

"I know."

"Then why did you add to it?" I can finally breathe again.

Zal clears his throat. His black eyes look at me and he gives a sad smile, then he stares down at his clinched hands in his lap.

"Maybe I was jealous." His voice seems to run out of air as he speaks.

"Of what?"

And then it hits me. "You mean …"

"I don't know; yeah, maybe. I guess." Zal is almost whispering.

"Shit."

"Exactly."

"So …"

"So that was a long time ago."

"So what now?"

"I think that we stop competing. I think we forgive each other … and ourselves."

"How do you do that?" I really want to know; I have no clue.

"I say I'm sorry." Zal's chest heaves as he forces out the words. His eyes catch mine then dart out over the Sound.

"You win, man," I say. "Ah, man … . You win!" I feel some brown, prickly ball breaking up in my chest. To tell the truth I want to hug him, but I guess I still don't feel comfortable with Zal's other side yet. So I just sit here for a while and listen to his breathing and the deer snuffling in the fairway.

My hurricane is over, mostly, and soon enough I'll have to deal with the damage. But for now I can just sit on this knoll with my friend, look out at Vineyard Sound, and picture a sea of schooners running before the wind with a trail of diamonds in their wake.

Nick Madrid Mysteries
by Peter Guttridge

No Laughing Matter
Tom Sharpe meets Raymond Chandler in this humorous and brilliant
debut. Meet Nick Madrid and the "Bitch of the Broadsheets," Bridget
Frost, as they trail a killer from Montreal to Edinburgh to the ghastly
lights of Hollywood.
ISBN: 0-9725776-4-5, ISBN13: 978-0-9725776-4-9

A Ghost of a Chance
New Age meets the Old Religion as Nick is bothered and
bewildered by pagans, satanists, and metaphysicians. Seances, sabbats,
a horse-ride from hell, and a kick-boxing zebra all come Nick's way
as he tracks a treasure once in the possession of Aleister Crowley.
ISBN: 0-9725776-8-8, ISBN13: 978-0-9725776-8-7

Two to Tango
On a trip down the Amazon, journalist Nick Madrid survives
kidnapping, piranhas, and urine-loving fish that lodge where a man
least wants one lodged. After those heroics, Nick joins up with a Rock
Against Drugs tour where he finds himself tracking down the would-
be killer of the tour's pain-in-the-posterior headliner.
ISBN: 1-933108-00-2, ISBN13: 978-1-933108-00-1

The Once and Future Con
Avalon theme parks and medieval Excaliburger banquets are the
last things journalist Nick Madrid expects to find when he arrives at
what is supposedly the grave of the legendary King Arthur. As Nick
starts to dig around for an understanding, it isn't Arthurian relics, but
murder victims that he uncovers.
ISBN: 1-933108-06-1, ISBN13: 978-1-933108-06-3

Peter Guttridge is the Royal Literary Fund Writing Fellow at Southampton University and teaches creative writing. Between 1998 and 2002 he was the director of the Brighton Literature Festival. As a freelance journalist he has written about literature, film, and comedy for a range of British newspapers and magazines. Since 1998 he has been the mystery reviewer for *The Observer,* one of Britain's most prestigious Sunday newspapers. He also writes about—and doggedly practices—astanga vinyasa yoga.

Praise for the Nick Madrid Mysteries

"Highly recommended."
—*Library Journal,* starred review

"... I couldn't put it down. This is classic Guttridge, with all the humor I've come to expect from the series. Nick is a treasure, and Bridget a good foil to his good nature."
—*Deadly Pleasures*

"Guttridge's series is among the funniest and sharpest in the genre, with a level of intelligence often lacking in better-known fare."
—*Balitmore Sun*

"... one of the most engaging novels of 2005. Highly entertaining ... this is humor wonderfully combined with mystery."
—*Foreword*

" ... Peter Guttridge is off to a rousing start ... a serious contender in the mystery genre."
—*Chicago Tribune*

"[The] Nick Madrid mysteries are nothing if not addictively, insanely entertaining. ... but what's really important is the mix of good suspense, fast-and-furious one-liners and impeccable slapstick."
—*Ruminator*

"... both funny and clever. This is one of the funniest mysteries to come along in quite a while."
—*Mystery Scene*

Inspector DeKok Investigates
by Baantjer

DeKok and the Geese of Death

Renowned Amsterdam mystery author Baantjer brings to life
Inspector DeKok in another stirring potboiler full of suspenseful
twists and unusual conclusions.
ISBN: 0-9725776-6-1, ISBN13: 978-0-9725776-6-3

DeKok and Murder by Melody

"Death is entitled to our respect," says Inspector DeKok who finds
himself once again amidst dark dealings. A triple murder in the
Amsterdam Concert Gebouw has him unveiling the truth behind two
dead ex-junkies and their housekeeper.
ISBN: 0-9725776-9-6, ISBN13: 978-0-9725776-9-4

DeKok and the Death of a Clown

A high-stakes jewel theft and a dead clown blend into a single riddle
for Inspector DeKok to solve. While investigating a jewel theft
DeKok is called to check out the death of a clown found floating in a
raft down the canal, an enormous knife protruding from its back. The
connection of the crimes at first eludes him.

1-933108-03-7

DeKok and Murder by Installment

Although at first it seemed to be a case for the narcotics division, it
soon evolves into a series of sinister and almost impossible murders.
Never before have DeKok and Vledder been so involved in a case
whereby murder, drug smuggling, and child prostitution are almost
daily occurences.
ISBN: 1-933108-07-X, ISBN13: 978-1-933108-07-0

A. C. Baantjer is the most widely read author in the Netherlands. A former detective inspector of the Amsterdam police, his fictional characters reflect the depth and personality of individuals encountered during his thirty-eight year career in law enforcement. He was recently knighted by the Dutch monarchy.

Praise for the Inspector DeKok Series

"Along with such peers as Ed McBain and Georges Simenon, [Baantjer] has created a long-running and uniformly engaging police series. They are smart, suspenseful, and better-crafted than most in the field."
—*Mystery Scene*

"… an excellent and entertaining mystery from a skillful writer and profound thinker."
—*Midwest Book Review*

"Baantjer's laconic, rapid-fire storytelling has spun out a surprisingly complex web of mysteries."
—*Kirkus Reviews*

"This series is the answer to an insomniac's worst fears."
—*The Boston Globe*

"DeKok's maverick personality certainly makes him a compassionate judge of other outsiders and an astute analyst of antisocial behavior."
—*The New York Times Book Review*

"It's easy to understand the appeal of Amsterdam police detective DeKok; he hides his intelligence behind a phlegmatic demeanor, like an old dog that lazes by the fireplace and only shows his teeth when the house is threatened."
—*The Los Angeles Times*

"Shrewd, compassionate and dedicated, DeKok makes a formidable opponent for criminals and a worthwhile competitor for the attention of Simenon's Maigret fans."
—*Library Journal*

Boost

by Steve Brewer

Sam Hill steals cars. Not just any cars, but collectible cars, rare works of automotive artistry. Sam's a specialist, and he's made a good life for himself.

But things change after he steals a primo 1965 Thunderbird. In the trunk, Sam finds a corpse, a police informant with a bullet hole between his eyes. Somebody set Sam up. Played a trick on him. And Sam, a prankster himself, can't let it go. He must get his revenge with an even bigger practical joke, one that soon has gangsters gunning for him and police on his tail.

"… entertaining, amusing … . This tightly plotted crime novel packs in a lot of action as it briskly moves along."
—*Chicago Tribune*

"Brewer earns four stars for a clever plot, totally engaging characters, and a pay-back ending … ."
—*Mystery Scene*

ISBN: 1-933108-02-9 | ISBN13: 978-1-933108-02-5